HEAR ME CRY

by Eileen Wharton

HEAR ME CRY
Copyright 2022 © EILEEN WHARTON
All Rights Reserved.

No part of this publication may be reproduced, distributed or transmitted in any form or by any means, or stored in a database or retrieval system, without prior documented approval of the publisher. Red Dragon Publishing LTD. This book is a work of fiction.

ISBN; 978-1-7392127-0-4

Names, characters, places and incidents either are the products of the author's imagination or are used fictionally. Any resemblance to actual persons, living or dead, businesses, companies, events or locales is entirely coincidental.

Dedication

For Ariana and Khaleesi.

Chapter 1
KATIE 2019

A clatter from downstairs told me he was here. In my house again. In the kitchen. Now. But by the time I crept down, brandishing a weapon, he'd be gone. Just like every night since I'd returned to Northumberland. How he got in and how he left, I didn't know. Sometimes I caught sight of his shadow in the garden; sometimes the shape of a face at the window. Why hadn't he just killed me and got it over with? It was almost as though he relished the terror he instilled in me night after torturous night.

On mornings like this I wished I'd stayed in my city flat. Still lonely but surrounded by people. I could have thrown open a window and called for help. Out of the hundred passing by, averting their eyes to pretend they hadn't seen or heard anything, there'd be someone whose conscience might scratch enough to assist. In this house the only ones to hear a panicked cry were the seagulls.

A loud thud and my heartbeat thumped in my ears. I picked up my phone to check the time. The light from the screen cast eerie shadows on the bedroom ceiling. I reached to switch on the bedside lamp with shaking fingers. The orange glow chased the shadows away. I clicked on social media and tried to relax, but the news updates warned of murder and mayhem. I placed the phone face down on the bedside cabinet, turned over, and pulled the covers over my head.

Something scraped on the bedroom wall. It called to mind childhood ghost stories. Sitting round the campfire with school friends, telling eerie tales about the hand that wandered streets and broke into houses to strangle people in their sleep. My heart boomed.

I reminded myself about the tiny brown torpedoes I found in the master bedroom. Evidence a small rodent had taken up residence. The scratching was probably nothing more sinister than mice in the wall cavities. I needed to buy traps.

A thud. Another clatter. My heart gave flight again. Pressing against my ribs, fluttering like a caged bird. I threw back the covers. I could no longer hide from the knowledge that someone was in the house. The time had come for me finally to confront him. 'Who's there?' I called out. 'I have a weapon.' I sat up, swung my legs round, and planted my feet on the floor. I picked up the baseball bat I kept propped against the wall, stood, and tiptoed towards the door. The landing creaked from my tread on the floorboard, warning the intruder I was on my way. I crept down the stairs and flicked on the big light. Another clank. Nausea washed over me, my knees folded, and I sat on the bottom step. *Deep breaths, deep breaths. Compose yourself.* If he had come for me this time, I might need to fight for my life.

Another clank came from the direction of the utility room. I descended the steps to the cellar and a shiver ran down my spine. It happened without fail every time I came down here. Another clang – and I realised what the noise was. The drier had started up again. It had a mind of its own. A pair of jeans tumbled round and round. I'd forgotten to remove my belt. Relief escaped in a short blast of air, and I smiled.

I jumped at the shrill cry of my ringtone. Blood flashed round my head, my pulse throbbed in my ears. *Please don't let it be Mark. Please don't let it be Mark.* It wasn't. Of course it wasn't. I accepted the call from my boss.

'Kovacs, I want you in my office as soon as you get here. And don't be late.' He'd cut the call before I managed to tell him it was only 6 a.m. and, even though I now lived over an hour away, I was never late.

When the car rolled up to the office building, a scrap of moon fought with a thread of cloud and a light drizzle smothered the streetlights. The security guard flicked up his collar, blew on his hands and nodded good morning.

I didn't have time to hang up my coat before Brightman called me into his office. 'Close the door, Kovacs,' he said, his glasses perched on the end of his nose, his dyed hair swept over to conceal a bald spot. 'Siddown.' He didn't take his eyes from the papers in front of him on his desk. 'Give me one good reason why I shouldn't sack you.'

'I don't understand,' I said, sitting down. 'I haven't done anything.' There were others in the agency who'd been caught in compromising positions in the stationery cupboard or on top of the photocopier, but not me. I hadn't so much as had one too many ciders at the work's Christmas party. I'd been feeling tired. The noises kept me from sleeping properly, but I'd never been late and I'd always done my job to the best of my ability.

'When was the last time you signed a decent author?' he said.

'Well ... I ...'

'This pile of crap is not going to sell.' He pointed to the manuscript from my latest client.

'It's a great book.'

'It's been done to death. It's completely irrelevant.'

'I don't think you can say it's irrelevant. Fairy tales and folk tales have a place among great literature. They help us break boundaries of time and culture. They feed the imagination. They're didactic.' The stories were very personal to me. I'd spent hours with the author; developing the words, changing them, improving them. Manipulating them into poignant and profound passages. Teasing out a metaphor, severing the adverbs until it was tight and precise and as near to perfect as we'd ever get. It felt like he was criticising one of my children.

'This one about the Little Mermaid, it's nothing like the story I know.'

'The real tale was much more tragic.' It was also close to my heart. The mermaid sold her soul and her voice to the sea witch in exchange for legs, but every step she took was like walking on sharp knives. She would only obtain a soul if she could win the love of the prince and marry him, for then part of his soul would flow into her. Otherwise, at dawn the day after he married someone else, she'd die with a broken heart and dissolve into sea foam upon the waves. The mermaid was given another chance. If she killed the prince and let his blood drip onto her feet she could become a mermaid once more and her suffering would end. She couldn't bring herself to kill him, though, so her body dissolved into foam. She became an ethereal spirit who could earn back her soul by doing good deeds for mankind for 300 years.

'I just need a chance to prove myself,' I told my boss.

'You've had chance after chance,' he snapped.

'Okay. But I'm sure there will be great interest in the next book. It's a fascinating story.'

'What story? I'm beginning to think you wouldn't know a good story if it jumped up and bit you on the arse.'

'With respect…'

'Fuck respect, Kovacs. We need a big sale. We want commercial. No one wants to read a feminist rant. Your ballet book isn't going to generate a six-figure auction. There's not a story worth printing here,' he said. I curbed the resentment and hit him with my grand achievement.

'I'm working on my own book. A story no one else has managed to get. You won't believe it if I tell you, but it's true.'

'You're right, I don't believe you. What is it?'

'She's agreed to talk to me. She's agreed to tell me, and only me, her tale.' I deliberately didn't tell him who.

'Who has, Kovacs?'

I left a pause. Just long enough for dramatic impact so that when I said her name his mouth dropped open and his eyes screamed shock.

Chapter 2
HEATHER 2019

I knelt, head bowed, in front of Our Lady. She stood, arms wide, her blue gown the colour of cornflowers, her eyes sad at the loss of a son. Every morning I could be found there before the rest of the congregation awakened. I usually left prior to the other sisters arriving. They'd come armed with mops, buckets and polish, ready to clean the church. That morning I was lost in my thoughts as the music of the violins slid through the chapel. Soeur Francis sashayed across the altar, lighting candles and singing the hymn in a low, sweet voice, 'Nearer my God to thee, nearer to thee.'

She realised I was there and jumped. 'You gave me a fright. You're here early.'

'I'm just leaving, Soeur Francis.'

'You've a busy day in the kitchen today.'

'Yes, Sister.'

'And you are busy writing something, I hear.'

'Yes, sister.' The congregation thought I was journaling about the lack of new sisters to the congregation and the need to close homes because there was no funding. That couldn't be further from the truth. I was telling my story. A story the other sisters knew nothing about. If they knew who I was I would never have been accepted into the congregation.

I glided back to the room where I slept.

I looked through the tiny cell window and watched a small bite of leftover moon disappear behind a curl of cloud. A daddy longlegs sprang from the cream brick walls to the Bible for my use, legs trailing like jellyfish tentacles. I lifted my black mule, waited for it to settle, but my hand trembled.

I remembered the fourth death, and sobs overtook me.

Chapter 3
HEATHER 2019

Katie couldn't be more different than me. And it isn't just that she looked different. Though she did. Last time I saw her the navy-blue skirt suit swished like only expensive clothes do. Her heels showed a red sole and her blonde hair was pulled into a tight ponytail, glasses perched on her head. She carried a briefcase. In contrast, I floated in the black habit, sashaying along corridors. My hair, if I had any left, was tucked into the grey veil. A band of white framed my lined face. The cracks of age had opened at the corners of my eyes and mouth. Battle scars.

Little Sisters lost our given names and took on those of saints. Mine was Soeur Anthony.

I wandered through the vegetable patch, past the kitchen where I usually worked. The dinner was prepared there for the old folks and the community. I strode down a corridor lined by stone pillars and passed through the oak door at the end, stepping down a stone staircase and into my cell. It was a sparse room with its simple bed and wooden chair. A single hook on the back of the door was the only evidence there was somewhere to hang clothes. Almost like a prison cell. But it was the life I chose.

The Little Sisters vowed to live in poverty in order to look after the poor and elderly, just as our founder, Jean Jugan, had done over 200 years before. It was a vocation. And some might say a penance. Some form of restitution perhaps?

Katie was very excited about my story. I couldn't tell you how long I'd been trying to find a way to tell it. I'd been thinking about what I would say about this for a long time, but when the moment came, my tongue felt stuck in some strange limbo. It felt like the tongue of the mute or the dead.

She would know about tongues of the mute. I would know about tongues of the dead. I sat and stared into the distance. The tick of a clock. The ring of a bell.

I couldn't speak but finally I began to write.

Chapter 4
HEATHER: LETTER TO KATIE 2019

Dear Katie,

I should go back to the beginning, painful though it is to tell the tale. But what is the beginning? Would you want to know where and when I was born? Who my parents are? Might you be interested to know that my great-grandparents came to Durham from Ireland on a boat? Tossed by stormy seas, emaciated by famine? Is it relevant that my father was born during the Jarrow March? Family history has it that Grandmother O' Flynn gave birth while following Red Ellen to London, wrapped her newborn in a shawl and carried on to the Palace of Westminster where they gave her £1 for the train fare home.

My own delivery was less dramatic. I arrived to great excitement on 25th June 1968. The Rolling Stones' 'Jumpin' Jack Flash' was number 1 in the UK music chart, Enoch Powell had delivered his Rivers of Blood speech two months previously, Martin Luther King had been assassinated, the Kray twins had been arrested, though not yet convicted, and the price of a pint of milk was ten old pence.

I was the long-awaited daughter of Neville and Eileen Parnell. Milk floats jangled across town, and 'Heather' by The Beatles drifted from the radio as pains ripped through my mother. I appeared fourteen hours later while the midwife sang the same Beatles song. Mother said it was a sign, so Heather was my given name.

After seven boys, my birth was celebrated with a King Edward cigar and a glass of Mackeson Stout. The former being given to my father, the latter to my mother, to build her up after her ordeal. No marching to Downing Street for her. She took to her bed for three weeks until Granny dragged her out, telling her there was no time for the baby blues. There was washing to be done and socks to be darned.

I was a chubby, solemn baby if the photos are anything to go by. I wore my brothers' hand-me-downs. Apart from the pink matinee coat, the looped-bonnet gifts soon dried up when the novelty of a female child's arrival had worn off.

School was a Catholic village establishment with a strict headmistress and fierce parish priest. I know what you're thinking, but this is not one of those misery memoirs, tales of neglect and abuse. This is a story of secrets. Secrets, smoke screens, and lies.

Chapter 5
KATIE 2019

I couldn't believe it when I received the phone call from the solicitor to say the house was mine. Left to me in his mother's will. I could only wonder about her motivation for doing this. Maybe she realised I wasn't all bad. Perhaps she wanted me to relive old memories. Or did she just want me to suffer? I'd never know the truth. My friends thought I was mad for giving up my flat, eighty seconds' walk from work. The journey from the Old Parsonage took seventy minutes, and that's not accounting for rush hour. It didn't matter. As soon as I received the details and scanned the photos, the building spoke to me like the image of a long-dead acquaintance. A ghost from the past. One with which I had unfinished business. A shiver ran the length of my body and a flood of memories came gushing back.

I was eager to get home and type up the pages. For a moment I allowed myself to daydream about prizes and promotions: a seat at the dinner table at the Booker awards; a spot on *This Morning*, interviewed by the silver fox and a busty blonde. I imagined the headlines in the *New York Times* and the *Guardian*: 'Literary agent turned author steals the spotlight'.

When I opened my front door, I could tell someone had been here. There were no obvious signs, but the house had an unsettled air as though it had just breathed out. The umbrella was still in the hall stand where I'd left it, my slippers sat side by side at the front door, the TV was off and the hall light dimmed. But I left it lit every morning to save coming back to the dark.

'Mark?' I called into the expectant air. The silence shouted back at me, jostling with the sounds of the old house settling round my presence. The creak of the floorboards, the clang of the water pipes, the hum of electricity. I wouldn't give in to the fear. I couldn't give in to the fear.

I opened the kitchen door and a rectangle of light seeped onto the tiled floor. I'd left the fridge open. Shit! Dust motes spiralled in the shaft of light. Particles of me dancing into the next life before me. A faint odour of sour milk greeted me. Reaching in, I grabbed a carton, opened the lid, and sniffed. Fine. There must have been a spillage somewhere. I lifted the kettle to fill it, almost dropping it again; my heart pounded and my stomach churned. I hardly dared to put my shaking hand on the side, but even before I did so, I knew the kettle would still be warm.

Rattling open the knife drawer, I pulled a bread knife from its compartment, holding it in front of me as though pointing it at an unwelcome intruder. The end shook as I inched towards the sitting room and opened the door.

Empty.

I reasoned with myself that the sun must have been shining through the kitchen window onto the kettle. *Why am I cursed with such a vivid imagination?*

I crept up the stairs and stepped onto the creaky landing. The gush of running water from the bathroom startled me. I was certain I had turned off the taps that morning and I'd definitely removed the plug.

The bathroom was so full of steam from scalding water running into the bath, I couldn't see a thing. I calculated how long I'd been out of the house and worried about how much the hot water running down the drain had cost me. I consoled myself that at least the overflow was working, or I'd have been wading through a flood. I was meticulous about turning off taps. Maybe it was the plumbing issue the agent had talked about. A loose washer or something. I was ignorant about these things.

I inched forwards and switched off the flow, opening the window, the cold air stealing the steam. The icy blast raised pimples on my arms.

As I spun round to leave, the thought of a soothing glass of claret on my mind, I caught sight of my reflection. My heart stopped, and I blinked, trying to erase the sight before me.

Written in the condensation on the mirror: a single word.

YOU.

Chapter 6
HEATHER: LETTER TO KATIE 2019

They say the sign of a happy childhood is never being able to remember the rain. I wasn't sure how true this was, but the days had all seemed sunny until the summer of 1975. After that, when I looked back, angry storm clouds gathered and rain battered off dormitory windowsills, while I listened to Freddie Mercury singing about killing a man.

The commune stole our traditions. It stole our happy life. It stole my family.

Christmas was always very special in our lives before. We spent weeks in preparation, feeding fruit with brandy to make the Christmas cake. It was almost as though the cake was a prized pet or a prodigal child. My mother fed it, sang to it, talked about its breathing. I imagined the cake transforming into a giant entity which splurged round corridors and swallowed us up. consuming us in its giant, cakey sludginess, like a *Dr Who* villain. But the cake was eventually married together, turned into tins and baked, then fed again to retain the moisture. 'It's all in the feeding,' my mother used to say.

We were burgled one Christmas and they ate half of the cake. You'd think they'd murdered one of her children. She never got over it. Every Christmas she told the tale to anyone who'd listen. She stayed up nights to guard the cake, as though it were the crown jewels. She sat in the pantry holding a stick. A night patrol by a rebel soldier. She'd appear dark-eyed and bad-tempered the next morning, shuffling us off to school to sing carols and make ornaments out of pinecones.

We finally broke up for the Christmas holiday, and spent hours trying to avoid jobs our mother created for us. 'Just run along to the shop and buy string...' 'Just pop to the post office for stamps ...' 'Go and deliver these cards for me ...' As the time for Santa to arrive got closer, I dreamt I awoke to an empty sack. In other dreams the presents filled the house so we had nowhere to sit.

We'd go to bed on Christmas Eve having hung up my dad's socks. We used his welly socks, because they could hold more fruit and sweets.

We put out empty pillowcases, which were plump with presents the next morning. Church began with carols and ended with smoke and boredom, and then home to dinner. Dad carved the turkey and took all the credit for Mam's days spent in the kitchen. Pigs in blankets, roast potatoes and mash with extra butter and cream. Piles of Brussels sprouts, mashed turnip, and honey-roast parsnips. This was the seventies. You ate it or you were served the food up at the next meal, cold and congealing. There was no pudding for those who didn't eat every bite of dinner, and I was one of the few people who loved Christmas pudding.

Nan fell asleep eating her dinner, gravy seeping into her red paper hat which had been prised from the inside of the toilet roll cracker after a glass of sherry. We were poor in comparison with many of my friends, but Mam always claimed we were rich. 'We're rich in love,' she said. And she made sure to tell us we were much better off than a lot of people. Just round the corner there were people surviving on potato skins and handouts. 'Just round the corner' was like another world. Mam always made sure we knew to be grateful for what we had. And we always were.

Then everything changed.

Chapter 7
KATIE 2019

The girl is being dragged by her hair. Blood trickles down her face as though she's been pierced by a crown of thorns. Her eyes plead for help. My heart thumps. Fear surrounds me, filling my chest until it feels like it will burst. I must help her. I must.

I leave the safety of the bushes and run towards her. I lash out at her attacker. Punching, kicking, biting, screaming. Running footsteps die away, and the girl and I are left on the ground. Her mouth froths with blood. She opens it and screams. When help arrives, she tells them it was me. I attacked her. Shock steals my voice. I want to tell them it wasn't me. I tried to help. It wasn't me. But my tongue lies still. Why am I being blamed?

I woke, with my heart pounding. For a second, I wondered where I was. I imagined I was back there. The horror. The fear. Terror ebbed away, but the guilt remained like a stain on the bedsheets.

Heather's letter had awakened something in me. Something I'd rather have kept buried.

Hear me Cry

It was still dark. Something tapped at the bedroom window, making me jump. I didn't dare to look. Terrified at what might be staring back at me. The moon had slipped through a crack in the curtains and painted a stripe of pale blue across the bedroom floor. I stepped into it and pulled on my dressing gown. I needed a cup of tea. I felt around with my toes for my slippers. I left them beside my bed every night. My toes failed to find them, so I crouched on hands and knees, feeling for furry softness. There was dust and the earring I'd lost the night of the agency summer ball. I had searched the house high and low. I was sure I would find it when I was looking for something else. My hand rested upon something furry, cold and hard. I screamed.

I raised the valance and the small corpse lay there. Bile rose in my throat and I grabbed it by the tail. I ran down the stairs with it held at arm's length. I didn't want to put it in the kitchen bin so I fumbled with my left hand to open the French door lock. The door creaked open and cold air rushed in. I padded barefoot and lifted the bin lid. It was full. The stench of decomposition made me nauseous. I dropped the poor dead mouse on top of yesterday's newspaper, let the lid fall onto it, and turned to go back inside. A movement from the kitchen. A flash of grey and it was gone. My imagination was playing tricks on me again. I stepped inside, closed and locked the door, then washed and dried my hands. I flicked the kettle switch and popped a tea bag into a mug. I picked up a magazine and read an article while I waited for the water to boil. The hoot of an owl, the scream of a creature from the beach, and the rhythmic tap-tapping of branches at the kitchen window. *I must arrange to have the trees cut back.* I squeezed the tea bag and plopped it in the bin, poured milk into my mug, and stirred.

I sipped the welcome brew and climbed the stairs. I padded back into my bedroom. My legs weakened, my heart thumped, my breath caught in my throat. There on the bed, where I had lain minutes earlier, was the dead mouse.

My heart quickened. The rodent's nose was squashed and bloodied, the unmistakable marks of the trap on its face. I clasped my hands over my mouth to stop me from screaming. This mouse hadn't died a natural death. Which meant one thing and one thing only. Someone had definitely placed it there.

Someone was in the house.

Chapter 8
Regression Therapy: AUGUST 1975

I dream I'm swimming in the sea. I take gulps of the water, and the salt feeds my thirst. I wake on the stone floor, and it's dark. I'm naked and ashamed. My tongue is stuck to the roof of my mouth, and I crave water. The scrapes on my legs and hips are screaming with pain. One eye can barely open, and my cheek is swollen. I'm relieved to be alone, but then comes the rattle of a key in the lock, and I know he is back. Fear crawls from my stomach to my mouth, and I retch. There's nothing there to come up. I can't remember the last time I ate. It was before I came here. Before he dragged me by my hair. I kicked and I screamed, but he was far too powerful. He threw me into the back of a van with the ease of a farmer throwing a dead chicken to his dogs. I banged on the walls and the back doors, but all that did was bruise my knuckles. They're throbbing now. Even if I'd had the energy to attack him, I doubt I could land an effective punch. I'm too small, and he's too mean.

A slice of light appears on the wall as he opens the door and descends the steps. His shadow spreads across the wall, and the steps creak beneath his weight. I want my mammy.

'You gonnie behave yersel'?' he asks. 'Or do I need to skelp ye again?'

I pull my knees up to cover my nakedness.
'I want my clothes,' I say.
'Ye'll get them when ye've earnt them,' he says.
'I'm cold.'

He pushes me, and I fall to the side, putting my hand out to stop me from falling flat. He stands on my hand, grinding his heel into it. The bones crack and I scream in pain.

He raises his fist, and I flinch. I nurse my broken hand, but he grabs it and squeezes. I retch from the pain. I scream. He disappears back up the steps, and the door closes behind him. I cry until there are no tears left and my head bangs.

The door opens again, and he's carrying a chunk of dried bread and a glass of water. He has a scratchy grey blanket under one arm. I fall on the food and drink greedily. The water first. I've never been this thirsty. Not on hot summer days at the beach, not on sports days at school.

'I need more water,' I say. 'Please.'

He throws the blanket at me, and I cover my nakedness.

'If you don't behave yersel', I'll take it back and you'll freeze to death.'

He withdraws again, and I'm hoping he's gone for more water, but the light is switched out and I'm left alone in the cold and dark.

Chapter 9
HEATHER 2019

I awoke to a disturbing memory. I was running through a forest. Rain slashed my face, wind whipped up branches, and they tore into my flesh. I didn't know what or whom I was running from, or why I was running. I was unsure whether it was a dream, a nightmare, or reality. Was it a story I'd been told and then adopted as part of my own personal history? Who was the shape in the shadows? Why was I running? Why did that memory flash into my mind every time it rained?

It was raining now. Needles pattered on the window. I pulled the scratchy blanket round my ears and listened to the howling wind. The moonlight cast eerie shapes, and I imagined axe-murderers lurking in the trees that surrounded the Georgian building. My bladder cried to be emptied, but I closed my eyes and tried to fool it until morning when the safety of sunlight would light my way. There was a body in the single bed beside mine. Her snores rolled round the cell, the moonlight morphing her face into the mask of a demon. It reminded me of a face all those years ago. A face etched on my memory. Printed in blood and carved in shame.

Katie wrote to me. She'd tried her best to remain impassive, but her words revealed her shock at what had happened. I wasn't sure whether I would tell her the truth, but when I sat down to write it all came out.

Dear Katie,

The trouble began after I met Jovano. The circumstances of our meeting were unusual, to say the least. As the saying goes, 'Don't judge a man until you've walked a mile in his shoes.' I'm sure the same goes for a teenage girl and the love of her life.

My parents had decided to abandon convention. It was, after all, the 'swinging seventies'. We were withdrawn from the village school and we took to the open road in a camper van emblazoned with the dictum, 'If it feels good, do it'. My mother dressed in a floaty turquoise dress with wizard sleeves, a band of flowers round her head; my father in denim flares and a waistcoat, love beads buried in the hairs of his chest. My eldest brother, Charles, decided not to come. He went off somewhere east to find himself. I never knew he was lost, I said to Mother. She turned her wet eyes to the horizon as though searching for him there.

There was no TV so we read books. Books about love and lust, about intrigue and betrayal, about adventures in foreign lands. We built fires and sang to the strains of my father's guitar.

We eventually came to a field where a woman with matted locks met and welcomed us, her freckle-peppered face split by a smile. 'We've been expecting you,' she said. 'What a beautiful child.'

My youngest brother, Tom (older than me by two years), stuck out his tongue, and I kicked him on the shin. Before the bruise had turned blue we were introduced to a large group of people in a field. They congregated around a fire beside the crumbling mansion. Moss sprang from the gaping roof and climbed in at the windows.

As the strangers hugged us, my nose filled with the damp scent of twigs and pine forests. 'This is our new family,' Mother said.

'I don't want a new family,' I said.

'Shhh,' she said. 'Be polite.'

We were shown to a dormitory. 'I'm to share a room with them?' I asked, incredulous.

'We're all to share,' Mother said.

I later learned a new word: 'Commune'. It was a warm word, filled with the smells of baking bread, the sounds of children's laughter, and the sight of flowers and freedom. It soon swelled with pettiness, self-serving egos, and backstabbing. What happened there was to change my life forever. Twist it into gnarled shapes with hidden nooks and broken branches.

Chapter 10
KATIE 2018

I peer through the trees. She's being dragged by her hair. Her feet dig into the soil, trying to make purchase. Her face is disfigured, black holes where her eye sockets should be. I shout at him to stop, and he looks towards me, fear filling his eyes. He drops her and runs. I leave my hiding place and approach her battered body. Her hair is matted and thick with blood, her clothes dirty and torn. I turn her gently. Her face becomes Oliver's face. A snake slithers from his mouth, its tongue flicking towards me. Screaming.

I woke in my bed, shaking. The feeling of doom closed in around me. A canvas being painted black. My heart raced, sweat stood on my brow and ran down my face, and my stomach roiled. I must curb the panic. I must stop the attack.

After five minutes of deep breathing, I rang the solicitor and asked if I could pick up the keys. I was passed on to one of the junior clerks who said she would meet me at The Old Parsonage at three.

'I can't get there until five as I'm working,' I said.

'I don't want to be out there after dark,' she said. 'I mean, the roads are bad, and I hate driving in the rain.'

Dusk hung around the edges of daylight when we met at the gates at four and, as she offered her hand, I felt it shaking.

'Sally,' she said, looking behind her as though she was worried she'd been followed. 'Lovely to meet you in person.'

'Likewise.'

'It's a popular location. Do you know anything of the history of the house?' she asked.

'A little,' I said.

She was trying to communicate something with her eyes. A warning perhaps. Torn between professionalism and a desire to save a fellow female.

'It's a noisy house,' she said.

'Most old ones are.'

'The plumbing and electrics need work. I'm told the old lady was waiting for the warmer weather. Sad.'

Scruffy trees besieged the feral lawn; the veranda's paint flaked in patches like lichen. The windows seemed to sigh at me. It was a far cry from the first time I'd ridden up the driveway to view the house in all its splendour as an innocent bride.

'I'm about to look around. Would you join me?' I asked. I turned the key in the lock and said, 'After you.' I could tell she was torn between being polite and being desperate to leave. Manners won.

The door creaked open, and the musty scent of muddy boots and a trace of floor polish hit me, transporting me back to that time long ago. I swallowed a sense of trepidation and embraced the excitement rising within me. I could hardly believe I was back here in this house where so much had happened.

Sally entered every room as though she expected a burglar to jump out at her. Her voice was plump with false enthusiasm. I showed her through to the drawing room. Our heels click-clacked on the shiny wooden floor and echoed round the room. The fireplace wall had been taken back to the original stone, and chopped wood rested in uniform piles at either side of the hearth. The log burner sat in the middle, cold and black. I'd imagined it roaring, orange flames dancing across the walls as I sat nursing a glass of red with my feet tucked under me on the sofa.

The kitchen was just as I remembered it: roomy, uncluttered, beamed ceiling and granite island. 'The utility, laundry, and games room are in the cellar,' I said.

'Don't ask me to go with you.' Her voice quivered, and her lip trembled.

'What's wrong?'

'You must have heard the stories,' she said. 'Please don't mention this to anyone at the office. I'll be in big trouble ... I'm not supposed to gossip ...'

'It's fine,' I said. 'I know the history of the house.' I was indeed part of the history of the house.

'And you're still going to stay here? Knowing what happened?'

I nodded.

'Alone?' she said, her eyes widening in horror.

'Yes,' I said. 'Alone.'

Chapter 11
KATIE: NOW

Your office is sparse. A single window, desk, a couch, a filing cabinet where I expect you keep details of all your mad patients. No pot plant or exclusive lamp you might expect in the office of an eminent psychiatrist.

'What do you want to talk about today?' you ask me.

'I don't really want to talk at all if I'm honest,' I tell you.

'How about a sentence starter?'

'Oh, one of your games,' I sigh, annoyed. 'They bore me.'

You ignore me and continue.

'How about, I was struggling with …?'

'Boring,' I say.

'Try it,' you say. 'Let's see where it takes us.'

'I was struggling with …' I pause. I could make something up and beat you at your own game, but surprisingly, I feel like telling the truth.

I was struggling with feelings of grief, guilt, and remorse. As I walked into town, I thought I saw Oliver in the distance. The same age, same build, same blond hair. My heart thudded, and my body shook. I strained my eyes to see. He was holding the hand of a woman in a beige mac. I hurried my footsteps to catch up with them. The woman spun, her eyes resting on me, wondering perhaps why I was staring at her son. I was desperate to look into his face, willing him to turn round. The woman tugged at his hand, as though to show ownership. 'Yes?' she said. 'Do you want a photograph?'

'Sorry, I thought you were someone I know,' I said.
'Clearly not,' she said.
Rudely, I thought.
'Your son reminds me of …' She tutted and yanked her child aside. He turned towards me now, and I could see the resemblance to Oliver was confined to the back view. His eyes were too close together. His front teeth intact. And, of course, he was far too young. He was the age Oliver was then. Not the age he'd be now.
'Come on, Caleb,' she said, crossing the road and stepping onto a bus.
'That must have been quite a shock for you, to see a child you thought was Oliver?' you say interrupting me from my thoughts.
'It was,' I say. You lean forwards and touch the photograph of your son. An involuntary movement, I think, and for a second I believe you sympathised with me. 'It was a terrible shock. It took a while for my heartbeat to return to normal. I wandered the streets aimlessly for a while, holding back tears. My heart yearning for Oliver. Seeing his face in every shop window, hearing his voice in every boy's chuckle.'
'That must have been very distressing, but perfectly natural given what you suffered. How did you deal with it?'
I don't really know how to answer you. I'm not even sure you want me to. Your questions resurrect memories. Some of them I'd prefer to keep buried.

I'd long since stopped practising my Catholic duties, but I chanced upon a church and stepped inside. The priest was lifting an errant Bible from the floor and asked if he could help me. Hot tears ran down my face and he took me into his quarters to make me a cup of tea. He was a gentle soul and so easy to talk to I found myself telling him all about what happened in Prestwick.

It all started on holiday. We spent whole summers there. My three brothers and I. We stayed with family. Aunt Isobel was a seamstress, and she took in ironing. Her flat was a cave filled with other people's clothes. We made forts from Mr Murphy's oversized shirts. We piled up the black plastic bags, erecting walls to keep out our foe, armaments against the marauding Sassenachs. I was most disappointed when I realised we were the marauding Sassenachs.

The black sewing machine with the huge pedal whirred all day, and the needles darted through the cloth, chugging like a train on a track while Aunt Isobel puffed on her cigarette until the ash grew long. Wedding dresses hung from door frames, each a promise of a new life filled with Silver Cross prams and televisions from Radio Rentals. I wondered how many of those dresses danced their way to the divorce courts.

You weren't allowed to mention divorce in our house. It was a dirty word. One followed by black silences and whispered snapping. Mam believed marriage was for life. Life. No matter what. 'Till death do us part. What God hath joined, let no man put asunder.'

I remembered the journeys in Dad's Morris Marina, through green fields and over grey roads, hugged by mountains wrapped in mist. Sick bags stuffed under seats. Sandwiches of tinned salmon and Tunnocks snowballs. Stopping at Dumfries for flasks of coffee. Seagulls wheeling and arcing across the sky. Swooping down to steal crusts, leaving behind their mocking screech.

Just when it felt that the journey would never end, we'd arrive at Aunt Isobel's block of flats. Bladders bursting, we'd race up the concrete stairwell which boasted lewd graffiti and the scent of Jeyes Fluid. The odour of burnt toast and stale smoke greeted us as Aunt Isobel threw open the door to welcome us with a happy Scottish squeal. A homely flat with tartan carpets and mismatched furniture. Miniatures of Scotch lined the walls in various shapes. Golf balls and Scottie dogs, bells, jars, and boots. Kilted men ready to kill the English.

'Come away in, hen, come on, ma wee darling,' Aunt Isobel used to say. Uncle Peter sat by the fire, knocking muck onto the hearth from the pipe he never lit and speaking unintelligible Irish. In the whole of my childhood, I never understood one word he said. If he stuck his thumb in the air, we knew he was happy. If the thumb curled into a fist, we knew to run.

It was on one of the most fun-filled days that the terrible thing happened.

Chapter 12
HEATHER: LETTER TO KATY 2019

Some of the group hugged trees. I thought they were bonkers at first, but Dad told me to hold my tongue when I voiced my opinion. 'It's okay for her to feel that,' said Adrik, a bearded man in a kaftan and dark glasses, who smoked herbal cigarettes. 'Let the child speak freely.' He wasn't so keen on free speech when I called him a creepy bastard as he tried to hug me. 'The child has issues,' he said.

'Yeah, I hate BO,' I said.

Gone was the old-fashioned discipline. When we lived in the house, a mouthful of cheek resulted in a clip around the ear or a wallop on the backside. In the commune we were 'listened to'. We were allowed to make our own choices so we could learn from our own mistakes. Only we didn't. My brothers ran wild, and I ran wilder.

When I met *him* for the first time, I wasn't hugging a tree but climbing it. The branches were streaks of black lightning across a silver sky. A raven sat on the highest twigs, a portent. My wild curls danced as I climbed higher and higher. He stood underneath with a sketch pad and pencil. 'What are you fucking doing?' I shouted down. He ignored me and continued to scribble. Silver moonlight wriggled through the leaves. 'I said –'

'I heard what you said.'

'So?'

'What's it look like?'

'Looks like you're too sissy to climb a tree, so you're sitting there drawing like a girl.'

'Like a girl?' he replied.

'Yeah,' I said.

'Michelangelo, Rembrandt, Picasso, Dali...' And to prove me wrong again he threw down his sketch pad, put the pencil between his teeth, and clambered up the tree, sitting in a branch opposite me, his blond head a new moon against the darkening sky.

'How long you been here?' I asked him.

He tucked the pencil behind an ear.

'Couple of years.' His accent was the strangest I'd ever heard. He obviously picked up lilts from every town he'd visited and mixed them with the English countryside. An eclectic swirl of stretched vowels and tentative glottal fricatives.

He told me how he'd been born in Athens to British parents who had dropped out of mainstream life and travelled with a commune to Istanbul and eventually to India. They'd partied on the beaches of Goa and went on to a place called Freak Street in Kathmandu, where ganja was in constant supply. I had no idea then what ganja was, but I wasn't about to expose my ignorance.

'Was it filthy, like this place?' I said.

'This is a palace compared to some I've been to. One place in the Surrey countryside had no toilet doors.'

My face must have shown my disgust.

'Exactly,' he said. 'Freaking perverts removed them all.'

'What the hell for?'

'Something to do with freedom.'

'What's that you have there?' I asked, pointing to a small transparent plastic dish he'd taken from his dungaree pocket.

'This is Dylan's house.'

'What the hell is Dylan?'

'A daddy longlegs. Fascinating creatures.'

I shuddered. Unlike my brothers, I didn't get pleasure from pulling the legs off them, but I hated the way they drifted and lolloped, vacillating over your head like an octopus treading water.

'I've seen boys pull the legs off them.'

'They don't need to be pulled off. A simple pinch is enough to trigger their internal system that discharges the leg. It's a way to stay alive if something is trying to devour his limb.'

'Does it hurt?' I asked him.

'It's up for debate. They can recover a surprising degree of mobility by learning to walk differently. In some species the males wrap their legs round the females to keep them in place and even shake her during sex. Females are often more dominant because they're bigger and stronger. I've seen females tear the legs off a male because they don't want to mate with him.'

'I don't blame them,' I said.

The boy was an artist. He wanted to sell some of his paintings, but his parents wouldn't allow it. They had shunned capitalism and all its entrapments. All commune members were expected to take a vow of poverty. We weren't allowed to own personal possessions other than clothing and tools. I secretly wished for pink princess dresses and hair ribbons, musical jewellery boxes, handbags, and sparkly shoes.

I tried to believe in it all for my parents' sake, but then I found out the secret. The weight of it was far too heavy for one so young.

I was about to write all about Jovano, but Mother's footsteps echoed down the corridor, and my story fizzled out.

I imagined Katie's disappointment. She was impatient to read the truth, but I had no more time as it was my turn to clean the chapel that evening. Mother called to me and swished away from the cell door, leaving behind a waft of authority and disapproval.

It was strange, but now that I'd begun to write my story, I found I didn't want to stop. I wanted to confess it all.

Chapter 13
KATIE 1976

I stopped talking altogether sometime after it happened. I woke from a troubled sleep and couldn't speak. My dad asked me if I wanted a morning roll, and I nodded in response.

'Cat got your tongue?'

I shook my head.

'What's the matter?' he asked.

I shrugged. Mam felt my brow with a cold hand.

'Have you got a sore throat?'

I shook my head.

'But you've lost your voice?'

I nodded. They discussed me later that day. They must've thought because I couldn't speak that I couldn't hear, too.

'Do you think she's putting it on?'

'I'm not sure. What do you think?'

'Maybe she's seeking attention.'

Attention was the last thing I wanted. I'd have been happy to become translucent and to fade completely into invisibility. I didn't want to die as such, but I wanted my existence to fold in on itself until no one noticed my presence. Like a caterpillar returning to its chrysalis. The slow curling of the wings, the split repaired, me a quiescent insect pupa.

There began a round of visits to different professionals. It started with our GP, who initially referred me to an ENT specialist. He did various tests and concluded there was nothing physically wrong. It was probably psychological. It was a difficult age. I'd been through a lot. If they ignored it, it would probably go away.

It didn't go away.

Then came the round of psychologists. Each believing they held the key to open my voice box. Each failing. Finally, Mr Anand, who said I was selective mute. Probably brought on by trauma. It didn't feel selective. I wasn't choosing to be dumb. I just couldn't speak.

I was the strange silent child. The one others elbowed in corridors because I never fought back. I had no unkind words with which to defend myself, and physical fighting just wasn't part of who I was. There were, of course, the teachers who were convinced they could cane speech out of me and those who thought bags of sweets might elicit a verbal response. None of their techniques worked. They served only to determine whether I liked them or hated them. The worst thing was they turned a blind eye while I was bullied. Bashed in the face with a lunch tray, shoved into the mud in the yard, head held under water in the toilets. They weren't particularly inventive forms of torture, but the bullies weren't particularly intelligent.

There were times when I tried to force out my voice, but it remained trapped. I tried to squeeze it between my lips, sneak it between the gaps in my teeth, but it could not be forced. Sometimes a syllable leaked out. Sometimes the merest of whispers escaped, and sometimes a squeak burst through and the whole class looked at me as though I'd run naked across the room. The school day was one long cringe, one long, drawn-out torturous squirm. I winced the days away. Mr Donnelly, my teacher, made it his business to ask me whether there were problems at home. I'm sure he was desperate for me to confess to all manner of abuse and neglect, just so he could be my saviour. They all wanted to solve my problem, the do-gooders in their long-collar shirts and sickening sideburns.

The only person I could talk to was Aunt Isobel. I asked her not to tell my parents because they'd think I was choosing not to speak, and I wasn't. She said she understood and she did. She was the only person in the world who did. It was only on her twice-yearly trips to visit us that speech came and only when there was no one else in the room.

Every night as I slept, his face invaded my dreams. I imagined he was coming for me. I started to wet the bed. I woke in the early hours in a warm pool which soon cooled. I tried to go back to sleep perched on the dry edge, shivering, a growing sense of shame spreading like the wet patch. After I woke stinking and shivering, I'd cover the stain with a blanket. Mother discovered it later that day and cast her worried eyes over me before catching me alone and asking me what was wrong.

I shook my head and shrugged.

'You've never wet the bed since you were three years old,' she said.

Making my mortification a deeper stain on my conscience, I shrugged again.

'You have to tell me when you've done that so I can change the sheets.'

That night, I slept on the camp bed, my mattress propped up to dry, my humiliation scrubbed with washing powder, the stain fading to sepia. The next night as I got into a newly made bed, it crinkled beneath me.

'I've put you a waterproof sheet on, just in case it happens again.'

It was like sleeping on a crisp packet. Every turn was evidence of my secret shame. It did happen again. Night after night. Doctors were consulted, drinks were stopped at bedtime, my urine was measured and tested. There was no physical cause. It had nothing to do with my kidneys. My bladder let me down night after uncomfortable night, yet it was in perfect working order.

I could never stay at friends' houses in case it happened there. Imagine the shame! Not that I got invited anymore. I was the quiet, shy freak who didn't speak.

Chapter 14
HEATHER 2019

I watched the sun rise while tears turned to ice on my cheeks. Mother Mistress insisted on walking with me to confession. She wanted to talk to me about the vows of obedience. Sisters must ask permission to do even simple things like bathe.

'I don't think anyone should have to ask permission to bathe,' I said.

'But that's how it is here. If you want to belong to this community, you must respect the vow of obedience.'

I sighed. 'Yes, Mother.'

I'm ashamed to say I hurried my duties so I could get back to writing the pages. I wanted to remind Katie about the time before the commune. At home in the village. I'd been thinking about it a lot.

We went to a lovely school. The dinners were even better than my mother's culinary delights. Lamb stew with the sweetest, most orangey carrots you've ever seen. Jam roly-poly and custard. Real comfort food.

The priest, Father McMahon, was an old man with a mainly bald head and a kindly smile. I'm saying he was old, but he was probably younger than I am now. I imagine he was only in his early forties. Everyone over thirty seemed ancient in those days.

I remember the shape of his head in the confessional, like a foetus against the black mesh. An umbilical cord to the Lord. I could never remember any real sins so I used to make them up. 'Bless me, Father, for I have sinned. It has been two weeks since my last confession. I hit my brother, I was cheeky to my mam, I made my bedroom a mess.' Unlike the previous priest, instead of making us say three Hail Marys and ten Our Fathers, he gave me a practical penance.

I imagine your face, Katie. Its pained expression. You have no need to worry. I'm not going to tell you he touched me up. Nothing as clichéd as that. No, by practical penance I mean he told me to buy some sweets for my brother, or make my mother a cuppa, or tidy my bedroom. I liked that he was different. Modern. I didn't buy my brother anything or make my room neat, so I'll probably go to Hell. I did make Mam a cup of tea. She said it was 'Water bewitched and tea begrudged,' and poured it down the sink. Father McMahon never asked me whether I had completed our penance; he said that was between God and me.

I marvelled at God being everywhere and seeing everything. I wondered how fast he could run and whether he watched people having sex and, if so, whether that made him a pervert. Nigel Jenkins told me that Mr Bolton from number sixty-three was a pervert. He knew because his dad's brother-in-law had seen him watching a couple in a car parked in Doggie Wood.

Father McMahon sat behind the grille, his sad face turned towards the light. He clung on to the last hairs on his head like a drowning man clinging to reeds on the riverbank, white wisps swept behind an ear. I could see the thin tube leading to his hearing aid, and the irony struck me that the person who listened to my sins was deaf. Criss-crosses of light seeped along the floor and up the walls. He detected my presence in the confessional, and turned towards me. The corners of his mouth curled upwards. His eyes remained untouched by the smile, though; the melancholy still sat in their irises.

I wondered why he became a priest. Guilt perhaps? The need to atone? But for what? Undoubtedly, he was as messed-up as the rest of us, and maybe listening to our tragic confessions made him feel better about his shitty life. I wondered whether he'd tell anyone about the pitiful case of the girl and her confessions.

I imagine, Katie, you're dying to know what I confessed. I can almost taste your impatience.

My teacher, Mrs Brownlow, had a daughter with callipers on her legs. She was born with some deformity. Mrs Brownlow spent every spare minute in church. I imagined she was praying for her daughter to walk normally. God never answered her prayers. I'd been praying for a pony for three years, and He hadn't answered mine either. I wondered whether, like Father McMahon, God was deaf. I asked Mrs Brownlow one day if she thought the Almighty might be hearing impaired, and she threatened to slap my face. She said it was blasphemy.

She made me stand in the corner of the yard at playtime with my face turned to the wall. A daddy longlegs crawled out of a crack in a brick and bobbed along the wall, like some kind of alien craft landing on the moon. I held on to a leg to stop him escaping, but he just left the limb behind and flapped away. I wondered how many legs he could lose and still survive. I wondered why he had six legs and Mrs Brownlow's daughter didn't even have one that worked properly.

She was called Anne, with an E. She was most insistent about the E. We were friends for a short time until I was asked to their house for tea. Something happened, and I was never invited back.

Some of the quacks thought it was connected to the suicidal thoughts. They're still there. Every day. It's a way out. An easy way. Only I can't bring myself to do it, and then I feel even more of a failure than I already am.

I don't have any plans as such, but I imagine doing it. I picture the sisters finding me hanging from the ceiling. Or sometimes I think about stealing drugs from the pharmacy and taking an overdose, or taking a sharp object from the kitchen and cutting my wrists.

A door clashed interrupting my train of thought. Footsteps approached, running faster.

'Sister, come quick. It's Mr Fraser. Hurry, bring Father. He needs the last rites.'

No rest for the wicked. I made the sign of the cross and stood.

I might have reassured Katie I wouldn't act on my suicidal thoughts. The truth was, I wasn't sure myself whether I'd act on them or not.

Chapter 15
KATIE: NOW

We're sitting in your office. The sun shines through the gaps in the blinds, fanning across the desk and lighting up the paperweight with the picture of your son. He's not unlike Oliver. Surprising when you're so dark. There are no pictures of your wife, but I'm assuming she's a little blue-eyed blonde thing who melts whenever you flick those black lashes.

'So tell me about a time after the trauma.' You sit back, hands tucked behind your head. 'Tell me about the nightmares.'

I sigh, not wanting to go back there, but knowing I must if I'm ever to move on. I pick up the paperweight, and you reach nervously towards me.

'Sorry,' I say, placing it back on the desk but making a mental note to use this in future if we have a session about Oliver and you fail to understand me being overprotective. You couldn't even bear me to pick up a paperweight containing your son's photo, I'll say. So don't bloody lecture me about getting to grips with things.

I remember my childhood bedroom. Lilac door, Holly Hobbie wallpaper. Jewellery hung from a mug tree, clothes spread across a chair, my dressing gown draped from a hook on the door. After dark the same clothes became dead bodies, the orange beads viscera strewn from the branches of a tree, Holly Hobbie the Grim Reaper, and my dressing gown a man hanging from a gibbet. As cars passed on the road outside, the headlights cast trapezium shapes in the shadows. The man dangling from the gibbet moved, and I swore I could hear him moan. I lay with the blankets pulled up to my eyes, not daring to move, not daring to make a sound, not daring to sleep in case the Grim Reaper took me.

Sleep was some children's saviour. Their sanctuary away from a cruel world. A place where reality could be forgotten, and a world of wonder could be explored. Classmates told tales of dreams about unicorns, rainbows, fairies, and houses made of gingerbread. My dreams were places of torture, death, disease, murder. And then the waking nightmares began.

I woke to the sound of dripping and the feeling of weight on my feet. As though rain was leaking from the guttering outside my bedroom window and someone was sitting on my legs. Then there was the sound of metal grinding on metal. I opened my eyes and a creature sat at the end of my bed. Its body was black like a huge cat's, but its face was that of a devil. Blood dribbled from its eyes onto the top sheet. It held two knives which it ground together, the metal grating. The bedroom was vivid around me. I was awake and not dreaming. I tried to get up, I tried to scream, but I couldn't move. I couldn't make a sound.

'Were your dreams very lucid?' you ask when I tell you about them.

'They weren't dreams,' I say. 'They were real. I know how mad it sounds, but it wasn't a dream. I was awake. I used to wake with blood on the sheets.'

'Maybe you just got your period?' you say.

'No, my mother thought the same thing, but I hadn't started yet, and the blood was at the bottom where the beast sat. Not where I slept.'

'Okay. Let's leave it there for today.'

Chapter 16
Regression Therapy: SEPTEMBER 1975

I've already examined every wall, every nook and cranny for an escape route. The walls are thick stone, and there are no windows. It's like an underground cave. I have no toilet, so I have to use a corner of the room. I squat like an animal. The stench is unbearable.

My hand throbs, the swelling has gone down, and the black bruises are fading to yellow. My fingers are a different shape from what they once were. My back and hips are sore from sleeping on the floor. It's always too cold to sleep properly, and I can never find a comfortable position. I find some straw in an old wooden box and pile it under the blanket to create a makeshift mattress. It's more comfortable, but then I'm cold because I don't have a blanket to go over me. I try to fashion it so I can have some straw under me and some of the blanket over me, but the blanket's too small and the straw just ends up spreading all over. I'm cold and hungry and thirsty and I want my mammy.

My own heartbeat pulses in my ears. Terror runs through me. I'm waiting for him to come.

The key rattles in the lock, a splash of light hits the wall as the door opens, and his feet clatter on the stone steps. Fear crawls up my spine, panic grips me and my whole body shakes. I feel like I'll be sick but there's nothing in my stomach to come up. He's carrying water and a bowl of something on a plate with a slice of bread next to it. It smells like soup. Am I really getting something hot to eat? I will him to fall and injure himself. Even if it means the soup spills and I don't get to taste it. Trip, slip, fall, smash your head wide open. Go on. Fall. Please God make him fall. I will run up the steps and out into the world. Someone will come and help me. They'll take me back to my mam and dad, and I'll never have to see him again. I'll sleep in my warm bed surrounded by my family.

Every step is assured. He doesn't fall. My heart aches. I'm not sure where I find the courage to speak. Before this I've never been cold or thirsty or hungry. I've never wanted for anything.

'Please can I have another blanket?' I ask.

He places the water on the floor, throws the bread at me, and walks back up the steps with the bowl.

'Is that soup? Is it for me? Please can I have it? It smells nice. Please. I'll behave. I promise.'

He ignores me. Tears of frustration burn my eyes and burst down my cheeks. I hate him. I scream. He puts down the soup and rushes towards me with his fists clenched and a murderous look on his face. I crouch in a ball, protecting my face with my arms.

'Yell as much as ye like. There's naebiddy tae hear ye,' he snaps. 'No one around for miles. The only thing ye'll get fae calling out is a sair throat. They're no' looking for ye. They think ye drowned in the sea.' Panic fills me. I'm trying to remember what my mother looks like. I see her face. Anxious, crying, calling my name. I see my dad with his arm around her comforting her. I see a police officer telling them there's no hope. I'm gone for good. I try to imagine them looking for me. Tears sting my cheeks.

I turn my face to the wall.

Chapter 17
HEATHER: LETTER TO KATIE 2019

Dear Katie,
One of my favourite memories of home before communal life was lying in bed with my dad sitting at my feet, reading me tales about the North country. He smelled of Old Spice and Halls Mentho-Lyptus, and his stubble grazed my cheek as he pecked me good night. His deep tones, like the scrunch of boots on gravel, lulled me to sleep with stories about witches and wanderers, fairies and fishermen.

I realised they weren't allowing us to talk with affection of anything that had gone before. All stories of our prior life were to be negative, filled with the sickness and corruption of the outside world. Reinforcing why we'd eschewed it in favour of communal life.

It was 1983. We sat round the campfire, and Dad told tales of the mines. The veins pulsing beneath the skin of the land. Seam upon seam coughing out tonnes of hard coal. How the cavernous mouth swallowed up him and his marras, and the claustrophobic tunnels suffocated them. Their lungs burning with dust, their muscles aching, tasting nothing but coal at every meal. Men whose bones were crushed under runaway carts. Men whose lungs turned black from decades of inhaling dust. Men who were buried under falling coal, sliced by its razor-sharp edges. Digging, drilling, blasting. Dying.

There were no tales of the camaraderie between the men. How they drank together in the working men's club, raised pigeons in their allotments, and kept chickens that provided us with eggs. Nothing about the Big Meeting in Durham, the parade of banners, the brass bands, the speeches. We loved to go and ride the carousel, eat toffee apples and hot dogs while baking in the July sun.

When Dad went to the club it was merely to show his face and have two pints with his marras. He always returned promptly and tipped up his pay packet to Mam, who budgeted to the nearest half-penny for the week. There were stories of the siren screaming through the village, signalling a disaster at the pit. The women running, aprons still tied to their middles, babies glued to hips, worry etched into their faces. Pulling out bodies of boys too young to marry and evermore to lie in a cold cemetery with flowers wilting and wind chimes jangling. Then there were the songs. Eerie tunes, and lyrics about blood dried on pit-black meat. Bairns and bones buried beneath mountainsides. The hard face of the coal board and mine owners who cared more about profit than people.

One day, Dad was feeling particularly maudlin. Staring into the terracotta flames as he poked the kindling with a stick. Sparks scattered across the dark sky, dancing and flashing like female fireflies luring unsuspecting males to their death. We were begging for a story. The tales helped stitch the old life to the new. The boys wanted him to tell about The Lampton Worm or the Pollard's Boar, but I asked over and over for the tale of the Fairies of Rothley Mill.

'Once upon a time there lived a worthless boy named Ralph,' Dad began.

'Aw, Dad, she always gets her own way,' Tom said.

'Hush,' said Dad. 'I'll tell the Pollard's Boar another night.'

My brother sulked and poked the fire, but he listened intently to the story anyway.

'The worthless boy was the Miller's son, but he was as lazy as his father was hard-working. He was a mischievous boy, and he was a cruel boy. He took great delight in hurting all the little creatures of the woods. He stole the eggs from the linnet's nest and beat the field mice to death with beech sticks. He caught young wild rabbits and kept them in boxes until they fretted and died. He pulled up the bluebells and scattered them throughout the wood. He kicked frogs as they hopped by on their way back to their spawn.

'Many a time his father scolded him and beat him for his cruelty. He warned his son that one day he'd be punished, but the boy ignored him and continued to bully. Every evening he sat at the top of an old kiln near the mill and threw stones at a squirrel that scampered in the chestnut tree, and the thrush perched on a branch singing as the sun set.

'One night he sat practising his cruel sport and heard an unusual noise. A tinkling sound. Like all bullies, he was afraid. The sound came nearer and nearer, until he saw a procession of fairies, tiny and perfectly formed, with long golden hair and dresses made from daffodils. They rode horses with saddles, bridles and reins made of daisy petals, and each horse's bridle had a bell, no bigger than a raindrop, which tinkled prettily. Ralph watched them dismount, tie their horses to the rushes, and enter the kiln. Through a spyhole he saw them light a fire with twigs and fill a large pot with water from the burn, then add porridge to it. Some fairies stirred the porridge and sang while it bubbled, some played pipes that they made from hollow stalks, and some danced in the light of the fire. Then they each took an acorn cup, dipped it into the porridge pot, and feasted. They finished feasting, dancing, singing and put out the fire, then rode away, the bells once again tinkling.

'The next night the same thing happened, and the night after that. Ralph hated the peace and the pleasure these small creatures were providing and vowed to find some way of hurting them. The next night, before he climbed on to the top of the kiln, he put a large stone in his pocket. He waited until the fairies were gathered around their porridge pot, tasting it to see if it was ready, and flung down the stone right in the middle of them all. Hot porridge splashed in all directions, and the fairies jumped backwards, rubbing their eyes and crying out in pain. 'Burnt and scalded!' they cried. 'Burnt and scalded!' They hopped around, holding their hands up to their faces.

'Ralph laughed.

'When they heard the laughter, a hundred tiny pairs of eyes were upon him, and a hundred tiny fingers pointed towards him. 'Burnt and scalded! Burnt and scalded!' They were so angry that Ralph shivered in fear. He jumped down from the kiln and ran home, but the fairies leapt onto their horses and galloped after him. Under the trees, over the grass, through the wicket. On and on they chased Ralph. Long before Ralph reached home, they had caught up with him. The fairy at the front of his posse came right up to Ralph and dealt him a blow at the bottom of his back. Ralph fell and lay trembling in the grass. The fairy riders retreated and all became still and quiet again. Ralph lifted himself up and walked the rest of the way home. He felt no pain but he was limping. He could no longer walk like an ordinary boy. Although he told himself he would soon be well, he always walked with a limp. The fairies had justly punished him for all his bad deeds against them and their fellow creatures.'

Just as Dad finished telling the story, his voice no more than a whisper, Karma's stick tapped the ground, and his limping frame came into view.

'Burnt and scalded! Burnt and scalded!' we chanted under the light of the moon, then burst out laughing.

Karma's lip curled in distaste, and he beat the fire with his stick until it was nothing but glowing embers.

Chapter 18
KATIE: 2019

Since what had happened to Oliver, I'd been going to church. Not the Catholic church of my youth but a spiritualist church in town. I always imagined someone from the other side would be able to tell me what had happened. Spirits were supposed to see everything, right?

The church was in a Victorian terraced house behind Tittybottle Park. Identical stone buildings sat side by side. The gate squealed open, and I strode up the path, my heels click-clacking on the ground, my umbrella used like a walking stick in time with the clack. I opened the door and walked straight in, pretending to feel confident but actually feeling shy and a little afraid. A woman in a turquoise hat bid me hello. A feather in her headwear fluttered, and I imagined the bird was still alive but pinned to the felt and anxious to escape.

'Ye're one of our parishioners?'

I wasn't sure whether the woman was asking or telling, but I nodded, and she marched me through the inner door into a room which looked like my granny's old parlour. A parrot sat in a cage in the corner, pecking at a block of cereal. Green velvet curtains surrounded the bay window. I was dizzy at the sight of wallpaper bearing peacocks, and a gaudy carpet. Chairs were arranged in a circle, and a man in a black suit who resembled an undertaker placed leaflets on the unoccupied ones. A strange collection of people sat: a young man with a ginger beard who wore braces to hold up his jeans, a pale woman in a striped jumper, an old woman with grey curls hanging in links like butchers' sausages. We sat. The suited man stood at the fireplace.

'Divine spirit of the pure white light of love and truth, we call upon you to shine down your light onto this gathering of your servants. Take our hands and lead us on a journey beyond the mystic veil of our two worlds. We ask for your protection from the dark forces. We ask in the name of the Lord. Amen.'

There followed a stilted 'Amen' from each of the congregation. I coughed in embarrassment. The man at the front nodded to the woman wearing the dead bird, and she closed the curtains, enveloping us in obscurity. He spoke, his voice a curl of Scottish vowels, stretching and turning in the dark air.

'I have Valerie here. Does anybiddy have a Valerie in the spirit world?'

The man in the braces stood. 'It's my mum,' he said.

The man at the front, who I had learned was called James, turned to the younger man.

'She said you have to let her go. She's at peace. She's with Belinda, and they're laughing together.'

'Belinda's her sister,' the young man said.

'Who's Gerry?'

'That's my father,'

'She says to take care of Gerry and make sure he gets his heart checked.'

'Aye, he's had angina. We have an appointment at the hospital on Monday week.'

James jerked his head to the side and shook his head. 'Hauld on, you're talking too quick.' He paused. 'Is there anybiddy here who knows Charlie?'

Two people stood. The woman with the sausage curls and the woman in the striped jumper.

'It's for you,' he said to the woman in the striped jumper.

The other woman sat, disappointment making her mouth a crescent.

'Charlie says you've no tae pawn the watch. Does that make sense?'

Her face reddened.

'I'd never pawn it, tell him,' she said.

'He says yer a lying wee shite, and he's seen ye checking out the prices in the windae at Ramsdens.'

At this, the woman paled and sat.

'Sorry, I'm only telling ye whit he said.'

I thought it was pretty humdrum. Anyone could have made things up. People believed what they wanted to believe.

And then he faced me, and I couldn't believe what he said.

'I have someone here for you,' he said. 'He says he knows what happened. He knows, and you're in danger. You need to leave. You need to get out of that house.'

My hands shook, tears poured down my cheeks. The man's eyes rolled. His face transfigured into the weirdest mask. The nose protruded, the jaw widened, the eyes turned red. The woman in the striped jumper grabbed my right hand. The man on the other side of me grabbed my left. His hand was clammy and I let mine go limp so I had as little contact with him as possible. I squirmed inside. When everyone in the circle was holding hands, the woman with the dead bird chanted, and everyone except me joined in.

'Lord, by the faith we have in Your merits, protect us from evil, protect us from Satan's attacks and afflictions. Fill us with the gift of the Holy Spirit. We praise You, we thank You, we adore You.' The man continued to change, his whole body shaking as he fell to the floor.

They chanted. No one lifted a hand to help James. They just uttered the words over and over until he lay still and his face returned to normal. He slumped, limp, spent.

Dead-bird woman stood at the fireplace and said, 'All rise.'

The circle of people stood.

'Divine Spirit, we offer thanks for all the work You have done today. Thank you for bringing us further evidence of life in the everlasting realm. We thank Your guides and those who inspire us. We ask for positive energy to be sent to those in need. We plead for protection on our earthly journey until we meet again in the everlasting realm beyond our world. Go in peace and love.'

The circle broke, and people chatted as though what had happened was an everyday occurrence. Striped-jumper woman must have noticed my pale face and scared eyes.

'Don't be afraid,' she said. 'We're protected.'

'What was that?' I asked. 'I've never seen anything like it. He looked like a demon.'

'We try our best to protect from bad spirits, but sometimes they get through. That was a bad one. It's a shame, but don't let it put you off.'

What terrified me most about the whole thing was that I knew who the bad spirit was.

Chapter 19
HEATHER: 2019

I barely had time to splash my face with water and run a brush across my teeth. I'd squeezed the toothpaste until it was flatter than a sheet of paper. Sisters took the vow of poverty seriously. Nothing was wasted, nothing thrown away. Possessions were forbidden. They were merely things for our use. The pen for my use. The Bible for my use. Sister Rose joked about her false teeth, calling them the teeth for her use.

Katie had left me a note asking questions: *What name did you give to them when you entered? You can't have given your own.* My eyes narrowed and my mind closed. That wasn't something I was willing to divulge. I didn't want to tell her. She wouldn't insist. She needed the story.

Please will you tell me about the commune? I'm sure people would be fascinated by your unusual way of life.

I placed the pen between my teeth, smoothed a stray hair, and tucked it into my headband. I slid the pen from my mouth and sat poised, ready to write.

Dear Katie,

All grown-ups considered themselves our parents. It didn't stop my brothers from getting up to mischief while I was doing the dirty work, cleaning out the goat, Mountain Girl. She had a wicked glint in her one remaining eye, the other having been extracted with a stick by a feral youth called Griffen Liberty. I always kept my back to the fence in case she decided to run at me and butt me. I had nightmares about being impaled on those horns.

It was also my job to feed and water the chickens and collect the eggs. Ember Heggarty, the largest of the brood, pecked at my fingers as I tried to extract her precious clutch.

The grounds were surrounded by trees. I began to love trees the way other girls loved dolls, or pretty dresses, or boys. Trees were my friends. I loved the shape of them, the smell, the way they whispered secrets in the breeze and rustled in the wind. My favourite was the beech. Tall, broad and sturdy, with limbs that were made for climbing. His leaves green with wavy edges, igniting in autumn to coppery bronze. I hated it when the men severed one of his limbs to make a walking stick.

I realised why these people hugged trees. Trees were far nicer than the people in there. I'm not ashamed to say I hugged that tree, I talked to it, told it my dreams, and shared my secrets. I climbed its branches and hid in its leaves. I even had nightmares about it. I imagined all kinds of horrors: aphids attacking, borer infestations, mildew, beech bark disease, and bleeding canker. I lay awake at night, worrying about brown liquid oozing from the trunk; wilting leaves and dead branches piled up in my mind; a stack for November 5th. In hot summers I saw it scorched; in cold winters frost-bitten and solitary. My dreams were coloured pale ochre, burnished copper, and blood red. I pictured it growing with mature dignity, hosting moss, ferns, and climbing plants; developing lumps on its trunk like calluses. I'm not sure whether this was an unnatural childhood obsession or merely a distraction from the horrors of the commune. The things I eventually had to get away from.

It was 1983. I can't remember the month. Jovano had a plan. In 1976 he'd trekked the hippie trail with his parents. From Europe they'd journeyed to Turkey: Istanbul, Erzurum, then into Iran to Mashhad, across the Afghan border into Herat through Southern Afghanistan, over the Khyber Pass into Pakistan via Rawalpindi and Lahore to the Indian frontier. He wanted to travel like his parents. Together. In freedom, he said, silver moons rising in his eyes.

For months he plotted and planned our escape. We eyed my parents' old camper van, watching where the elders hid the keys after the infrequent times they'd used it to leave the commune. Some of the community hand-sewed bedding and clothing to sell at the market, so we could buy anything we needed but couldn't make or grow ourselves. Jovano was tasked with loading and unloading the van. He was able to ferret away pennies so we'd have petrol and food for our journey. When I dreamt of our flight, my feet were glued to the ground while we were chased by demons. I imagined bearded boffins and concubines in kaftans who dragged us back to the cold kitchen, tied us to a table, and tortured us with medieval devices, chanting incantations about wood spirits.

I lay on my bunk in the dormitory, looking at a sketch Jovano had done for me of an acorn which had fallen from the largest oak in the grounds. He had expertly caught the way the scales on the cupule caught the light. The little nut put me in mind of a Scotsman with a feather tucked into his Tam O'Shanter.

A rhythmic dunk, dunk, dunk chopped through the air and seeped through my concentration. My heart missed a beat when I realised what the sound was. I must have looked like some kind of weird phantom, running across the grass, my hair wild, my arms outstretched, my fingers curled like bare twigs in winter. The noise escaping from me wasn't a scream or a moan but a mixture of the two. There were six wounds that I could see; injured flesh exposed to the elements. Adrik was swinging back the axe, ready to take another swipe at my beech tree. I pounced, aware of the salt on his brow.

'What are you doing? You mad bitch. Get off me!'

I gripped the arm that held the axe, my teeth sinking into his shoulder. I could taste metal, and the material of his shirt was bark on my tongue. He rolled onto the ground, and I rolled on top of him. The axe fell onto the grass with a muffled thud.

'Leave him alone!' I screamed.

'Heather, stoppit,' a voice called. Jovano stood in the shadow of the beech. 'Stop fighting.'

I picked up the axe and flung it into the hedgerow, dislodging an empty sparrow's nest. Adrik skulked away, muttering about the insane child, and Jovano disappeared into the shadows.

I sat at the base of the beech's trunk, staring at the moon through his leaves. His branches stretched across the sky. I stroked his rough skin, patted it and whispered apologies. A warm breeze flickered through his highest branches, I stole back to the house in his shadow and crept up the stairs. I stole a last look at him from the bedroom window, silver moonlight wriggled through his leaves. The next morning brought red eyes and hot tongues. I found Adrik in the kitchen with the sketch pad. One page was crumpled like parched foliage; others bore the scratches of jealous blue ink-gaping wounds across the jagged surface.

'How could you ruin my drawings?' Hot tears sprang.

'You want to give your head a shake, girl. Crying over pictures of a bloody tree.'

'They were my pictures,' I said. 'You had no right.'

Insults stabbed the filthy air; resentment sat among the breakfast things, and I vowed I would leave as soon as possible.

And then the worst thing happened, and I was left with no choice.

Chapter 20
KATIE: NOW

'You were going to tell me how you met Mark originally.'

'Was I? I don't remember mentioning that.' As usual, you're manipulating me, but I find myself wanting to tell you.

I'd always wanted to work in London. I thought it was the most exciting place in the world. My first trip was truly thrilling. I couldn't afford the train, so I paid fifteen pounds for the overnight bus. The seats reclined so you could sleep on the way. Not that I did. I was far too exhilarated. The Pet Shop Boys sang about West End girls and suburbia in my earphones, and I anticipated my new life as I watched the rain trickle down the fogged-up windows.

For months I'd pored over books and magazines about London life. One book, borrowed from the library, told me about every pub in London. I imagined sitting at the Ritz, meeting my favourite authors and actors. Authors were my rock stars. I imagined we'd converse over half a lager (I hated wine) about the prose of Alice Walker and Pat Barker. I'd confess to enjoying Douglas Adams and Tom Sharpe, and they'd concur these were brilliant authors. I'd strike up friendships with literary types, and we'd go to the theatre and ballet at weekends, travelling the Tube together to the West End.

I pored over the underground map, trying to make sense of its warren of lines and colours, connecting and disconnecting like veins, little realising what it was like to travel the Tube in real life. I initially loved the smoky, noisy, dank tunnels with their whistles and warnings to 'mind the gap, please'. I loved the buskers and the bustle, the thrill of the escalators, the buzz of rush hour. The cards slotted into slots and the myriad new faces.

I'd applied for so many jobs in publishing, only to be turned down without explanation. Many didn't even deign to reply. I couldn't even get an interview for an unpaid internship. In desperation, I applied for anything London-based. At least I'd be there at the heart of things. Maybe then I could find a way in to the world where I wanted to be. I applied for mother's help positions advertised in *The Lady* and thought that could be my ticket to living and working in London. How naïve I was! I scheduled the interviews for the same day so I didn't have to fork out the fare more than once.

It was 1986, September, I think. I arrived at a draughty King's Cross station, expecting to see the Queen and Prince Philip alighting from first class. I inspected every face in case it belonged to someone famous. None of them did. There were stern faces, grim faces, black faces, white faces, faces with scars, and faces with scowls. None of the eyes rested on mine. I felt as though I was invisible.

A girl in a short skirt slipped in and out of a red phone box. A man in a raincoat grabbed her shoulder, and she shrugged him off. I sensed danger and it was exhilarating.

One interview was in Wimbledon, another in Brixton, and another in Finsbury Park. I felt so grown-up being in London on my own. My parents' warnings rang in my ears: Don't make eye contact. Don't talk to strangers. Don't get in any cars. Don't loiter. Don't study the map in plain view.

I looked for the signs for a public toilet so I could study the map alone. Which line should I take? Which stop should I get off at?

The interviews were not what I expected. I imagined we'd take tea in the garden and the women would speak sweetly to beautiful children dressed in playsuits.

I soon realised the women basically wanted a slave. The wage was thirty-five pounds a week to live in. I'd be looking after the children, doing all the housework and laundry, with one night off a week. It put paid to the idea I could put myself through uni and work as a mother's help.

'You aren't NNEB-trained,' said one of the mothers, peering over the top of her glasses at me as though I was something she'd scraped from the bottom of a dirty plate. 'So what I pay you will have to be much less. I expect you to be on call all day and every day. You will have one night off and one afternoon a week.'

There was no way I could fit in a degree in literature around a job like that.

The woman from Wimbledon said, 'You wear too much makeup. Are you always dolled up like this?'

I felt like saying, *Well, I don't roll out of bed like this, but I was making an effort because I'm at a job interview, you fucking moron.*

Instead, I blinked and said nothing.

'Your earrings are too large,' she said. 'I don't want you to be wearing makeup round my husband. I want someone plain.'

I had no idea what this meant at the time, but now I realise her husband probably had a history of shagging the nannies.

Strangely, I imagined everyone who lived in Wimbledon to be tennis players. I expected them all to wear whites and be friends with Cliff Richard. The ones I met had tiled conservatories which held umbrellas and smelled of wet dogs.

'You didn't get a position as a nanny?' you ask.

'No. I might have been naïve, but there was no way I was going to work as someone else's slave. I would have to come up with a different plan.'

'So you became a literary agent?' you say.

'Yes, and I was a good one.'

'How did that happen? It can't have been easy for a working-class girl with limited resources to break into a middle-class dominated sphere.'

'I suppose I had what you'd call a stroke of luck. It depends on how you look at it. I mean, I made my own luck to an extent. I created opportunities, but then an opportunity came along quite by chance.'

Jane Franklin was my god. She was *the* literary agent. People spoke about her in hushed tones, like they spoke about a religious leader or film star. Every literary agent aspired to be as successful as her. With her floating scarves, red hair, and custom-made suits, she swooped into rooms and monopolised conversations. She had an air of someone you wouldn't dare approach. Like the Queen of England or Elizabeth Taylor. Editors respected her hugely, and authors would kill to be on her list.

She'd been stalked by a number of both over-eager and unstable authors. One hopeful client sent a dozen roses every week with the same manuscript. After a number of standard rejections, Jane eventually sent him a letter that told him the bare truth: he could not write, he could not spell, his grammar was atrocious, he should never be allowed near a word processor. The plot had more holes than Bjorn Borg's tennis racket, the characters were as wet as the Mary Celeste, and the dialogue was stilted and lame. If he didn't stop sending this drivel, she'd have him arrested for harassment.

Another potential author used to send her photos of his naked torso and offer to sleep with her if she got him a book deal. When interviewed at literary festivals, she often joked she could write a book about all the terrible submissions she'd received.

I met her in the toilets of a bar I'd started to frequent when I was told it was populated by literary types. She emerged from the cubicle and was washing her hands. I couldn't believe she was there, and I must have had the dumbest look on my face. Her bangles jingled, and her huge earrings caught the light from the chandeliers. She glanced sideways at me as she ran her hands under the tap. I passed her a towel. She smiled, and I tried to think of something intelligent to say. I failed and blabbered some inanity about the weather. She was remarkably friendly and not at all the huge bombastic character I had been led to believe she was. Perhaps being in the toilet made her vulnerable. It called to mind the old vulgarity my granddad used when someone was snobbish or had ideas above their station: 'All our shite smells the same'.

I'd attended a conference in Bloomsbury, where she was interviewed by her most successful author. She'd said that a good way into the agency was to introduce yourself to agents, then follow up with a letter to say where and when you met them. She said she met so many people she could only vaguely remember the specifics.

I took a chance. What did I have to lose? I didn't say 'Dear Jane, we met in the toilets of a pub in Covent Garden'. I just said we met briefly during a conference and I was looking to pursue a career as an authors' agent. She put me in touch with the recruitment department regarding an internship. And, to my great surprise, they sent me a very short, to-the-point letter, inviting me for interview and wishing me well. The rest happened in a dream, and I was finally appointed as an intern. I went out that night and drank my body weight in martinis to celebrate.

For a working-class girl this was a huge achievement. No one needed to know that I cleaned offices at night to pay my rent. The other interns were subsidised by Mummy and Daddy. Most had gone to public school, and all seemed far more worldly than me, though I could have taken on any of them in a street fight. Unfortunately, that wasn't a skill required around there.

My first day at Amell, Jasper, and Franklin was memorable. I thought I knew everything there was to know about great books. I thought my love of Austen, Dickens, and Du Maurier would be enough to propel me to the dizzy heights of senior agent in no time. How wrong I was. How naïve, how innocent.

It was an exciting time of my life. I was wearing a skirt suit with shoulder pads bigger than a 1980s soap star. My wild hair was permed and tied back with a banana clip. The excitement building inside me was as frizzy as my hair.

'It's a Sin' was playing on the internal sound system as I approached the reception area and told the girl with the sink-plunger mouth my name. I said I'd been asked to meet Angela Goldman. Ignoring me and checking one of the nails on her left hand, the girl pressed a button with her right and spoke into the intercom. 'Ms Goldman, there's a Katie Kovacs in reception to see you.'

'Send her up to floor five,' said the voice I recognised as Angela's. We'd only spoken on the phone prior to this. I'd been interviewed by a panel, but she was at Frankfurt that day.

'Lift's along there,' pointed the girl whose name badge said Sophia Ellis-Trent. 'Fifth floor.' My new heels clattered on the shiny floor, and my stomach rose along with the elevator. I felt so important and grown-up click-clacking along the corridors of the famous agency I'd only ever dreamed about working in.

I was fresh as toothpaste, bright-eyed and eager to face my new career. I stepped out of the lift on floor 5 to an open-plan office the size of a small country. Black-ash desks, swivel chairs, and rows of computer monitors. Old-fashioned by today's standards, they were space age to me at that time. I imagined myself sitting in front of one of those screens, writing reports, answering the telephone, scouring the World Wide Web. But the reality of my job was much more mundane.

I gazed around for someone I could introduce myself to, but everyone seemed so busy. Those passing were chatting or had such an air of concentration I didn't dare break it. Others were in conversation on telephones. Some typed. I stood around, feeling like a spare part and a girl about my age with glasses and freckles asked me who I wanted to see. She wore dungarees and a striped scarf, and I felt overdressed and gauche.

I held out my hand, 'I'm the new girl,' I said. She had her hands full of envelopes and shrugged to let me know she couldn't shake my hand. She smiled.

'Hello, new girl,' she said.

'I'm an intern.'

'Oh, you must be Katherine?' she said. 'I'm Lavonda. My friends call me Von.'

"'I'm Katie,' I said. 'Only my mother calls me Katherine, and only when I'm in trouble.'

'I preferred New Girl. Just kidding. Do you want to hang up your jacket? It gets warm in here.' I noticed the sun shining in at the windows and gazed at the view across the Thames. I'd dreamed of working in a place like this. I couldn't believe I was actually here.

'Lucinda, this is Katie,' she said. 'She's the new girl.' Lucinda turned, looked me up and down, shrugged, pointed to a closed door, and said:

'You can start with the slush pile. Your job is to turn everything down or find the next bestseller.'

The excitement at finding the next bestseller sizzled through me. I couldn't wait to get started.

Von opened the door onto the slush pile. A whole room, packed floor to ceiling with mostly brown envelopes, all filled with A4 sheets of typed chapters. It seemed to me that everyone in the country had written a novel and sent it in. How on earth did they get through all of these?

'The key,' Von said, 'is to read quickly. You can usually get a sense from the cover letter whether the person can write. If there are spellings and typos, you can be pretty sure the manuscript will be riddled with them as well. Read the synopsis to see whether they can tell a story. If it sounds good, then read sample chapters. When you know it's a reject, if they've provided a self-addressed envelope, we send it back. If not, it gets shredded.'

I loved the smell of paper, the sight of those envelopes, the potential they held. Each might be a hidden gem that I was allowed to polish. Each held a new world, new characters, new locations. In reality, though, many were badly written pastiches of Harold Robbins or A. A. Milne. There were tales of talking picnic baskets, written by grandmas whose grandchildren 'absolutely loved them'. There were stories from men who thought everything else that had been published that year was 'utter rubbish', and they were sure they 'could do much better'. There were submissions which ignored the guidelines and sent the whole manuscript. Pages unnumbered. Stapled together. Green pages, orange pages, pages in the shape of an elephant. One submission, written on the back of an envelope, claimed to be the next Booker prize winner. By the end of my first morning, my back ached, my eyes ran, and my head swam. I couldn't believe how delusional people could be. There were, of course, professional submissions written by 'real' writers, but nothing that sang. Nothing that made me want to shout and wave, claiming I'd found the next Judith Kranz.

It's now hard to believe I was so excited about being bestowed the job of wading through the slush pile, given that I soon realised this was the worst job an agent has to undertake. I was convinced, though, that I was going to find the next bestseller. I was sure I had the 'eye', that I could spot the next Charles Dickens, Emily Brontë, Jane Austen. As I picked up each envelope, I dreamt of boozy luncheons where I chatted with the editor from Penguin who was desperate to publish my latest client's romantic thriller.

Hodder are interested, darling. They've offered six figures.

We can top that, and the film rights are a given.

I imagined the bidding wars and the praise I'd receive from the partners.

'Katie.' Von's voice broke into my thoughts. I slipped a standard rejection postcard into an envelope. 'Are you okay?'

'Yes, I'm fine.'

'You seemed to be in a world of your own. You were talking to yourself …' Heat rose up my face, my cheeks had two crimson balls sitting there to show my embarrassment.

'Oh I do that sometimes when I'm deep in thought.'

'We're going for lunch if you want to join us.' I'd brought a packed lunch so I could save money, but I was eager to make friends with the other interns. I could always just have a coffee and eat my sandwiches later. I tried not to gush.

'I'd like that,' I said. This was what I'd imagined. Lunches with the girls, discussing our favourite writers. Again the reality was totally different to my imaginings. There was a five-minute discussion about books and authors, but the main topic of conversation seemed to be who was sleeping with whom.

Had they spoken about Dickens or Austen, King or Sheldon, I could happily have held my own. I had an opinion on the classics and on many different genres of popular fiction. I had nothing to say in a conversation of this sort. A virgin, the topic of sex both scared and fascinated me. When they spoke of someone giving blowjobs in the bathroom I had no idea what they were talking about. I just knew it was rude and it was something I should know. I eventually bought a book about carnal knowledge and began a whole new education.

The lunches with the other interns were little different from dalliances in the schoolyard. Peppered with bitching and competitive sniping. I sat and took it all in. People who met me often told me I was a good listener. I was one of those people who got on a bus and got the life story from the person sitting beside me.

They never held back. I'd know about the intimacies of their lives in minute detail. The granddad's Alzheimer's, the mother's alcoholism, the father's gambling debts, the insurance fraud, the piles, and the period pains. Was nothing sacred? I was always far too polite to say, 'I don't want to hear this.' So I heard everyone's secrets.

But no one knew mine.

Chapter 21
Regression Therapy: OCTOBER 1975

I want my clothes back, and he says the only way to get them is to behave, so every time he brings water and bread, I thank him. I don't scream or shout. I don't ask for anything else. I'm totally obedient.

I must be exhausted this morning, because I don't hear the key in the lock or his feet on the steps. I wake up, and he's standing over me. I jerk the blanket, tuck it round me and curl into a ball. I realise he's holding my clothes. I don't say a word. I'm hardly breathing.

'Which one?' he says.

'Can't I have them all?'

'Which one?' he repeats. It's so cruel and humiliating. He gets pleasure from degrading me. What kind of person is he? He isn't human. At least he isn't like any human I've come across.

I'm anxious he'll disappear and I'll never see them again. I point to my pants, and he throws them to me. I immediately regret my decision. The cardigan would have been warmer. I daren't change my mind in case he takes them all away out of spite. He's good at spite. I don't want to put them on while he's watching, but he doesn't move.

'On,' he says.

I stay under the cover and hook my foot through the leg hole. He tugs the blanket away and watches me. I feel sick. I'm anxious he'll take it away again and I'll freeze to death, so I say nothing. I rush to pull up my pants and then hold my arm across my chest.

'Behave yerself or I'll take 'em back,' he says, then flings the blanket back at me.

It seems ages before he brings the bundle of clothes again.

'Which one?' he asks.

I point to the cardigan.

'Wrong,' he says, then disappears back up the steps holding all the clothes.

I want to scream and shout and cry, but I stay silent, knowing this must be some kind of test. If I pass, he might give me all my clothes. He might give me soup. He might let me go.

I imagine my family sitting round the table. In some daydreams they're crying for me. Mam is badgering police officers to get out and look for me. Dad is gathering all his friends and our neighbours. They're searching for me with torches in woods and outbuildings. They find the house. I shout to tell them I'm here. They hammer down the door, kill the monster and take me home.

In some of my imaginings everyone has forgotten me. They've moved on with their lives and the space where I used to be is occupied by another girl. The same age as me but different. She wears my clothes and plays with my friends. She sleeps in my bed and hugs my parents. My brothers don't argue with her. They smile and share their sweets. I'm angry they've replaced me so easily. I feel like fury will set me on fire. But hopelessness dampens the flame and I just sit and wait.

For ages he doesn't come down. Every day he opens the door, stands at the top of the steps, throws a bottle of water and a few scraps of food. I've learned not to drink all the water at once. It takes all my self-control not to gulp it down but to sip it at intervals throughout the day. My tummy is bloated and sore because of the lack of liquid and the diet of only bread. I haven't been to the toilet in days. I'm curled up in pain and I'm worried I'm going to explode or something. I don't want to die here. The next time he comes down I'm going to tell him I need more to eat or I'm going to die of scurvy. We learnt about it at school. Sailors get it because they can't eat fresh food. And rickets. I'm going to end up with rickets. Then he'll need to take me to the doctor. Maybe if I tell him that he'll bring me fruit and vegetables. He won't want me to have to see a doctor. But would he care if I got sick and died? He'd probably just take me to the woods and bury me.

I need to find something I can use as a weapon. A rock I can hit him with. There must be something in this cellar. Maybe something I can sharpen. If it's here, I will find it. I have to get out of here.

Chapter 22
HEATHER: LETTER TO KATIE 2019

It was an otherwise ordinary morning. I was dodging Ember Heggarty's beak while planting cabbages when Father trod on a rusty nail. We didn't realise the enormity of this seemingly trivial event. Father cried out, took off his boot, and examined the tiny wound. After rubbing the site for a while, he put the boot back on and we continued as normal, working the whole day until it was time to light the fire and make tea. My brothers pestered our father for a story. 'Tell us about the boar,' they said. So, as he had done many times before, Father told us the story of Pollard's Boar.

Something about it gave me the chills, but Dad's voice was so hypnotic I couldn't stop listening. We sat round the campfire, jacket potatoes cooking in the embers while Dad's gravelly voice rolled across the night air.

'Once upon a time, in the heart of County Durham, there lived a wild boar so big and so fierce no one could catch it. It so troubled the Bishop of the Oaklands that he offered a generous reward for its capture. Many tried and many failed to apprehend the enormous beast and were gored to death for their trouble.

'One day, a man called Richard Pollard decided he would catch the monster and claim the reward. He knew he'd have to use guile and cunning, because the brute was too strong for him. He stalked the boar. He watched its habits; he discovered where it liked to roam and what it preferred to eat. He found it liked to wander into a certain beech wood and feed on the beech nuts that fell from the trees.

'One day, Pollard climbed the branches of the finest beech and shook the branches until the ground underneath lay thick with nuts. He hid in the leafiest part of the tree and waited. And waited.

'Eventually, the boar came into view, sniffing the ground. His snout led him to the piles of beechnuts. It devoured the nuts until Pollard thought it would burst, then lay down to sleep after its sumptuous meal. Pollard climbed back down the tree and attacked the animal with his falchion, knowing the boar was full from its meal and unlikely to be able to fight back. The boar had been slowed down, it was true, but it was still a mighty adversary. On and on they fought, hour after hour until the sun went down and the birds stopped singing. On and on until the sun rose again, sending its first rays into the wood. By the light of that first ray, Pollard plunged the falchion into the boar, flooring the beast. It rolled onto its side, and its tongue hung out. It had finally died.

'Pollard was too exhausted to drag the boar to the bishop to claim his reward, so he cut out its tongue, put it in his wallet, and lay down to sleep. While he was sleeping, a stranger came upon the sight of the dead boar and the sleeping knight. He couldn't believe his luck. He cut off the boar's head and took it to the bishop to claim his reward. Pollard awoke and was most disturbed to find the head of the boar missing. He realised what had occurred. He rode swiftly to the bishop's castle where the stranger was claiming his reward.

'"Stop!' he cried. 'It was I who slayed the boar.'

"Nonsense!" said the bishop. 'This man has rid us of this terrible pest and has brought me the head. What proof do you have that you slayed the boar?' Pollard drew the tongue from his wallet and presented it to the bishop. The bishop looked in the boar's mouth and saw that the tongue was missing.

"I am satisfied you are the killer of the boar,' said the bishop. 'And now for your reward. I am going to dinner. Ride around my land and when dinner is over, I will give you the land you have ridden around.' While the bishop was at dinner, Pollard rode once round his castle. The bishop realised Pollard had not only outwitted the boar but had also outwitted him as well. He rewarded the knight with pastures and meadows and woodland.'

'What's a falchion?' I asked when the story was finished and my father stared into the embers of the fire.

'It's a sword capable of cutting off the limbs of an opponent with one stroke,' Father said.

'Why would anyone want to do that?' I asked.

My dad reassured me, 'It's just a story. A folk tale. There's no truth in most of them.'

My brothers re-enacted the fight between Pollard and the boar. They used sticks for a falchion and charged at each other. I sat silent, imagining the boar with his missing tongue. His mouth an empty cavern. I shuddered.

Father's foot failed to heal. The wound became green.

'It's septic,' Mam said. 'He's going to get blood poisoning. He needs to see a doctor.'

'There's no need,' Adrik said. 'Karma will see him.'

Karma who had once been a GP called Dr Johnson, had been struck off after some sex scandal involving a woman with alopecia. Father swelled and trembled, vomited and shook. Mother insisted they take him to hospital. Karma and Adrik said we should just wait for the fever to break. Father's toes turned black like charred stumps, and a fever raged within him.

We buried Father in the spring when new buds formed on fresh stems and lambs frolicked in the field next door. His organs had failed. There was nothing to be done. They dug a hole in the orchard, and he was lowered on an old door. My brothers held the rope, tears boiling behind their eyes. Mother wept and wailed, blaming Karma for father's demise. Then she blamed herself for changing from a homely mother into a tree-hugger. We hoped this might mean we could return to our village, but Mother said we'd burnt our bridges. I don't remember burning anything, I said. She just looked at me through misted eyes and shook her head.

'Granny has disowned us,' she said. 'We can never go back there.'

It felt wrong that Father was buried without a priest. Moonjava blew eerie tones on a wooden pipe, and Willow lamented an elegy. We made a wind chime which marked the spot, but I was worried for his soul. This wasn't sacred ground. It was an orchard in the grounds of a derelict mansion. What if his soul was trapped underground? Stifled by soil. Polluted. Mother and Adrik discussed it.

'What about the authorities?' she said.

'How will they know?' he said. 'It's what we do with our dead.'

'But it's a crime,' she said.

'We're exempt from the laws of the land. We have thrown off the shackles of our society,' Adrik said. Mother chewed her lip until there was a permanent lump. A raised, purple bruise. A plum.

Many lights went out when Father died. Some days it was difficult to make my limbs move just to get out of bed. At night, Adrik, smelling of ganja and barley wine, blew into our dorm with the cold north wind. He'd hump and grunt and paw at my mother, fading away like a traitorous moon before sunrise, and I wanted to kill him.

I didn't want to leave Mother, nor could I bear to behold the grubby thing growing between Adrik and her, or the hatred simmering inside my brothers. It was a cancer, a malignancy, a disease. I told Jovano I'd go with him. But the world around us had changed beyond recognition. Where we ended up and the fate that met us, we could not have imagined.

We set off early the next day. A grim autumn morning. Dry leaves blew in our faces and scratched us as we crept out in the dark and slipped into the van. Our plan was to try to get work in cafés and shops in every town we travelled through, so we'd have enough money to survive. We wouldn't need much. We were used to having nothing, so it needn't be much of a sacrifice. Or so we thought.

A slow turn of the key in the ignition was met by a roar: a violent storm growling across the night. Jovano left the headlights off until we'd left the grounds of the orchard, afraid we'd disturb the elders.

We'd travelled only a few feet when the van coughed out smoke and slid to a stop. We both alighted, Jovano lifted the bonnet, and his head was eaten by its jaws. My heart jumped in my ribs at the unmistakable tap of a walking stick on the ground. Karma coughed into a handkerchief and glowered at us with one rheumy eye.

Sprightlier than his crooked frame suggested, he bowled towards us, a finger wagging. 'You young people. No respect.' He spat the word young as though it was unwelcome phlegm. 'What are you doing with that? Why are you outside?'

'Why are you outside?' Jovano asked.

'You impertinent young scoundrel.'

He raised the cane above his head and brought it crashing down on Jovano's arm. A crack split the air. Jovano grabbed for the rod. There was a tussle, and Jovano was now in possession of the stick. He pulled back his arm, and the weapon sliced through the air, whistling. It connected with a crack on bone. Again and again. Blood spattered in rows across the van's paintwork. My own feral howls reverberated round the lane.

'What have you done?' I wailed.

'He was asking for it. He started it.' Breathless. Wide-eyed. Wired.

'You've killed him!' I said.

'I didn't mean to,' he said, dropping the cudgel.

'He's dead,' I said.

I'd watched TV programmes where people gave the kiss of life. Perhaps I could bring him back. Maybe he could be saved. If I just blew air into his lungs… But his lips were like two dead slugs, and I couldn't bring myself to touch his with mine. His body lay still and pale. I reached out with a shaking hand to feel his fingers. They were turning cold already. I felt I'd left my body and floated above the scene. Powerless to intervene.

'We've got to get out of here,' Jovano said.

'We can't leave him here,' I said.

'What else are we going to do?'

'We can't just leave him.'

'We'll have to lift him into the van, take him somewhere and bury him, otherwise the police will come after us.'

My heart knocked against my ribs, my legs faltered beneath me. I watched Jovano loop his hands under the old man's arms and drag him to the van door, his eyes bulging, his face contorted with the pain of the weight.

'Make sure no one's coming.'

The sky was the colour of murky ponds, and a mist slithered through the trees and settled on the roads. Deep, thick fog. We couldn't see the length of a laid-out corpse.

'Grab his feet,' Jovano said. 'Let's get him in the back of the van.'

'This is a bad idea. A really bad idea. I don't like this. I don't like this one little bit.'

'Heather, snap out of it. Open the door.'

I turned the handle on the back door and pulled it towards me. It creaked open.

'Shhhhhhhhhh.'

'You shhhhhh. I'm being as quiet as I can.'

'We don't have time to argue. Get his legs.'

'Oh God.'

'He isn't going to help us now.'

'Oh Jesus.'

Jovano slammed the door and snapped at me to get in the front. 'Come on. We have to get out of here.'

'Which way do we go?'

'Haven't a clue.'

'Right,' I said.

He turned the key, and the old banger whimpered into life.

Then a door opened, and a voice I recognised said, 'What have you two done?'

Chapter 23
KATIE: NOW

'I have always loved stories. I preferred books to people in some respects. Books were my escape from reality. I loved the smell of the pages, the look of the ink, the words marching across the page. I was never a writer, though. I've always had an enquiring mind. Nosy parker my mother called it, but I was constantly fascinated by the reasons why people do the things they do. Maybe I was born like that, or maybe it's because of what happened in Prestwick.'

'So tell me what happened in Prestwick,' you say.

I was seven years old, and it was the summer holidays. I'd gone to the beach with my brothers and my cousins. We played on the sand and splashed in the Firth of Clyde. We'd gone home in dribs and drabs. When one of us felt hunger pangs, they peeled themselves from the pack and sauntered back to the flat. Monica and I were the only two left. We watched the tide being lugged to the shore, the rippling laps becoming angry whitecaps that rose and smashed against the sea walls, spitting at us in disdain. The mist rolled in, cloaking the promenade as dusk curved into dark. The benign beach was now bleak and hostile.

'Let's go back,' I said to Monica.

'I want a fish supper,' Monica said. That meant she wanted to go to The Cod Almighty, which was all the way along the other end of town. Curls of foreboding made me yearn for the comfort of the smoke-filled flat, but I couldn't leave Monica on her own.

Aunt Isobel had said, 'Stay taegether and dinnae leave naebody alone. See you dae an a'll skelp ye.' Nobody wanted a skelpin' from Aunt Isobel. She had the hardest hand in the whole of Caledonia.

Streetlights smouldered beneath the haze. Our feet padded on the pavement, and I imagined my mam calling my name into the fog, worry lines etched in her forehead. We ran through the empty park. A swing squealed as it swung in the breeze. A scream pierced the night, and we both jumped. 'What was that?' I whispered.

'Ah dinnae ken. Up here,' Monica said, yanking me to a tree. She shoved me from behind and I clambered up its branches, skinning my knee on a gnarled limb. I gulped down the pain and scrabbled higher until Monica and I sat side by side at the top of the tree. We watched in horror …

A girl in a T-shirt and shorts was being dragged by her hair. Her face was streaked with blood, and her mouth was open in a scream. My heart thumped, my whole body shook so much I was sure the tree would collapse with the vibrations. The frayed moon was reflected in Monica's wide eyes, her hands clasped over her mouth to prevent the escape of a shocked cry. The girl below fought, lashed out, hands and feet flailing like a fish on the end of a hook. The man's hands were round her throat, squeezing the life from her. Her feet tore at the dank earth, her body undulating, arms thrashing. His knee was on her chest now and his hands were squeezing. Her eyes popped, her face turned blue. Monica and I saw everything and said nothing. The girl's hand reached for something, rested on a stone. She swung it in a frenzied arc and bashed him on the side of the head. He faltered, fell to the side a little, which afforded her time to get up. He punched her across the jaw. A crack split the air. His hands were in her hair again, and he hauled her away, her feet slipping in the mud. Monica sat open-mouthed, her breathing ragged, her eyes wide and full. I shook my head over and over, trying to rid myself of the image. We sat. And sat.

Monica and I gazed at each other in disbelief. Something passed between us. Something I can't describe.

'We can never tell,' I said. 'Never.'

Chapter 24
HEATHER: LETTER TO KATIE 2019

Nobody went to Mrs Brownlow's house. She was our teacher, you see, and teachers were above us. They didn't like us to know they were ordinary. That they didn't live in classrooms and sleep in stationery cupboards. They didn't want us to know they had lives and families and toilets and pets.

Mam had to go to the hospital, and there was no one to take care of me, so I was to go to Mrs Brownlow's with Anne after school. Instead of travelling on the school bus over hill and down dale, I was to go in the back seat of Mrs Brownlow's mini. I felt important climbing into the car that afternoon and waving at Michelle Gallacher who stared through the bus window at me, disbelief turning her mouth down at the corners, steam misting the window in front of her, until all I could see was the shape of her bobble hat. She looked like an acorn.

Mrs Brownlow's house didn't smell of chip fat; it smelled of fresh paint, and everything gleamed white. They had a special cupboard for shoes and vertical blinds at every window. Only posh people had vertical blinds. My mam wouldn't even have horizontal ones on account of them being dust collectors. Mam said that about most things she couldn't afford.

Mrs Brownlow made us pork chops for tea. She asked me whether I liked peas, and I said I did. I later learned the only ones I liked were called processed peas. Mrs Brownlow served me garden peas. They tasted of farts.

'Eat them up, you asked for them,' she said.

I asked for ketchup to drown them in and held my breath while I chewed. They still made me want to throw up. Mrs Brownlow collected the plates and tutted at the amount of ketchup left on mine. 'Was something massacred?' she asked.

We were then allowed into the playroom. Anne with an 'E' had her very own room just to play in. My bedroom could have fit inside it five times. She had a blackboard and a desk, a bike, and all the latest dolls. Spoilt rotten my mam would have called her. I'd have liked to have been spoiled rotten. Anne had a rabbit in an inside hutch and a hamster which ran round and round and round on an orange wheel.

'Let's get the hamster out,' I said.

'I'm not allowed,' she said.

'Why not?'

'Only Mam and Dad are allowed to touch him.'

I ignored her, opened the small metal door, and reached inside. The beige-and-white thing darted to the corner of the cage, burrowing under shredded loo roll. My fingers felt soft fur and then a sudden, sharp pain. I pulled my arm away. Two red marks on my fingertips showed where it had bitten me.

'It bit me,' I said, tears springing into my eyes.

'I forgot to say it bites.'

'Bloody vicious thing,' I said. 'It wants putting down.'

'It doesn't get handled much,' she said.

'I'm not surprised,' I said. 'Get me some gloves.'

Anne sighed and hobbled away to find some. She returned with her dad's gardening gloves.

'Perfect,' I said. Anne beamed, having got something right for a change. I reached in again and this time couldn't feel the savage little thing sinking its teeth. I plucked it from its bed and placed it on the playroom floor but didn't let go.

'It has a ball it can go in so it doesn't get lost,' Anne said.

'Go and get it then.'

She hobbled off again, but by the time she got back the hamster was gone.

'It bit me again and ran off,' I said. 'I think it's under the toy box.'

We shifted it together, but there was no hamster.

'I'm going to get killed now,' Anne said. 'My parents will hang, draw and quarter me.' Her parents were like mine. They wouldn't hurt a fly.

'Don't tell them,' I said. 'It'll come back. Let's go into a different room, then they won't know we've been in here.' I wandered into the hallway and into the room opposite. Books lined the walls, and a desk sat in the middle.

'This is Daddy's study,' she said. 'I'm not allowed in here.' I pointed to a sword in a case above the desk.

'What's that for?' I asked.

'It's Daddy's. He used to fence.'

'Let's play a game,' I said.

'What game?' she said.

'The Pollard's Boar,' I said. 'I'll be the boar, and you have to catch me and take me to the bishop to get your prize.' She pointed to the callipers on her legs.

'I won't be able to catch you,' she said.

As if I needed reminding. Anne was the slowest person in school. On sports day, we'd all have to applaud her for coming last, just because she didn't give up and managed to cross the finish line ten minutes behind everyone else. I always came first, and I didn't get as big a round of applause as she did.

'Okay,' I said. 'I'll catch you instead, but I'll give you a head start. You run, I'll count to a hundred, then come and find you. Ready, steady, go.'

She went.

Anne didn't come back to school. I didn't see her again. Someone said she was ill.

I was never invited back.

It was an accident.

Chapter 25
KATIE: 1987

It was the summer of 1987 when Shelly came back into my life. She stayed with me in the flat and left bossy notes dictating what I should do and where I should and shouldn't go. I was angry this morning to find one on the table which said:

STAY AWAY FROM THE OTHERS IN THE OFFICE. THEY'RE BAD NEWS, S.

Who the hell did she think she was? I scrunched it up and left it on the top of the wastepaper basket for her to see. She was just protecting me, but I was sick of her trying to control my actions. She didn't approve of Von either. I think perhaps she was jealous of our friendship.

Von maintained that the only way to get on in this business was to sleep your way to the top. As a naïve virgin, I was horrified. The thought of sleeping with someone who wasn't my husband, fiancé, or long-term partner, was abhorrent. I said as much and she laughed at how old-fashioned I was, but said it was cute.

'Some bastard's just gonna eat you up,' she said. 'We've got to get you some streetwise smarts pronto. I'm gonna introduce you to my friend, Omar. What he can't teach you about the *Karma Sutra* isn't worth knowing. Lord, your eyes are like saucers, girl. Calm down. It'll be fun.'

She picked me up that evening and took me to a bar in the West End. She introduced me to a group of friends, and Omar was among them. He was the kind of beautiful that you know is way out of your league. A vest top accentuated his perfectly defined muscles, and his hair was cropped short all round, but on the top of his head, long curls sprang in wild tendrils. I couldn't take my eyes off him. He barely glanced in my direction. Von elbowed him.

'Say hello to Katie, Omar,' she said. He turned his back on me.

'Hello to Katie,' he said.

'I don't care how handsome he is, he's rude.'

'He's not a fucking object,' he said, then turned and scanned me from head to toe.

'Neither am I.'

'Ooh, your friend's a spicy one,' Omar said.

'Your other friend's rude,' I said.

Von seized my arm and drew me away from her group of friends. 'Come on, Katie, make an effort.'

'*Me* make an effort?' I asked, incredulous. 'Your friend has no manners.'

'He's only joking.'

'He isn't funny.'

'Don't be so uptight. Relax.'

'I'm going home.'

'Come on, man. I wanted you to have a good time tonight. Maybe get a little action.'

'Von, I'm fine. I don't need to take my clothes off to have a good time.'

'No, but it helps,' she laughed. 'Okay, if you aren't going to fuck Omar tonight, I am. I'm not letting that hottie go to waste.'

'I'm going to get home. I'm tired and I have the beginnings of a headache. I'll see you tomorrow.'

A fog of loneliness descended on me. I was leaving the bar and heading towards the Tube station when a dark figure ran towards me and I felt my arm being jerked. Before I could figure out what had happened I was on the ground, and a hooded figure was running in the opposite direction holding my shoulder bag. I was too shocked to cry out. I dragged myself to my feet and noticed a hole in my favourite leather trousers, where a small patch of bloody knee peeked through. A number of passers-by averted their eyes in case they might have to come to my aid.

The robber was going to be disappointed with what he found in the purse. There was a packet of Wrigley's gum, ten pounds in cash, and a single Durex Von had slipped in there at the beginning of the night. I choked back tears, realising I now had no money for the cab home and I'd have to walk. What a nightmare ending to a rotten day. I was hobbling up the street and a voice shouted, 'Hold on, there.'

I turned and a suited man who carried a briefcase ran in my direction. I clenched tight fists and raised my arms, stood with feet apart and warned him, 'Don't come any fucking closer.'

He held his hands up in a surrender motion.

'Whoa, it's okay. I was coming to help you. I saw what happened, but I was upstairs and couldn't get to help you.' He pointed to the upstairs window of the Ritz. 'Let me call the police. Are you hurt?'

I relaxed a little when I realised how good looking he was. Surely serial killers couldn't be this pretty? His hair was dark, his eyes piercing and his face looked like it had been sculpted in clay by an Italian master.

'I'm fine,' I said but new tears sprang.

'You're not fine, are you?' he said. He plucked a handkerchief from his pocket and handed it to me. 'It's clean. I never use them. My mother makes me carry one in case I bump into a beautiful damsel in distress who needs to dry her tears.'

'Shame you've given it to me then. What are you going to do when you bump into her?'

He laughed, and I dried my eyes and blew my nose on his handkerchief.

'I'm Mark,' he said.

'Katie.' I was so grateful for a friendly face I felt like hugging him.

'I'll need that back clean. So you better give me your address.' He opened his briefcase and handed me a mini Filofax and pen.

As chat up lines went, I'd known much worse. I felt that familiar tingle that comes with new encounters. The quiver of expectation.

'I'll give you my work address,' I said, wary of giving the address to my digs to a stranger. He could have been anyone.

He glanced at the address and laughed. I didn't understand until later what he found so funny. He pulled a device from his briefcase, tapped buttons on it, and proceeded to call a cab. I'd heard about mobile phones, but I'd never seen anyone use one. It was what we call a house brick these days, but then it was futuristic. I was embarrassed because everyone was looking in our direction as he spoke loudly into the device. They mouthed, 'What an arsehole!' 'Pretentious wanker!' 'Who does he think he is?'

'I have no money for a cab,' I said.

He waved a hand as though knocking the notion away.

The cab arrived and he helped me inside, then handed a small bundle of notes to the driver and told him to take me wherever I wanted to go.

'See you soon,' he said. 'Probably sooner than you might think.'

I couldn't stop thinking about the handsome stranger all night. My insides tingled as I thought about him asking for my number. I loved the way he was so self-assured and protective. I went to sleep daydreaming about him kissing me and us walking hand in hand along the South Bank.

I didn't expect to see or hear from him again, but the very next day I opened the door to my digs for a delivery from Interflora. The biggest bouquet of flowers I'd ever seen. The card read: TO KATIE FROM MARK X.

How the hell did he get my home address?

Chapter 26
HEATHER: 2019

I was supposed to be praying, but I rushed through the rosary so I could get back to writing my letter. Katie would be waiting to read what happened to Adrik, and I didn't want to keep her waiting for too long.

Shock prevented me from closing the door as Jovano revved the sleepy engine and drove away. The car juddered forward a yard, then spluttered and stalled.

'I saw everything,' Adrik shouted, wrenching the door of the van. 'You're going to Hell. You're going to jail. Delinquents. Reprobates.' He grabbed my arm, dragging me from the seat.

I bumped onto the dusty road, pain hitting my hip and shooting down my leg. The engine shuddered, coughed out smoke and died. By the time I'd managed to scramble to my feet, Jovano was out of the driving seat. He leapt at Adrik, his arms round his throat, his finger ends white as he pressed on his windpipe. Adrik's eyes bulged, and he wriggled like a shark. He managed to tug Jovano's hands free, pulled on his arms, bent his back, and threw Jovano over his head so he landed in a heap, his leg twisted underneath him, his face contorted in pain. Adrik lurched forward and stamped on the side of Jovano's head. Jovano rolled sideways, howling, then lay still and silent.

Adrik grabbed at me, mauling me, ripping my clothes. 'You little slut. You're going to get exactly what you deserve.' He untied the rope holding up his trousers. He grasped my wrist.

Bile rose in my throat, and I retched, a hot spring of vomit spewing onto the ground. He shoved me backwards, the weight of him on top of me, crushing the air from my lungs. He pawed at me, his dirty fingernails gouging the skin of my thigh. I tried to scream, to push, to fight; my fists thudded on his back.

And then, behind him, Jovano rose, mountainous against the waning moon. A clunk, a crack, and the beast was still. I shoved Adrik away from me, my eyes bulging with the effort. Blood leaked from his ear in a sorry path down the side of his head, staining the dirt beneath. I scrambled to my feet, tugged down my dress and slapped the dust from my legs.

I jumped into the passenger seat, and Jovano took his place in the driving seat. In the rearview mirror a dark shape emerged from the road, slowly, unsteadily, teetering on woollen legs. The engine roared into life and Jovano drove away, his teeth clenched, eyes wide and wild. Without warning, he slammed the car into reverse, the damaged clutch squealing before engaging properly. The taste of burning rubber added to my nausea. The wheels spun and then the van raced backwards. My stomach heaved; my heart rattled.

In the rearview mirror, a tuft of hair, eyes, round and scared, the mouth a capital O. There was a huge bang. Adrik vanished under the back of the vehicle. Crack. Bones crunched as we powered forward again, leaving his bloodied carcass lying lifeless in the road.

'Oh, Jovano! Oh no. What have you done?'

'What choice did I have?'

Trees, fields, cottages, hedgerows and hawthorns, ponds and ponies whizzed by. I moaned softly, rocking in my seat all the way to Upperton Woods.

'Pull yourself together,' Jovano said. 'We have to bury Karma.'

'They'll be after us now as soon as they find Adrik.'

'No they won't. Police will just think it's a hit-and-run. Adrik is a dropout. He doesn't exist. I doubt they'll even be able to identify him.'

'Jesus, Jovano. What are we doing? This can't be happening.' I moaned again.

'Get a grip on yourself.'

My whole body shook. Jovano wasn't who I thought he was. Tears streamed down my cheeks, and I sobbed as I gazed out of the window, searching for answers on the disjointed horizon. A police siren nee-nawed in the distance, and the bottom fell out of my stomach.

'I had no choice, Heather,' Jovano said.

'You killed them both.'

'There was no other option. We had to escape. We were being held prisoner in that place. What I did, I did in self-defence. I defended you. He was going to rape you. Any judge would acquit me.'

I wondered if this were true. I'd watched Crown Court as a small child when I was off school with scarlatina, and my mother had bought flat fish to tempt me to eat. My throat burned, and everything I swallowed felt like broken crockery.

Solemn, wigged men with serious faces fiercely cross-examined people in the dock, and a jury of members of the public made a decision about their fate. With every painful bite of the Dover sole, the accused moved closer to incarceration.

There was no way Jovano was going anywhere other than a prison cell. My boyfriend was a murderer.

As though reading my mind, he said, 'It's not murder, Heather, it's self-defence. I wouldn't hurt a fly, you know that.' He wouldn't hurt a crane fly, but he had battered a person to death. Thrashed him hard round the face and head with his own walking stick and had then driven deliberately into a defenceless man. Without mercy. Adrik might have been a vile human being, but did he deserve to die under the wheels of a van, mowed down like a dog in the road? We didn't even lift his body to the side out of respect.

As we drove deeper into the English countryside, I tried not to look at the corpse in the back. I imagined it decomposing by the minute. The lips turning black, the skin slipping from the bones, maggots pouring from the eyeholes and mouth cavity.

Jovano's foot on the accelerator took us further and further from the scene of destruction we'd left behind. I'm ashamed to say that the more miles Jovano put between us and Adrik's body, the more cheerful I became. Calm lapped at me, and I had a sense that everything would be all right.

That was until I heard the noise from the back of the truck and realised Karma was still alive.

Chapter 27
KATIE: 2019

The first time I met Mollie I was juggling two bottles of rosé, a carton of milk, and a bag of potatoes when I backed into her trolley at the checkout.

'Sorry, I should have got a basket. I only came in for milk.'

'Snap,' she said, pointing to her trolley where ten bottles of the same rosé sat. 'Got to take advantage of the offers. Are you here on holiday?'

'No, I've moved into The Old Parsonage. I work in the city.' I think I saw a frown pass her face, but just as quickly it was gone and her face was severed by a broad smile.

'Then I'm your next-door neighbour,' she said. 'Mollie Gent. Our place is about a mile up the coast from you.'

'I know where to come for a cup of sugar then,' I said.

She smiled again.

'And is everything okay?' she asked. 'With the house, I mean.'

'The heating won't come on, but apart from that, no problems so far.'

'It's not noisy?' she said.

'You're kidding,' I said. 'It's as quiet as the grave. You should come for dinner.' For all I'd come here to get away, I was relishing the idea of company. The kitchen aglow, the stove heating stew, and homemade bread rising in the Aga. The friendly chatter of new neighbours, and the flow of red wine: glasses clinking in friendly salutes.

'Oh, you know, babysitters,' she said.

'Bring the kids,' I said. 'It'll be good for me to be surrounded by youngsters again.' It would. I missed Oliver more than I could ever express.

The pip of a horn whipped her into a flurry of activity. She threw her shopping onto the conveyor belt and dumped it in bags at the other end.

'That would be lovely,' she said but she was gone before we could swap phone numbers or email addresses.

After a ready meal for one and a glass of wine in front of the telly, I woke to the sound of moaning. The fire had long since died, and a chill sucked the air. A single scented candle still burned on the coffee table. Someone was in the house, and someone was in pain. I could barely make out the words, but it sounded like 'Help me', and 'Katie'. My stomach flipped over and my heart dashed against my rib cage.

'Who's there?' I called out.

The strange guttural gurgling became a scream.

'Help me, Katie.'

I sat, not daring to move. Hardly breathing and waiting for the next cry.

'Mark? Is that you?'

'Katie, help me.' The voice came from the cellar.

My phone was dead, so I picked up the candle and crept towards the cellar door. It groaned open, and I descended the stone steps. The kitchen light fanned out onto the wall, but when I reached the bottom step it went out. Damn. It had tripped again. The orange flame cast eerie shadows on the stone walls. My legs shook and my heart thundered. At the bottom of the stairs, I held the candle lower to see if anyone was lying hurt or in pain. There was no one there.

One wall was lined with old orange boxes and another held racks of dusty wine bottles. A scuffle came from the corner, and a rat ran across the floor in front of me. My shriek reverberated around the room. *I must buy poison.* Mice were bad enough, but rats... I shuddered. A shiver ran up and down my spine. A single rope swung from the beam closest to the far wall, yet there was no breeze. The moaning came again. This time above me. It was coming from the house. A juddering and knocking sound, then cracks split the air. The juddering began again, and the house shook.

Relief ran through my veins. It was the central heating coming on at last. The screaming and gurgling was the water rushing through the pipes for the first time this year. The workmen told me to expect strange noises as the system might need to be bled. I vowed to call the plumber in the morning. I retired to bed and slept again, dreaming of demons and banshees.

I woke to a ghostly moaning and frenzied cry. It took me a few moments to realise where I was. The window was open wide, even though I was certain I had closed it the night before. My heart returned to normal when I realised it was the seals on the beach, crying out in their eerie way to one another.

The phone rang. A withheld number. I pushed to decline. It could be someone ringing from the office; sometimes the Ed's office showed as an unknown number. It rang again, so I accepted, slipped on my dressing gown and padded to the bathroom.

'Katie, how've you been?'

It took me a few moments to recognise the voice. When I did, my hands shook, my mouth dried up, and my knees buckled.

'Mark? How did you? How could you …?' I cut the call and sat on the edge of the bath, my heart jumping, my legs shaking.

Chapter 28
KATIE: 1987

You can imagine my surprise when I was called into Mr Amell's office the next day. My heart thundered and my hands shook. I was terrified I'd be dismissed for some gross misdemeanour I knew nothing about. Had I rejected an outstanding work of staggering genius? Had they figured out I was an impostor? I rehearsed an apology for some random mistake in my head. I imagined myself begging for forgiveness and explaining that I couldn't go back to Durham a failure.

The huge desk was strewn with papers, and the computer screen showed a spreadsheet. I smelt the coffee before I saw the tray with the percolator and two cups. The swivel chair was turned away from me, his blurred reflection both looking out across the river and staring back at me. The white shirt strained against his pectorals and the dark tie cut his body in two. His face was familiar.

'You wanted to see me, Mr Amell? I'm sorry if I did something wrong. I haven't been here long and I'm learning every day. I love working at the agency and ...'

The chair swung round, and my knees almost gave way at the shock of him sitting there.

'Hello, Katie,' said Mark, a smile crossing his face and lighting his eyes. 'It's lovely to see you again.'

It wasn't the first time in my life that shock had stolen my voice, but it was one of the most embarrassing. No wonder he'd laughed when I gave my work address. The handsome stranger who'd rescued me was my new boss.

'I took the liberty of ordering you coffee. Will you join me?'

My tongue was eventually set free, and I stammered that I'd love a coffee.

'Did you receive the flowers? I hope you don't mind. I had my assistant look up your address.'

'They were beautiful,' I said. 'The nicest I've ever had.' In truth, they were the only bouquet I'd ever received, unless you counted bunches randomly stolen from gardens by boys who wanted to sleep with me.

'I just wanted to let you know that we aren't all bad in London.'

'Oh I know,' I said. 'Everyone has been so welcoming and …'

He laughed then.

'No need to be nervous,' he said. 'Come and sit down.' He leant forward and picked up the coffee pot, pouring the dark liquid into both cups. 'Milk?' The fact he was so self-assured only served to make me more uneasy.

I nodded.

'Sugar?'

I nodded again.

He took a cube from the sugar bowl and added one to my cup. 'Two?'

'Yes, please, I'm definitely not sweet enough.'

'Oh, I wouldn't say that,' he said, and handed me my coffee.

I sipped at the hot liquid. It had that tobacco flavour of proper filter coffee and it was far too strong for me. I'd be up all night if I drank this.

'I hope you're feeling a lot calmer after your ordeal,' he said.

'I'm fine.' This wasn't completely true. I'd slept with a knife under my pillow. Every sound woke me. Every stir in the flat and I imagined someone was coming to rob or attack me.

'It can be disorientating. It takes a while to get over something of that nature,' he said. 'But you'll get there. We're very happy to have you here.'

'I'm so happy to be here. It's an absolute dream come true for me. It's what I've always wanted to do. Ever since I was a little girl I've dreamed of coming to London and working in publishing.' I was gushing, but it didn't seem to bother him.

'Let's have lunch,' he said, and flicked through his diary. 'I'll have Janet send you a memo.'

'Janet?' I asked.

'My assistant. She'll let you know when I'm free for lunch.'

'Ah, okay. And I'll let her know if I'm free then,' I said.

He laughed again. 'You really are quite something, Katie Kovacs.'

'I am?' I said, and then with conviction, 'I am.'

The memo arrived much quicker than I'd been expecting. I came back from lunch to a Post-it note, asking if I was free to have lunch with Mr Amell the following day. I thought about saying I was busy, but I was worried he'd sack me so I sent a message via his assistant saying I was available. She sent a note detailing the time and place that warned me not to be late as Mr Amell was a very busy man.

I made the mistake of telling Von. She squealed with excitement and told me I had to sleep with him if I wanted to 'get on.'

'I'm not going to sleep with him,' I said. 'I'm just going for lunch.'

'Why do you imagine he's invited you for lunch?'

'Because he enjoyed my company?'

'Girl, you have so much to learn. Mark Amell can have the company of any girl he chooses. His last girlfriend was a model. He's dated Allie Clinton from daytime TV. You gotta do what you can to get ahead. Staying on the right side of Mark Amell is the way to get ahead in the literary world. You get to know him, girl, and he'll open doors, and I don't mean the door to the slush pile.'

I couldn't stop thinking about Von's words. What if he did want to kiss me? What if he wanted to sleep with me? My skin was clammy and my heart raced. Surely not. Like Von said, he could have any woman he wanted. He'd dated models and TV personalities. What was he doing with little old me? Maybe he thought it was funny to play with the office junior. If he thought he could play with me he was mistaken. Mark Amell was in for a shock if he thought I was a pushover. I let my mind wander and imagined what it would be like to be in a relationship with such a man. I saw us walking hand in hand. Saw people suddenly take me seriously when they realised who my partner was. I pictured him laughing at my jokes and bending to kiss my forehead, a look of love in his eyes, taking me to bed, stripping my clothes from my body with the self-assurance of a practised lover. I visualised our first argument where he admitted he was wrong, apologised and made it up to me with expensive presents and breakfast in bed. Excitement and terror overwhelmed me.

Chapter 29
KATIE: 1987

Von walked me home that night and fussed around me like an old mother hen. 'You gotta wear the right outfit: slutty but not too slutty.'

'I'm not going to lunch dressed like a tart,' I said.

'You ain't goin' dressed like no nun neither,' she said. 'Let me come up to your flat and help you choose something.'

'I'm going in my usual work clothes.'

'Aw, man, at least put some heels on and make an effort with your hair.'

'I always wear my hair up for work.'

'Wear it down. It's sexier.'

'I read that men don't take women seriously if they wear their hair down for work,' I said.

'*What?*' Von shrieked. 'What kind of rubbish are you reading, girl? You don't want him to take you seriously. You want him to take you to bed.'

'I don't,' I said. 'I really don't.' The thought horrified and thrilled me in equal measure.

'You'll need a sexy outfit and get rid of that school girl hairstyle.'

'Okay, okay. Anything to get you off my back. But I'm not wearing anything too revealing. I want to be smart and business-like. Maybe he wants to talk to me about a job. I don't want to presume this is anything other than a working lunch.'

'Honey, for what reason would Mark Amell invite the intern to a working lunch? It's never happened.'

'Maybe he wants to find out about my hopes and ambitions.' She rolled her eyes and said,

'You have so much to learn.'

I picked out a royal-blue skirt and white blouse. I hung them in the bedroom and had a long soak in the bath.

I sang along with the sweet voice of Karen Carpenter as I dried myself and applied body lotion. I picked up a brush from the dressing table and noticed the letter in Shelly's handwriting.

KATIE,

NOTHING GOOD CAN COME OF YOUR DATING MARK AMELL. YOU ARE MAKING A HUGE MISTAKE. STOP THIS NOW WHILE YOU CAN, OR I ASSURE YOU, YOU WILL BE SORRY. SHELLY.

There was no kiss to soften the blow, no apologies, no reasons. The letter sounded ominous and threatening. I wasn't going to allow Shelly to control me like this. She had no right.

I didn't sleep well as the letter had angered me. I woke tired and irritable. When Von called, I wasn't quite ready and I wasn't in the best of moods. I buttoned my blouse right up to the neck, and Von loosened three buttons.

'You gotta give him a little cleavage,' she said.

'I can't go to work like this and I'm sick of people telling me what to do.'

'I'm only trying to help,' she said. 'How about one button loosened for work and the extra two when you go for lunch?'

'Yes, okay.' I had to admit the skirt hugged my figure and made me look shapelier than the other things I'd been wearing to work. I'd bought it in a moment of madness, and it had been hanging in my wardrobe ever since because it'd cost a week's wages and I was scared to ruin it.

'Let me do your makeup.'

'Nothing over the top. I don't want to appear like I'm going clubbing.'

Von shushed me and patted foundation onto my skin with an applicator. I always just used my fingers. She busied about me with a brush, mascara wand, and lipstick, then swung me round to peer into the mirror on my dressing table.

'Voila,' she said.

'Not bad,' I had to admit. She'd used blue eye shadow, which brought out the colour of my eyes, and black mascara, which emphasised my long lashes. Poncho-pink lipstick completed the look. I combed my curly hair into a banana clip and was ready to go.

Von spotted the letter from Shelly.

'What's that?' she asked.

'It's just from a friend. She doesn't like Mr Amell.'

'Does she know him?' Von asked.

'She must think she does,' I said. 'She's very judgemental.'

'You've got to do what you've got to do to get on,' Von said.

When we got to work, a couple of the men from children's books whistled at me. One of the guys from sport opened the door and watched me down the corridor.

'Wow!' he said. 'Who let the minx out?'

'Oh no Von, I've overdone it. I look ridiculous. I'm going to give him the wrong impression. I need to wipe this makeup off. This is a mistake.'

'Nonsense.' Tracy looked me up and down.

'She looks good, huh?' Von said.

'Definitely,' Tracy said. 'What's the occasion?'

'I'm going for …'

'Never you mind,' Von said. 'It's for Katie to know and you to wonder.'

'I was only asking.'

Tracy caught me at the water cooler and asked me again what the occasion was.

'Nothing really,' I said. 'I'm just going for lunch.'

'Oh? You have a lunch date?'

'Not a date as such. Just lunch.'

'Who with?'

'Mark.'

'Mark from editorial?'

'No, Mark Amell. Mr Amell.'

Tracy's face turned red then white. You have thought I'd slapped her and she looked like she was going to throw up.

'Katie, don't go!'

'Whyever not?' I asked.

'I can't say. Just promise me, Katie, you won't go.' She clung on to my arm so that I had to shake her off. 'Promise me.'

'I can't. It's all arranged.'

'Oh God,' she said and wandered down the corridor towards the ladies. 'Oh no! Not again. It's Laura all over again.'

I forgot the name Laura until much later, and by then it was too late.

Far too late.

Chapter 30
Regression Therapy: NOVEMBER 1975

I forget about asking to see a doctor because the next time he comes down the steps he hands me all my clothes and tells me to put them on. I dress quickly before he can change his mind.

'Up the steps,' he says, gesturing to the door.
'Me?' I ask.
'There's naebiddy else here.'
I worry it's a trap and he'll pull me from behind and beat me. My legs shake as I climb the steps, and my eyes scream at the glaring light at the top. I squint.
'Yer eyes'll get used to it,' he says. 'There's naebiddy around for miles, so there's no point in shouting or screaming, so you best behave, or I'll take yer clothes back and put you back doon there.'
'I won't,' I say, and he eyes me. 'I mean, I won't make a noise and I will behave.'
I'm in a large room with a cooker in one corner and a table covered in beer tins, chip papers, and bean cans. The room I've been kept in must be the cellar. The windows are covered with boards, so no natural light comes in. There's a bare bulb in the middle of the kitchen, dazzling compared to the darkness of the basement. My eyeballs burn.
'Make me something t'eat,' he says. 'Whit can ye make?'
'I can make sandwiches,' I say.
'Ah'm sick a sangwiches,' he says.
'I'm not allowed to use the cooker,' I say. 'I've never made anything hot before.'

'Well, ye best learn,' he says.

My eyes are adjusting to the light.

'The toilet is upstairs, and ye can sleep up there. If ye make so much as a sound or go near the windaes, ye'll be straight back doon there. Ask if ye want to leave the room.'

'I need the toilet,' I say.

'Go on then. Top o' the stairs.'

The bathroom is a long room. The bath stands on its own, its curled feet reaching into a cracked floorboard on one side. The toilet has rarely, if ever, been cleaned, but it's infinitely better than squatting in a corner and having to live in the smell. I flush, and part of the chain comes off in my hand. Panic grips me. His voice travels up the stairs.

'Hurry up and get down here and make me something to eat.'

I turn on the tap to wash my hands in the filthy sink. It squeals and water drips from it. I wipe my hands on my cardigan and go back downstairs. He's emptying things from a large cupboard. He's searching for something. He's plonked eggs, beans, and a pack of bacon on the table.

'I think I can fry bacon and make an omelette,' I say.

'Go'an then.'

I've watched Mammy do it so many times I'm sure I can do it. The bacon sizzles in the pan, and my mouth waters for a taste of it. I wonder whether he'll allow me to have any. Or whether I'll just have scraps. I whisk the eggs in a bowl using a fork and add it to the pan. All I can think of is happy times in the kitchen with Mammy. I yearn to see her. Long for her hugs and kind words. Is she missing me? Has she forgotten all about me? Tears spring into my eyes and I wipe them before he can see my weakness. Cooking it is harder than it looks, though, and one side of the omelette is black and smoking before the bacon is ready. I then remember that Mammy melts oil and butter before adding the egg mixture. I'm not ready for the blow and when a crack explodes on the side of my head I'm knocked sideways.

'Ye fucking useless cunt,' he says. 'Ye've burnt it.'

More tears come, but I blink them away. I don't want to give him the satisfaction of knowing he's hurt me.

'I'll make another one,' I say.

'Don't bother,' he says, shovelling the food straight from the pan into his mouth.

He disgusts me. If I had a knife I'd plunge it in his eye. I'd stab him and stab him until he stopped moving and I could run away from this hellhole and back to my family.

I don't want to die here. I need to get out. I must find a way to escape.

Chapter 31
KATIE: 1987

Tracy was at the coffee machine, crying. I asked her what was wrong but she just cried louder and ran to the ladies. Part of me wanted to go after her to make sure she was okay, but I got called into a meeting – and when the meeting was over, Tracy was gone. All her belongings were cleared from her desk, and she never returned. A rumour circulated that she'd been caught stealing. Which made no sense because Tracy's parents were loaded.

A Post-it note stuck to the screen of my computer said:

SHELLY CALLED AND LEFT A MESSAGE: DON'T DO IT!!!!

I scrunched it up and threw it in the bin under my desk.

The dinner date with Mark went better than expected. He called it a lunch date. It was queer down here. They called dinner lunch and tea dinner. Supper wasn't a piece of toast or a bowl of cereal. It was all very confusing. I'd started to talk like them. It made things easier. I didn't listen to Von about the shirt buttons. I didn't want to come across as easy. That was the worst thing a girl could be. My stomach crawled as I approached the upmarket restaurant. I'd never even been there for a drink. A meal cost the equivalent of a month's wage. There was a queue round the block when I got there. After standing for only two minutes, a man in a uniform came out of the restaurant and called my name.

'That's me,' I said.

Perfectly manicured and coiffured ladies turned to look at me. Their eyes scanned my cheap clothes and childish hairstyle. I shrivelled in embarrassment.

'Mr Amell has asked me to collect you, madam.'

The man led me in through a private entrance, past a bar surrounded by red velvet seats, through another door marked 'Members', through a vibrant and sumptuous dining room to the table where Mark was sitting reading a newspaper. He stood as soon as he saw me, thanked the man, and pulled out a chair for me. I flailed like a small fish on the bank of a large pond.

I just stared at the menu but Mark put me at ease by ordering the food and wine, and chatting about the latest Sydney Sheldon novel. He claimed his newest client was going to outsell him.

I felt sure all the well-dressed ladies were looking in our direction and wondering why a man of such class was having lunch with someone like me but I was pleased I hadn't gone for the slutty look when Mark remarked how classy I always dressed. He said he didn't like women who made themselves obvious.

'I suppose you've heard about that nasty business at the office?' Mark asked.

'You mean about Tracy?' I asked.

'Yes, it's all very disappointing.'

'I can't quite believe it,' I said.

'Things and people aren't always as they seem on the surface.'

This couldn't have been more true, and I'd remember those words many times over the years.

The waiter placed our food on the table with a flourish. It looked like a work of art and tasted incredible but I'd have enjoyed it more if I wasn't so anxious about using the correct cutlery and spilling sauce down my front. After we'd eaten, Mark told me he was going to ring the office and tell them I was taking the afternoon off.

'I can't do that,' I said. 'I'm on the slush pile.'

'What's the point of being the boss if you can't do exactly what you want?' he said.

He always did exactly as he wanted no matter what the consequences were.

It soon became apparent that staying on the good side of Mark could advance my career in publishing. He was *the* man to know, and, as he was extremely handsome and charming, I was very happy to get to know him.

Chapter 32
KATIE: 1987

We spent many lust-filled nights at Mark's city apartment. It made me feel grown-up. That feeling of pride when he slapped books in front of me and waited while I read the blurbs of his top authors and then stroked his ego. I wanted to be as successful as him. I wanted to be able to spot literary talent the way he did. He'd made millions from the success of his authors. He went to award ceremonies. He was invited to premieres. He was somebody. I wanted to be somebody, too. And not just because of my association with him.

I was in the flat alone. Mark had an important meeting with international clients. I grazed his bookshelves for something to read. One of the authors he represented had written a book about child murderers. I slid it from the shelf and opened it. A sheet of newspaper fell out and floated to the floor. I picked it up and scanned the extract. It was about the case of Heather Parnell. As I read, my heart thumped and my legs gave way.

The Evening Star
15th April 1983
Investigations have opened into the suspicious death of an unidentified elderly man found in Haworth, Yorkshire, on Tuesday evening.

Police were called to the site when a body was spotted by children playing on the edge of the woods. The body is said to have been mutilated. Questions have been raised as to who would commit such a gross and callous crime against a vulnerable member of society.

The land borders a dilapidated mansion, which is said to house members of a commune. A visibly shocked Ethel Jones, a resident of Keighley, said, 'I always said no good would come from that place. They should have torn it down years ago after that fella killed his wife. There's strange goings-on in there.'

Arnie Baker, the local greengrocer, said, 'The place has been overrun with weirdos. You can hear them chanting until all hours of the night. We see lights in the trees, and there's weird screaming. Nothing good's been happening there, you mark my words.'

Our reporter tried to speak to one of the leaders of the commune but could not gain access as a human chain barred his entry. Women wearing long white robes with flowers in their hair spoke incantations and warned him to stay away. Calls have been made for the authorities to raid the site and arrest members of the odd cult.

Police have asked the public to remain calm and say they are making enquiries and hope to bring the perpetrators to justice very soon. They warn against vigilante attacks on the community at Longmuir Manor.

I didn't ask Mark why he had it. I folded it, put it back in the book, and placed the book on the shelf I'd taken it from.

Chapter 33
KATIE: 1987

A junior agent position came up in the agency, and both Von and Mark encouraged me to apply for it. I was shocked when they rang me to tell me I'd been successful.

'I told you sleeping with Mark could work for you,' Von said.

It was like a slap in the face.

'I got the job on my own merits.'

'Sure ya did,' she said, sarcasm rolling in her eyes.

'Mark didn't have anything to do with the interview process,' I said, hurt by the insinuation.

'Just because he wasn't in the room doesn't mean he didn't influence the decision,' Von said. 'Hey, don't get me wrong. I'm happy for you, and I think you deserve the position, but that doesn't mean you'd have got it without some intervention. We all know how it works in this agency. It's not what you know, it's who you know.'

We went out on the town to celebrate my achievement, but I couldn't help feeling the shine had been taken off it.

It was Von who'd encouraged me to get to know Mark, to sleep with him, to ask for his help, so I was shocked when she told me not to get serious about him.

'Trust me,' she said. 'Don't get too involved. Keep it casual, keep it light. If it all goes pear-shaped, then your career does, too.'

I didn't listen to her. I fell as hard as it was possible to fall. Mark told me she was jealous, and I agreed with him. Why couldn't she just be happy for me? A real friend would be happy for me.

Shelly had left a note pinned behind a fridge magnet.

IF HE CAN MAKE YOU, HE CAN ALSO BREAK YOU, S.

On Christmas Eve, Mark took me out to dinner and produced the biggest diamond ring imaginable. It was like every romantic film I'd ever seen. A string quartet played 'Endless Love'; he went down on one knee and asked me if I'd do him the honour of becoming his wife. The honour was most definitely all mine. I couldn't have been happier.

When we went back to work in January, Von practically ignored me. Everyone else made a fuss. There were balloons and banners and champagne. I really wanted Von to share in my happiness, but it seemed she just couldn't. I decided to speak with her about it. I couldn't stand the atmosphere building a wall between us.

'You don't seem too excited about my engagement,' I said. 'Considering it was you who encouraged me to get to know Mark.'

'I'm happy if you're happy,' she said, but she didn't sound at all happy. She sounded seriously pissed off.

My feelings were so hurt when she cried off from having lunch with me, saying she had an appointment, and I saw her in Covent Garden having lunch with Tracy. I couldn't help but think they were talking about me. I never confided in Von again. Mark insisted she was jealous.

'Do you want me to let her go?' he asked. 'I will if she's making things uncomfortable for you.'

'God no,' I said. 'That would be a serious abuse of power.'

'What's the use of power if you aren't allowed to abuse it once in a while?'

I glanced at him, horrified.

'I'm kidding, Katie,' he assured me.

It was a short engagement, and the wedding was a small affair. Mark didn't want a fuss, and I was happy to go along with whatever he wanted. Truthfully, I'd have preferred the whole fairy tale – white dress and carriage – but that was just childish. It was the marriage that was important and not some silly romantic notion that cost ten fortunes. I still couldn't help but compare my dream wedding to what was in effect a glorified tea. I'd always imagined myself dressed in a white floaty dress, pearls in my hair, a white horse and glittering carriage. Family and friends gathered, poetic vows and humorous speeches, a toast with champagne, crystal glasses clinking. A flower girl scattering rose petals, stunning blooms on every surface. I envisaged a string quartet, a DJ and dancing into the small hours. My dress swirling as he guided me onto the dance floor, all eyes on the beautiful bride and her handsome groom. The toast of the town, the envy of all.

It was just the two of us, with Mark's friends, Cynthia and Tarquin, as witnesses. Mark wanted it that way. His mother was having surgery, so he said it wasn't fair to invite anyone else when his mother couldn't be there.

'Can't we postpone it until she's better?' I asked.

'The marriage is the important part, Katie, not the wedding,' he said. 'You've no idea how many couples spend tens of thousands on one day, with months and months of planning and preparation, for the marriage to fall apart before they've paid the credit card bill from the honeymoon. It's better this way.'

I couldn't really argue with that, but it didn't stop me yearning for a floaty white gown and a train of bridesmaids. I wore a white trouser suit and carried lilies which made Mark sneeze so I had to bin them. We went to the Ivy for lunch afterwards. In truth, I couldn't wait for Cynthia and Tarquin to leave so we could be alone, but they hung around for hours, drinking and chatting about obscure subjects. I felt like a gooseberry at my own wedding. I told myself not to be ungrateful. We'd have years of being together. Just the two of us.

I was wrong about that, too.

Chapter 34
HEATHER: LETTER TO KATIE 2019

I wish I could excuse my behaviour by saying I had a terrible childhood. Abused. Neglected. Ignored. I wish I could say that I didn't stand a chance in life. That my parents were drug addicts and dropouts, that we dragged ourselves up. That I turned up to school every day with cigarette burns on my torso, no food in my belly, and haunted eyes. But that wasn't the case. Terrible things happened. Tragic events that sat in the cracks, that prodded the wounds of my life and refused to allow them to heal. But on the whole my childhood was good. My parents were good.

I've tried to look from the outside in, but it's impossible. I've tried to analyse myself. Why didn't I do this? Why didn't I say that? How could I do the other? I wasn't yet nine when we entered the commune, and only fifteen when Father died. Did those events shape my future? Was the unstructured nature of the commune to blame? Had I become feral? I wasn't without a conscience, so I wasn't a psychopath. I was relieved about that.

During the three years I was incarcerated, I took books from the library. They were brought to me on the wheels of a rickety trolley by women called Barbara and Pauline, Karen and Janet. I swallowed the lives of child murderers, trying to find the answers between the yellowing pages of the sensational tomes.

Of course, when these things were leaked to the press, they'd say I devoured books by other killers because I worshipped evil. This was so untrue. So unjust. The headlines were ridiculous.

INSIDE THE MIND OF THE COMMUNE MURDERER
SADISTIC COMMUNE MURDERER RELIVES CRIMES
UNREPENTANT SADIST WORSHIPS OTHER KILLERS

Quite by accident, I read an article in the national press. My mother had apparently been interviewed and had given her 'side of the story'. She'd left the commune and was living on a council estate in Solihull. I thought my eyes would burn through the paper as I read:

'She was a good girl, mainly, when she was young. But she had a wilful side to her nature. If I said 'black' she'd say 'white'.'

This just wasn't true. I didn't dare to question my mother. I'd have felt the back of her hand, and she had hands like an Irish navvy's shovel.

'She had a wonderful childhood, so I can't blame myself for what happened. Me and her dad brought them up to know right from wrong. None of her brothers turned out like that. She must have been mentally ill.'

Wasn't it wrong to allow that creep to hump you in a dormitory when Father's flesh was still warm? Was it right to betray him before the skin had even shrunk and slipped from Father's bones? To throw him in a hole and leave him there to rot? Was that right?

Then there were the articles asking what it was that sent me over the edge. Saying that perhaps I'd killed two older males as a way of seeking revenge for atrocities committed against me.

Insomnia raged within me. I'd forgotten what sleep was like.

There was the inevitable research into my childhood. The stories from teachers, priests and my peers. There were those who said I'd always been a bit weird, a lone wolf, different. There were those who said I was just a normal girl. 'No harm to nobody.' Polite, respectful, cooperative. And then there were those who told the story of the dead cat.

We used to play together in the back street: British Bulldog, hide and seek, kick the can. We took picnics on bike rides and stayed away all day, the older kids looking after the younger ones or leading them into mischief. The tedium of the summer holidays rang out, stretching ahead of us when we had already used our whole arsenal of games. We were restless and bored. We fidgeted and scratched shoes along cobbles, the segs designed to prolong the life of our footwear generating sparks as we scraped, slapped, and tapped our way round the streets.

We'd stolen potatoes for spud guns and shot at pigeons. We'd had a chase from the security guards in the precinct, and we'd taken blue speckled eggs from a nest in the hedge surrounding the allotments. Moses Harrington had smashed them with a stick, resulting in a sticky mess of albumen, flesh, bones, and feathers, a single black eye staring into Hell. We'd flayed him then. Raked him over words of hot coal until he pared himself away and drifted home alone.

We found the cat quite by chance. It was stuck in a hole in the allotment fence, a cut in its side, a feral ball of claws and teeth. Michael Kelly had managed to release it, and he held it to his chest until it stopped flailing. Then began the discussion about a cat having nine lives.

'It's true,' Sharon said. A red-haired girl with freckles who always knew everything. Her uncle was apparently the security guard in the same block as the vets. Not many dared to challenge Sharon. She was rough.

'And if you throw a cat from a tower block it will land on its feet.'

'Bullshit,' Tony Thompson snapped at her.

We called him Teetee on account of his initials. He only had the guts to stand up to her because his cousin was two years older and built like a brick shithouse.

'It's the fucking truth.'

'Go on, then,' Tony said. 'Throw it off the garage.'

'I'm telling you it'll land on its feet.'

'Throw it, then.'

'I'm allergic. You'll have to do it.' She turned to me.

'How am I supposed to get up there?' I asked.

'Climb the drainpipe and I'll pass the cat up to you,' Tony said.

'I don't want to hurt it,' I said.

'It won't get hurt, I'm telling you, it'll land on its feet and run away.'

I scampered up the drainpipe, tearing my shin on the brick face of the garage. I have a scar today where a slither of my dermis was left on the wall. The wound leaked clear liquid that was much more painful than the loss of blood. The sun beat down onto the black felt of the flat roof, and it burned into my hands. I rolled to my feet, then crouched and reached down for the cat. Tony held it at arm's length. The thrashing started again as the animal floundered and flapped, striking out at me with protracted claws. I flinched and grabbed it tight, holding it to my chest until it stopped wriggling.

'Go on, throw it,' Sharon said.

I hesitated. Tony made noises like a chicken, flapping his bent arms, his hands tucked under his armpits.

'Go on,' they chanted. 'Throw the cat, throw the cat, throw the cat.'

I held it out and paused.

'Throw the cat, throw the cat, throw the cat.'

I didn't so much throw it as drop it. It happened slowly, like a film on pause. Then I wanted to press rewind, but it was too late. The cat fell. Shrieking, flapping, fluttering. It hit the ground with a thud. The skull cracked against the concrete, and blood seeped out, spreading in the shape of a heart. Its limbs lay outstretched as though it was playing dead. My eyes were as glassy as the dead cat's, and I realised I was alone; the sun had plummeted behind a cloud, and dusk had rolled up.

I willed it to get up, shake the blood from its fur, and wander off into the night, but it lay there still and bloody.

When the tale was retold to the papers, there was no mention of other children, no mention that I was coerced, bullied into it, no mention that I was told the cat would live.

They spoke of inherent evil. Of escalation. Of serial killers, bed-wetting, and fire-starting. They told lies. Lies that sold papers. And they wondered why I didn't trust journalists.

This time, though, they are going to get the truth. You are going to tell the truth.

My truth.

Chapter 35
KATIE: NOW

You're already seated at your desk when I come in. Your perfect eyes scanning the screen in front of you. I imagine you're reading through notes other psychiatrists have made about me. More lies and assumptions.

'Hello, Katie, take a seat. I've just got to dash off this email and I'll be with you.'

I sit, resisting the impulse to come round to your side of the desk and check your screen to catch you out in the lie. I know. I see you.

You look up from the screen after pressing the 'send' button and smile like I should be grateful for your attention at last.

'How have you been?'

'Fine,' I say.

'Shall we continue where we left off?'

'If you like.'

'I wanted to ask about Shelly. Did you hear from her after you were married?'

'Not as much, but she was always there in the background telling me, 'I told you so'.'

'That's not very helpful,' you say. 'Last time you were telling me about Mark. About your relationship. Your marriage.'

I shrug.

'Do you want to tell me when it went wrong? Or when you first realised the relationship wasn't what it seemed?'

'Is anything ever as it seems?' I ask.

'That's a good question,' you say. But you won't answer it. You never answer questions. You only ask them.

I organised a night out so Mark could meet some of my friends. He was his usual charming self. He opened doors, he gave them lifts home, he laughed at their jokes, he gave money to the homeless. Julia leant into me in the back of the car and said, 'I am so jealous. He's absolutely perfect.' I smiled and hugged her.

'You'll find someone equally fabulous soon,' I said.

'He's a real gentleman,' she said. 'I'm so thrilled you've met someone so wonderful.'

After we'd dropped her off, Mark said, 'Has your friend always been such a slut?'

I thought I'd misheard, so I asked him to repeat himself. I felt like he'd punched me.

It was such a shock. Though later I realised it was nothing like him punching me. When Mark punched me for the first time it hurt much more than that. I was so hurt by the things he was saying about my friend. I was indignant. I challenged him, of course. I asked him what he meant.

'She flirted outrageously with every man in the room, including me,' he said.

'Oh, she's just friendly,' I said.

'She's obviously a cock-teaser.'

'Mark, there's just no need for that.'

'You certainly won't be going out with her on your own again. I can just imagine what the two of you would get up to.'

It was our first major argument. That night he slept on the couch, and my arms ached for him. Instead of him apologising to me, I apologised to him and agreed that Julia could be a bit over the top at times. I felt so disloyal.

I was completely loyal to Mark, though. One by one my friends fell by the wayside as I made excuses not to see them for fear of upsetting him. Reflecting now, it was textbook controlling behaviour, but at the time I was so enthralled by him, I just couldn't see it. Our social life was restricted to his friends. I must say, I tolerated them rather than liked them. My needs were eroded on every level.

The first time he hit me we'd been to the opera to see *Tosca*. It had occurred to me that every opera we'd been to see portrayed women as victims. I made the mistake of voicing my opinions over dinner with Cynthia and Tarquin.

We were at Mark's favourite restaurant. It had pictures of rabbits and hares round the walls, and heads of deer and moose overlooked us. Shiny guns stood to attention in glass cabinets. The whole place made me feel uneasy.

Mark was tucking into a rare venison steak, and I'd ordered the turbot with saffron. Our guests had both plumped for ceviche.

'What did you think of the performance?' Cynthia asked me.

'It was interesting,' I said. 'The music was obviously beautiful, and the voices were powerful, but I can't help thinking that it's another vehicle to reinforce patriarchy.'

'Really?' Cynthia said. Her sarcastic tone wasn't lost on me. 'In what way?'

'Think about it. Tosca, like Carmen from last week, is a powerfully disturbing figure, but we aren't allowed to leave the theatre seeing women like her alive and breathing. It's like women who want to do something with their lives that don't include men, are somehow considered dangerous.'

'Oh, really?' Tarquin said, a flash of something like anger crossing his face.

'Ignore her,' Mark said. 'She hasn't a clue what she's talking about.'

'Oh, so because I'm a woman I'm clueless?' I said. Anger surged through me at being dismissed so offhandedly. 'I'm not entitled to an opinion? I rest my case.'

'There's no need to get irate, dear,' Tarquin said, his voice dripping with condescension. I might have known the three of them would gang up on me. Why couldn't they see how wrong it all was? I fumed.

'I'm not irate. I'm merely pointing out that women in opera who show that there are different ways of living, women who take lovers, women who don't seek the approval of men, are killed. What message are we sending?' I felt I should keep my mouth shut but frustration boiled over and I couldn't bite my tongue.

'Let's change the subject,' Cynthia said. 'Have you seen my new watch from Liberty? Isn't it darling?' I wanted to say, *For fuck's sake, Cynthia, help me out here. Where's the sisterhood?* Instead, I sat through the rest of dinner seething, and when we got home, Mark hit me for the first time.

'What the fuck was all that about?' he spat as soon as we were alone. He flung his gloves in the hallway and kicked off his shoes, shook his coat from his arms, and threw that, too. 'Why can't we just have a nice night at the opera without you turning it into a political rant?'

'I wasn't turning it into a political rant. I was merely voicing an opinion.'

'What the fuck is wrong with you? Why can you never just be happy? Why are you never satisfied?' His words bore into me, burned me inside. I should have just left it but I couldn't. Anger and frustration welled up and overflowed.

'What I said is true. The composers seem to be saying to us, yes, these women are fascinating, but we have to kill them off. It's misogynistic. Look at Gilda in *Rigoletto*, she gives up her life for a man who abducts and rapes her. It's absurd.'

Mark screamed in my face. He grabbed me by the throat and pinned me to the wall. Then I felt the slap. Stinging, burning, shocking.

'Jesus, woman, can you not just shut the fuck up? You're a philistine. I take you out. I take you to nice places, and this is the fucking gratitude I get. You show me up in front of my friends. What will they think?'

The next day he brought me flowers. He cried and begged my forgiveness for his 'outburst'. He was stressed, tired, overworked. I forgave him, because that's what you do when you love someone. I did, however, learn to bite my tongue. I stopped voicing my thoughts, my feelings, my wishes.

I'd got the message. It didn't matter what I thought. My feelings, hopes, dreams were irrelevant. As long as I didn't upset Mark and his friends, that was the main thing. If I didn't say or do the right thing, he didn't speak to me for a whole week. The silence burned me, ate me, tore me. Even more than the violence did. It was the first time I felt real regret. The first time I wondered what I'd got myself into.

'Just so you know, if a man hits you and tells you he's sorry, he's lying. Not just to you but to himself. If he's hit you once he'll hit you again and again and again until you put a stop to it.'

'And how did you put a stop to it?' you ask.

'Oh, that came later. Much later.'

Chapter 36
KATIE: 2019

A letter dropped onto the mat as I sipped my morning coffee. I recognised the writing as Shelly's. My stomach knotted as I ripped it open.

KATIE, YOU NEED TO STAY AWAY FROM MOLLIE. YOU DON'T KNOW ANYTHING ABOUT HER. SHE'S TROUBLE, S.

Why did she have to do this every time I made a friend? Why couldn't she just leave me alone? Sometimes I wished Shelly would just go away. Leave my life forever. Other times I felt like I couldn't live without her. She kept me right. Kept me safe. And then sometimes it was Shelly who hurt me the most.

I wrote to Heather asking her to tell me what happened when they stole the van and left the commune. The last pages had gone off on a tangent, detailing an incident in her childhood. I'd already read about that. It no longer held my interest. I wanted to get to the commune murders and what happened after that. I wanted to know how a 'normal' girl became a cold-blooded killer. Today's letter continued the tale.

Dear Katie,

It wasn't technically theft. The van belonged to my father, and my father was dead, so it was my inheritance. Before I tell you, I just want to point out that Karma was not a nice man. Just remember that.

We were driving down a country lane, and his bloody face appeared behind me in the van. My heart raced, and my face burned. Karma reached into my seat, and his hands gripped my throat. Jovano whacked him and the car swerved. Karma squeezed the life out of me. I could feel my eyes bulging as I tried to gasp for air. The car screeched to a stop and Jovano jumped out, raced round to the passenger side, and pulled at Karma's hands, but he couldn't budge them. Jovano disappeared. A clang, a scrape, a crack and Karma's hands released my throat. I gasped and gasped for air, my head light, my eyes blurred. Everything went black.

When I awoke, Karma's lifeless body lay beside a shallow grave where Jovano stood shovelling soil.

'You okay?' he asked.

'Yes, I think so.' I could barely speak for the pain in my throat.

'Help me,' he said.

'I can't,' I said. 'This is so wrong.'

'Heather, we need to bury him.'

'But the police will find him. Then they'll come after us.'

'So what do you suggest?'

I'd noticed a freight train passing, so there must be tracks nearby.

'What if we drag him to the railway line and leave his body there? A train will come and ...'

' ... And cut him in two?'

'And it'll delay identification. It'll at least give us time to escape.'

So that's what we did. We dragged his dead body onto the train track by the light of the moon and watched the train come, crouched under an embankment in the rain. I wasn't ready for the amount of blood there'd be, or how the body would look decapitated and mutilated. Jovano insisted we still bury it.

'It'll give us even longer to escape,' he said.

I helped him bury the body, but I didn't kill him. I think I was on autopilot. I don't think it registered what we were doing. My instinct for survival had kicked in, and all I could see was getting as far away as possible.

So we escaped in the van. We drove in silence down the motorway. The rain snivelled down the windscreen. Brake lights bled in streaks across the road ahead, and my heart beat in my ears like claps of thunder.

And then, of course, you know about Christina …

I did know about Christina and that's what stopped me from having any sympathy. Once is an accident, twice might even be explained as bad luck, being in the wrong place at the wrong time. But three times? Three deaths didn't happen by chance.

Chapter 37
KATIE: 1988

By the time I'd realised the relationship with Mark was abusive, I was powerless to stop the decline. It was long after I'd become hooked, like a smack addict chasing the dragon. Defenceless against the tide of love and lust. I was always making the same mistakes over and over again. There had been signs, but being head over heels, I'd chosen to ignore them. It was always done so cleverly. The manipulation was so accomplished, I always blamed myself. I always thought everything bad that happened was my fault. I always had since the incident on holiday. It defined my whole existence. It affected my whole life. And he was always so sorry. I think I became addicted to the rush of love when he was overcome by shame at what he'd done.

Of course, Shelly revelled in this. She'd been right all along, and I didn't listen.

One time, Mark and I had been for dinner in an exclusive restaurant, and a friend and colleague of his had joined us, enthusiastically chatting about a book he'd just read. I listened eagerly, but I couldn't contribute other than to say that it sounded quite wonderful, having not read it.

Later that evening at home, Mark had poured me a glass of wine and was tugging off his tie and flicking open the top two buttons of his shirt. 'You know, you really should read more intelligent texts.'

I felt a small wound opening inside me. Slowly it spread: a bloodstain on sheets. Feeding the paranoia I felt about being inadequate.

'I should,' I said. 'And I would if I had the time. You know how much I love reading.'

He opened the log burner and fed chunks of wood to the howling, orange flames.

'It's a poor excuse, not having the time,' he said, slapping the muck from his hands. 'What we should do …' He paused and looked out of the window and into the distance. 'What we should do is have a book for you to read each week, and we can discuss it on Thursday evenings after dinner.'

'That sounds like fun,' I said, the merest flicker of doubt lapping round the edges of my heart.

'And then you won't appear to be such a dullard in front of my friends.'

I turned towards him, hurt burning inside me. What did he just say? I couldn't believe it. My cheeks burned from so many emotions rushing through me. I wanted to scream, to hit out, to run.

'I'm just kidding, Katie. Lighten up.' Rather than making me feel lighter, his comment incensed me further.

How could he always turn everything around and make me believe I was in the wrong?

'I'd love to read Maya Angelou's *I Know Why The Caged Bird Sings*,' I said. 'That would make a great discussion topic.'

'It has to be something that suits us both,' he said. 'Or how could we have a discussion about it? And I said highbrow.'

'You're right, of course,' I'd said. 'What do you suggest?'

'Well, I suppose we could pander to your plebeian tastes to begin with. How about *Lord of The Flies*? It's a simple enough text to start you off.'

'I can read, Mark,' I'd said sharply. 'I'm not a dunce.' I wanted to say, *Just because I didn't go to Oxbridge doesn't mean I'm any less intelligent than you,* but I bit my tongue. Why did he call me those things? How could he just have no thought for my feelings like that? Rage burned inside me but I swallowed it.

'We'll examine it from a post-modernist perspective. Let's explore individualism versus community, and the dehumanisation of relationships.'

I didn't enjoy the text. It was far too brutal for my liking. Mark knew I was sensitive to violence, yet he still insisted I read the whole thing. I hated the bullying aspect, the mob mentality. It depressed me, but when I tried to tell him so, he accused me of being too sensitive.

'Maybe it's you who is too insensitive,' I said in an unusual display of defiance.

He didn't speak to me for four days to punish me. The worst thing in the world for me was to be ignored. Mark knew this. I would rather thrash things out. Argue. Say my piece and have it over with. I hated silence. Silence invaded the room. It stole my peace. It made me feel ill. Silence was cruel. It fed my insecurities. It reminded me of past trauma. Mark knew this. I read the book. I discussed the book. Yet still he made me feel like I'd done something wrong. I wasn't good enough. I was a second-class citizen.

'Can I read something light this week?' I asked.

'How are we supposed to have an intelligent conversation about a trashy novel?' he said.

'I don't mean Barbara Cartland or Catherine Cookson, just something less violent.'

'I thought you could read *Ulysses* by James Joyce,' he said. 'There's lots to discuss there.' He handed me the text.

'I'll never get through this in a week,' I said.

'Nonsense,' he said. 'If you stop watching trashy TV, you'll have loads of time.'

It was pointless arguing, but I rarely had time to watch TV at all, let alone the trashy programmes I enjoyed.

'I'm inviting Cynthia and Tarquin. We can all discuss it together.'

I groaned inwardly.

That night as I began to read *Ulysses*, my heart sank. There was no way I'd be able to read this in a week and understand what it was about. I rang my friend, Tania, and wailed like a small child.

'You need Cliffs Notes,' she said.

'What are they?'

'They're study guides which summarise plots, give character analysis, and explore relevant issues. It got me through uni. Didn't you use them?'

'No, I just read the books. Where can I get one of these?'

'Any good book shop. I've probably still got a copy on *Ulysses* somewhere. Hang on.'

The phone receiver thudded on the hall stand, footsteps faded, and a door opened. Seven minutes later, Tania was back.

'I found it,' she said. 'It's a bit dog-eared, but you're welcome to it. I'll drop it by in the morning after the school run.'

'Thank you so much. You've saved my life.'

'Why are you letting him dictate to you what to read? Where's the pleasure in that?'

'It's just something he wants us to enjoy together. It would seem churlish to refuse.'

'Enjoy, being the operative word. Where's the enjoyment for you?'

'I know, I know. I'll do this one and then it'll be my choice.' But my choice never seemed to materialise.

Tarquin and Cynthia had badgered and bullied me mercilessly. They'd treated me like the village idiot.

'What do you think about the themes of paternity in the piece, Katie?' Cynthia said.

'Oh ... em ... well ...Stephen's thinking about the Holy Trinity involves, on the one hand, Church doctrines that uphold the unity of the Father and the Son and, on the other hand, the writings of heretics that challenge this doctrine by arguing that God created the rest of the Trinity.'

'Katie has been reading the Cliff Notes. How quaint.'

'No I haven't,' I said. My cheeks burned and I wanted to slap her. I was so sick of their condescension.

Cynthia laughed nastily. When they'd gone, Mark turned on me, and I'd never seen him so angry.

'Humiliated, Katherine, is how I feel.' He only ever called me Katherine when he was angry. 'I cannot comprehend how a wife of mine could be so devious, so underhanded, so calculating.' He made it sound like I'd had an affair or murdered someone. I felt sick and ashamed, but angry and resentful.

'Mark, I told you I didn't have time to read such a book in a week, but you insisted.'

How did he always manage to make me feel guilty? Why did I always end up feeling like I was a terrible human being? I'd be punished for this transgression.

I wasn't aware just how awful the punishment would be.

Chapter 38
KATIE: 1988

I had had a particularly great day at work. An author I discovered had just made the *New York Times* best seller list. I couldn't believe it. It was so exciting. The Tube home had been a nightmare. There was a jumper on the line, and I was delayed by hours. I couldn't wait to get back to the flat to tell Mark all about my grand achievement. He was going to be so proud of me.

I could tell he was in a bad mood as soon as I opened the door. He didn't greet me with his usual, 'Hi, darling, how was your day?' He stormed past me to close the door, complaining there was a draught.

'You're late,' he barked.

'Yes, there was a suicide on the Northern Line. Awful business. Poor man.'

'Inconsiderate bastard,' he said. 'Why didn't you get a cab? I cooked. Dinner is ruined.'

'I'm sure it'll be fine,' I said.

'It won't,' he snapped. 'I told you it was ruined. Didn't you hear me?'

I reached up to put my arms round him, to placate him, but he shoved me away. I lost balance, knocked my hip against the hall stand, and cried out.

'Mark, that hurt!'

'Oh, don't be pathetic,' he said.

'I'm not being pathetic. It's really sore. Don't push me like that.' My earlier excitement had fizzled out like a damp firework, and tears boiled in my eyes.

'Oh, not the fucking waterworks!'

'I'm going to bed,' I said. 'I had good news to share with you, but I don't want to share it now.'

'You're so fucking childish,' he said. 'I'd never have started a relationship with you if I'd known you were going to be so immature.'

I felt so confused. I'd been so happy, so excited to share my good news, and it had all gone wrong.

'Let's not fight,' I said. 'I really don't want to fight.'

'If you don't want to fight, why do you always start?' he asked.

'I don't,' I said. 'At least I don't mean to. I'm sorry.'

He snubbed me for the rest of the night. I tried to make conversation, but he completely ignored me.

'Don't you think not speaking is rather childish?' I asked. 'Nothing will get resolved if we don't communicate.'

'This won't get resolved,' he said. 'Because I'm at the bottom of your pecking order.'

'What do you mean? That's just not true.'

'Yes it is. When did you last put me first?'

'I always put you first,' I said. 'I don't know how you can say that.'

'Because it's true. Your friends are more important than me.'

'That's not true. I hardly see my friends anymore.'

'Your job is more important than me.'

'It isn't, Mark. Of course it isn't.'

'Prove it,' he said.

'What do you mean?'

'What I said. Prove it. Prove your job isn't more important than me.'

'And just how am I supposed to do that?'

'Hand in your notice.'

'*What?*'

'You heard me. Hand in your notice. Stay at home and look after me.'

'You hand in your notice,' I said.

'And how, pray tell, are we supposed to live if I don't work? We don't need your paltry wage, but we most certainly need mine.'

'Mine won't be paltry before long. Kruegar made the *New York Times* best seller list.'

'And?'

'And Kruegar was my find.'

'Not your author, though.'

'But if I can spot one bestseller, I can spot another and another and another. I'm good at this. I *know* I can do this. It'd be nice if you had a bit of faith in me.'

'And it would be nice if just for once you acted like a wife. A proper wife.'

'Wow! I can't believe what you're saying to me.'

'And I can't believe that I come a very low last on your list of priorities. I thought when I married you …'

'What? I'd be your unpaid skivvy? I have a career, Mark, whether you like it or not.'

'You have a career because I made you,' he said. 'You remember that.'

It was then that I recollected Shelly's words. Mark could make me, and he could also break me. My life, my career, everything I held dear, was in his hands.

Chapter 39
Regression Therapy: DECEMBER 1975

I wake on the filthy mattress. It smells musty, but it's heaven compared to sleeping on the stone floor of the cellar. It's warm and dry, and I now have two blankets. There's no door on the room, so he can see me from his bed in the other room. He eyes me like a wolf eyeing a chicken. I've no idea how long I've been here. The miserable days and nights roll into one.

'I'm going out today,' he says. 'A man is coming tae stand guard outside, and if ye so much as make a squeak he'll have ye heart and liver ripped oot and eat it for his dinner. There's some square sausage in the fridge. I'll have it later. Make sure ye don't ruin it.'

'Can I have some, please?' I ask.

He doesn't say no. He just shakes his fist at me. Hunger has got the better of me, so I decide I'll risk it.

As soon as the door closes behind him, I start to plan my escape. If I can force one of the boards from the window, I can smash the glass underneath and climb out. He says we're in the middle of nowhere and that no one will hear me shout, but when he leaves, the roar of car engines and the chatter of voices bursts in. There are people out there, and one of them will surely help me. I try not to think about the man who he claims will eat my heart and liver if I escape.

The window boards are held in place by two planks nailed vertically like bars. They shouldn't be too difficult to prise off if I can find some tools. I rattle drawers and cupboards in the kitchen, searching for anything sharp enough to use. A screwdriver, a chisel. My hand rests upon a bread knife. Long and serrated. It might do. I wedge it behind one of the planks and push. Pain shoots through my hand. I shove again and again, but there's no movement. Maybe I should try and wrench the nails out. I press the point of the knife under the nail head and try to work it loose. Nothing. Maybe I could saw my way through the wood. After half an hour, I've made a dent about two centimetres in length, and my hand throbs like it's on fire. Maybe I can do a little every time he goes out. But what if he notices what I'm trying to do? No, I need to escape today. I can't stand another minute in this place. I want my mammy and daddy. I'll never be naughty again. I'll go to bed when I'm asked, I won't be too loud, I will do my homework, and I'll tidy up my toys. Please, please, please let me get out of here today.

I saw and saw with the knife. I pull and pull at the plank until I feel like my hand will snap again. With a crack it eventually gives way. I stick the knife in the corner of the board and work it in until I can feel the glass. I clatter the board backwards and forwards, and a corner lifts. Daylight peeks in. I keep working and working the wood until there's a triangular patch of light. Not big enough to crawl through yet, but I know I can get there. My heart thumps. I daren't hope. I keep working it. My hand stings, I feel sick with fatigue and fear. I can't give in. This is my chance.

Eventually, I've worked enough of the board free and I press my face to the grubby glass. Shapes are blurred, and I'm not sure what it is I'm seeing, until I recognise his moustache, his cruel mouth, and his evil eyes. He's there staring back at me. I scream. His key rattles in the lock, and I'm torn between running and banging on the window. Fear holds me and I run. I curse myself. I should have stayed and tried to draw attention to myself. Someone might have heard me and sent for help.

When he finds me I'm curled up in a ball, begging him not to hurt me. He stamps on my hand until he's smashed every bone. I retch and retch until there's nothing left in my stomach.

I must have passed out because I wake up naked in the cellar. Cold and in agony. I will never get out of here now.

Chapter 40
HEATHER: LETTER TO KATIE 2019

We took to the road and travelled south. Distancing ourselves as far as possible from the mess we'd left behind.

Mess conjures up spilt milk, or cornflakes scattered across the worktop in a rush to catch a morning train. Dirty washing splayed across bedroom floors after being discarded by their owner who was in search of love or sleep. It doesn't evoke the brutal murder of two elderly people.

The car swallowed white lines like a wild animal as we sped towards the horizon, the engine growling in protest.

Clouds in the shape of crocodiles swam across grey skies. We eventually ran out of petrol just outside a city. Jovano wanted to head to a city. They're anonymous, he said.

At a supermarket, Jovano bought scissors, hair dye, and hoodies. 'We need to disguise ourselves,' he said. 'In case the police are looking for us.'

He cut my hair and I cried. The curls fell. Golden, auburn, cherry red autumn leaves. My curly wild locks cropped right to my head. The black hair dye gave the impression I was trying to impersonate Elvis, and it took me back to the day he'd died.

The headlines screamed KING ELVIS DEAD. I couldn't understand how this figure, who was such a huge part of my childhood, was gone. I wondered where he'd gone to. I imagined his soul leaving his bloated body. The soul in my childish imagination resembled the bottom of a shoe with ghostly eyes. It floated upwards, singing 'Lonesome Tonight', and playing a harp-shaped guitar. That was my first experience of death.

The rest were so much worse.

An Elvis facsimile stared back at me from the mirror of a cheap B&B room. Jovano shaved his head to the bone. The same features which, when surrounded by hair, gave an angelic air, now appeared alien and freakish. The black circles beneath his eyes that had once been endearing were now zombie-like.

Our own mothers wouldn't recognise us.

We met Christina quite by chance, as so often happens. I write this matter-of-factly, as though brutal murder was a regular occurrence, like attending a birthday party or meeting an old school friend for coffee.

We'd ended up near the coast. We were sleeping in the van, because the money was running low. We made regular trips on foot into the nearest city centre to search for work. We both lied about our age, but still they wanted documents to prove who we were. We'd been to the village supermarket to buy food for that day, and I was waiting for Jovano to use the toilet. An elderly woman carrying shopping bags limped past me. She wobbled to the side with each faltering step as though she had one leg shorter than the other. I thought about Ralph, the miller's son, and wondered what she'd done to earn her limp. I watched, fascinated, as she struggled under her burden. Then a carrier bag burst, spewing tins and packets onto the ground. Cans and bottles rolled in arcs, a red one smashing against the kerb, its contents bleeding into the road.

I'm not sure what made me want to help her. I'm unsure what force drew me to pick up her items and offer to carry them to her home.

All I know is, if the carrier bag hadn't burst, Christina Widdecome would still be alive.

Chapter 41
KATIE: 1988

When I rode up to the house for the first time we were already married, but I was alone. Mark had just come back from the Frankfurt Book Fair, and I was taking some time off. I was desperate to go to Frankfurt, but he said he had back-to-back meetings and I'd just be in the way. He'd been trying to persuade me to give up work completely, so taking some time out was the compromise. He'd given so many reasons. He didn't want a wife who worked. He didn't want people to think he couldn't support me. I'd have enough to do running the estate. I had duties. Obligations. Why did he always make me feel like a second-class citizen? Frustration bubbled inside me but I forced it down and tried to look on the bright side.

Maybe it wouldn't be so bad. I could be a lady of leisure for a while. I could take up painting. Maybe write poetry. Plant flowers. This could be an opportunity for growth. It didn't matter how often I told myself all this, I didn't believe it. I loved my job. I felt like my career was on pause before it had even had a chance to begin. My nana's voice kept running through my thoughts: 'No good crying over spilt milk.' I'd just have to make it work. I had so much to be grateful for. I'd go back after a few weeks. I'd persuade Mark that a wife who worked was more interesting than one who sat at home arranging flowers and approving lunch menus.

Mark said he'd meet me at The Parsonage. He promised he'd be there before me as his flight was an early one, but his chauffeur rolled the Mercedes up the long driveway and his car was nowhere to be seen. I was nervous and with good reason. The house was an imposing building built with yellow stone, which reminded me of sand dunes in the sunshine. Ivy had begun to climb the walls, and wisteria fought with honeysuckle. A lazy dog sat on the veranda, lifting its head languidly when the car purred up the drive, then placing it back on its front paws and closing its eyes again, basking in the afternoon sun. I was so in awe at the size and beauty of the place I could barely breathe.

I knocked at the front door. A man dressed like an old-fashioned butler opened it and bid me welcome. I soon realised he *was* the butler. Mark's mother had the help lined up to shake my hand. She had the air of a duchess bringing her new daughter to her country residence. I'd never been in a home so large. You could fit my old city apartment in the hallway. I was filled with excitement and anticipation.

Mrs Amell was a formidable creature and not just in stature, though she did tower over me. Her grey hair was drawn back into an elegant chignon, pearls at her throat, and a Chanel skirt suit caressed her tidy frame. She invited me into the kitchen, but it felt more like a command. She bid me sit at the table in the adjoining dining room. She inspected me like she was examining an amoeba through a microscope.

'And what is it you do, darling?' she asked. The 'daahrling' would've sounded affected had it been uttered by anyone else, but from her mouth it simply sounded threatening.

'I'm a literary agent,' I said.

'How sweet,' she said.

You'd think I'd just told her I was running a raffle. And that's how it was. If I dared to mention a career, she rolled her eyes in a patronising manner and changed the subject. I'm sure she believed I should be seen and not heard. I could never understand women like that. Even if they had no aspirations of their own, why wouldn't they cheer on other women?

'Has Mark arrived?' I asked, eager to see my husband. I needed to feel his protective arm around my waist as I faced the in-law.

'He's been detained, but he shouldn't be long,' she said. 'Let's have tea.' There followed a stilted conversation about the weather. I was shrivelling under my new mother-in-law's gaze like a slug doused in salt. Her next words hit me hard. 'It'll be lovely to have another Mrs Amell here again.'

'Again?' I asked.

'Hasn't he told you?'

I felt a surge of an emotion I couldn't identify, like a cold tsunami rising and flooding me.

'Oh yes,' I said. 'Of course.' But he'd told me nothing. My thoughts whirled, and I couldn't concentrate on her conversation. Who was the other Mrs Amell? Had Mark been married before? Why had he not mentioned something this important? Cold crept inside me, filling my legs and my chest.

'Are you comfortable here, or would you prefer to take tea in the drawing room?'

I told her that I was quite comfortable. Huge sash windows looked out onto the beach. A large white bird pecked at something small in a shell.

'It's a stunning view,' I said.

'Yes, we take it for granted,' she said off-handedly. 'But you're right, it is quite pretty.'

'Have you lived here long?'

'Yes, not in this house as such, but my family is a very old one. We've been here in the village for generations. My husband bought this when he became ill. The old lady who had the house died, and her family just wanted rid of it. We thought the sea air would benefit Mark's father. Unfortunately, it didn't.'

I later learned Mrs Amell's family had made their money in mining. From the blood, sweat, and death of poor men and their families. Mrs Amell had a superior air as if she was always smelling milk on the turn.

She rang a bell on the wall, and a woman dressed all in white, excepting a blue-and-white-striped apron, entered the room.

'We'd like to take tea in the drawing room, Mrs Benson.'

'Very well, ma'am,' she said.

I felt like I'd stepped into a nineteenth-century novel.

'Will your guest be joining you?' She spat the 'your guest' like it was an insult. She might as well have said 'the slut', because her expression suggested it.

'Forgive me, Mrs Benson. This is the new Mrs Amell.'

The woman, who'd been missing from the line-up at the door, nodded to me, turned, and left the room.

Mark's mother ignored the woman's rudeness, and waving her hand in an offhand way, said, 'She will get used to you eventually. She was very fond of Mark's wife.'

I wanted to scream, *I'm Mark's wife!* but I swallowed my rage and frustration, which spun inside me. I couldn't believe Mark had never told me he'd been married before. How had that not come up in conversation? No wonder he didn't want a big wedding. Rage, humiliation and hurt burned inside me.

We'd just become seated in the huge draughty drawing room when the phone rang and the butler entered, holding a tray containing a note.

Mrs Amell took the folded piece of paper, read it, scrunched it, and threw it into the open fire. 'It seems there's only the two of us for dinner. Mark has been held up. He said we're to have dinner without him.'

Disappointment must have shown on my face.

'Don't look too upset at having to spend time in my company.'

'Oh I … it's not … I'm not …'

'I'm teasing,' she said without smiling. 'We'll be able to get to know each other.' She rang the bell again, and when Mrs Benson appeared asked her to take me to my room. 'We usually dress for dinner,' she said. 'Shall we say seven?'

Of course, I didn't dare to say I'd rather just go to my room and relax. I wanted to bathe and read and lie in bed thinking of Mark. How I longed for him to be there holding me and kissing me, reassuring me that everything would be all right. I wanted to ask him when his mother would be moving into the granny flat in The Lodge he'd had renovated for that purpose. I couldn't wait for us to be alone together in the house.

But of course, that was not to be. I didn't know then how manipulative Mrs Amell was. I didn't realise the hold she had over Mark. If only I'd known before the wedding it would have saved so much heartache.

Chapter 42
KATIE: 2019

I fell asleep after reading Heather's letters and awoke in a darkened room, muddled. A fuzzy haze held muffled sounds. I wasn't sure what woke me, but I had an unnerving feeling that someone was watching me.

'Mark,' I called out.

The howling of the wind answered me. I think I saw the shape of his face at the window, his brows meeting in a scowl at some imagined misdemeanour. The rational part of my mind knew it couldn't be Mark, but my heart still raced, and my frame shook. I could recall every detail of Heather's story. The words were so horrific they were etched in my mind. They were jagged and rough, like the bark of a tree. They were jammed so hard in my brain that even if they left, they would leave an imprint.

Chapter 43
HEATHER: LETTER TO KATIE 2019

Jovano came running to help as soon as he saw what had happened. He made a hammock with his jumper and stuffed some of the shopping in it. We walked home with the old woman, and she didn't stop thanking us. 'It's not often young people will stop to help an old codger like me. Young 'uns have got a bad reputation, but it just shows ye.'

Her house was a huge Victorian mansion on the outskirts of the village.

'Come in,' she said.

The hallway boasted the original tiled floor and a mahogany hat stand. A white cat shot from a room at the end of the hall and wrapped itself round Christina's legs, rubbing its face on her calves.

'Now, Tintin, let Mammy get in. One of these days you're going to break my neck.' She nudged the cat gently with her foot and led us through to the kitchen to dump the shopping. 'Let's get the kettle on and make you a nice cup of tea.'

I took over the tea-making and told her to go and sit down.

'You're so kind,' she said.

I made tea and brought it to her. She was sitting in a rocking chair by the fire in her front room and had laid a cloth over the coffee table.

'I've never seen you around here before. Have you just moved in?'

I opened my mouth to tell her we were from Durham but had decided to go travelling, but Jovano spoke quickly.

'We've fallen on hard times,' he said. 'Our parents were abusive, and we finally managed to escape.'

'Oh, how awful,' she said. 'Some people don't deserve to have children.'

'Oh, they weren't so bad. When they weren't beating us, we were mostly ignored.'

'That's terrible. No child should be ignored. Children should be cherished and loved and spoiled. Would you like to stay for dinner? I'm having lamb chops.'

'That'd be lovely,' Jovano said before I could say otherwise.

So we stayed for dinner. Christina told us about her children, who'd long since left home to pursue careers in the air force or had emigrated to Australia. She complained about the people passing and dropping rubbish that blew all over her front garden. It was more like a football pitch than a garden. A big, rambling walled garden you could get lost in. She waxed lyrical about the benefit cheats, the scroungers, the druggies and the ne'er-do-wells of the locality, while we nodded and tutted in the right places as we chomped on new potatoes and juicy lamb.

The dark rolled in so Christina lit the lamps in the front room, Jovano sighed and stood, shaking her hand and wishing her all the best.

'Are you staying nearby?' she asked.

Jovano coughed and dropped his head.

'We're hoping to find a comfortable spot somewhere …' He glanced up at her through his eyelashes. 'Somewhere out of the biting wind.'

'Whatever do you mean? Surely you have a hotel or a B and B?'

'Sadly not,' Jovano said.

I was embarrassed by him laying it on so thick.

'But we'll be okay,' I said. 'We'll find somewhere. There'll be plenty of hostels in the city centre, and they're cheap.'

'Just a shame they're so dangerous,' Jovano said. 'I heard of a girl whose throat was slit as she lay in her bunk. But I'm sure we'll be okay.'

'Nonsense,' Christina said. 'There's plenty of room here. There's no way you are spending a night on the streets ... or in one of those dens of iniquity.'

'Oh, we couldn't impose ...' Jovano said.

'Rubbish, I insist,' Christina said. 'I have seven bedrooms and I only need one.'

'Oh I couldn't,' I said.

'I won't take no for an answer,' Christina said. 'Anyway, I'll be glad of the company. You can stay as long as you like.'

And so it was decided. By being a good Samaritan, Christina Widdecome had sealed her fate.

Chapter 44
KATIE: 1988

Mrs Benson led me up the sweeping staircase and along the passage. She opened a door on the left and nodded at me to go inside. My luggage had been opened, and my clothes, I learned, hung in the dressing room wardrobe, and placed in drawers. French doors led out onto a balcony which overlooked the sea.

'I took the liberty of running Madam a bath,' she said.

'Oh, thank you.'

'Will that be all, ma'am?' Mrs Benson asked, her gaze running over me, her lip curling in distaste.

'Yes, thank you. And please call me Katie.'

'Ma'am,' she said and backed out of the double doors, closing them behind her.

I quickly turned the gold key in the lock and sat on the bed. At last I was alone. Being in the house felt like I was wearing someone else's clothes. Too tight, they caused constant discomfort. For much of my time at The Old Parsonage, I felt I was living in someone else's skin.

Dinner was stuffy and formal. The food was excellent. Apparently, the chef was French and capricious but incredible. Mrs Amell interrogated me about my background, my qualifications, and my family. I told her the good bits. The bits the tabloids had no interest in. The other bits, well, they were none of her business. The time passed slowly until it was time for me to retire to my bedroom.

I lifted the telephone to call Mark. I was so churned up about the fact that he hadn't told me he'd been married before, I could barely speak.

'What's wrong, darling?' he asked.

'Nothing,' I lied.

'There's something, Pudding. Come on, spit it out.'

I imagined him running a hand through his thick hair.

'Why have you never told me you've been married before?'

There was silence and a sigh.

'So Mother's told you?' he said.

I imagined him frowning. 'Yes, and I must say it would have been better coming from you. I felt humiliated. Your mother thought you'd made me aware.' Hot tears stung my eyes.

'My past is my past,' he said. 'I have no wish to relive it or to discuss it.'

'But what happened? When did you divorce?' I swallowed down a lump like an apple core.

'We didn't.'

For an awful second I had visions of our marriage being a sham. An illegal pairing. My husband a bigamist.

'She died,' he said.

'Oh! I'm sorry.' My hand flew to my neck. I wasn't sure why I felt my exposed throat should be protected.

'I don't want to talk about Laura,' he said.

'I'm sorry.' But my curiosity about her had been awakened, and I couldn't put her back in the box. I wish I had just forgotten her. I wished I had never heard her name.

My eyes were already heavy, and I must've fallen straight to sleep. I was awoken in the early hours by a terrible howling. I slipped out of bed and wrapped a silk housecoat round my shoulders. I padded in bare feet to the window and looked outside. The howling was coming from the beach below. A haunting, terrible noise that still permeates my dreams. The bedside lamp cast shadows across the room, and it was then that her face appeared.

How I hadn't noticed it earlier I'll never know. I'd sat in the window, watching the seals bobbing on the sea. How could I have missed that face? It hit me like a punch to the ribs. My hold on my husband, on my life, felt fragile, our love nebulous. When he was here with me, I felt more secure, but he was in a different country, and there was his beautiful dead wife smiling at me from my bedroom windowsill, framed in silver, her dark hair curled round her white face. Her perfect pink lips surrounding straight, white teeth. Her eyes shining, the merest flick of eyeliner sweeping their lids.

The pain I'd felt on seeing her stays with me to this day. My horrible mind told me over and over again: *You're the second one. Second best, second class, second rate. If she hadn't died you wouldn't be here.* Why could I never quieten the voices in my head? Why did my husband keep a photo of his dead wife in the bedroom? Had she slept in this bed? Did he wish she still did? Was I the consolation prize?

I jumped at a tapping on the window, and the howling began again. I opened the French door onto the balcony, and the drapes fluttered in the wind. Grass in the dunes wavered and a seabird swooped to catch its prey. It seemed like the howling was coming from the beach. It drew me in and I needed to follow it.

I turned and crept back into the bedroom, closing the French doors. I shoved on my overcoat and slipped my feet into flat shoes. I turned the key in the lock. The door creaked open and I padded down the hall. I held my breath as I passed my mother-in-law's room. I didn't want her waking and interrupting my mission. Though what my mission was, I hadn't a clue. I was compelled by the haunted howling. My heart was certain it wasn't just the wind.

I padded across the lawn and out of the latched gate. I trudged across the dunes. Clumps of grass bent in huddles, crouching to shelter from the wind. The silver sea, like mercury, bubbled on the shore. Light seeped from the horizon and bled into the indigo sky, reaching out across the tops of the dunes and bathing the hills in an orange glow. A single boat lay marooned on the sand, its mast reaching towards the heavens, the hardware rattling in the wind.

Glancing back at the house, I swore a face loomed at my bedroom window, but as I tried to focus, it was gone. The house seemed to mock me. The howling grew stronger. I believed it was coming from the rocks ahead. I crept along the beach until I reached the rocks. An opening on the other side revealed a cave. A light flickered from within as though someone held a candle.

'Hello,' I called out, entering the cave. 'Can I help you?'

The ridiculousness of the situation struck me. Who did I think was there? And why did I think I could help them? The howling stopped, and a figure came towards me out of the shadows. The clothes were dark, and it wore a cloak. The face was invisible.

And then it wasn't. The features hit me, and I couldn't move. The same face, the shining eyes, the perfect pink lips, and the straight white teeth. They weren't curled in a smile, though, but snarled in a sneer. It couldn't be. Laura was dead. I turned to run but tripped over a rock.

Pain shot up my arm, and my world turned black.

Chapter 45
HEATHER: LETTER TO KATIE 2019

So we lived with Christina quite happily for a while. We did little jobs around the house, cooked, cleaned, and helped her to decorate. Living in the commune, we'd been independent and hard-working. Christina was glad of us. She said I was like a daughter to her. Her son rang once a week, but she never heard from her daughter. She only went out to go shopping, to go to the bingo, or to collect her pension from the post office. I accompanied her, but Jovano would not.

It was only later I realised why.

I liked Christina. She got on my nerves at times but living in close proximity with anyone is difficult. She had annoying habits like sucking on her dentures after eating seeded fruit. She sang in the shower and as she was dusting. Trilling tuneless warbles that set my teeth on edge. I swallowed cringes because it was her house. She had every right to whistle the national anthem topless while ironing if it so took her fancy, though I'm pleased to say it didn't. I was a tolerant person, but Jovano was not.

Regret is a strange emotion. It's impossible to describe. The cliché is to want to turn back the clock. I imagine the hands rewinding and the scene playing backwards in slow motion.

I began to get terrible nightmares. I dreamt of murder. In slow motion. In reverse. The body was no longer slumped, the legs bent grotesquely under it. The limbs uncoiled, the chest inflated, the body twitched, the eyes opened, and the blood returned to the wound. The skull uncracked, the grey streak poured back into the brain. The mouth unfurled, the shock in the eyes returned to a normal expression, and everything was peaceful once again.

Jovano obviously had a plan, and I was so naïve. Whenever Christina went anywhere it was me who went with her. I took her to the post office, to bingo, to the community centre. Even when I was ill and unable to leave my bed, he refused to go anywhere with her. He would say he was poorly too, but I could tell he was feigning illness. No heat emanated from his forehead, and he moved with the speed of someone healthy, not the shuffling, lumbering gait of someone who was struggling to put one foot in front of the other, as I was.

The public saw only me. Remembered only me. When it came to the blame game, he was nowhere to be found. Very clever. I was a dumb stooge. A patsy. He knew exactly what he was doing with me. Christina and I were oblivious to his nefarious thoughts and deeds.

He had a way of cajoling me to do things I didn't want to do. Not the way an abusive husband does, with temper or with sharp words and put-downs. Jovano was a manipulator extraordinaire. He did it insidiously. Completely without my knowledge.

One morning we'd eaten breakfast, and Jovano was sharpening the falchion just outside the back door. The blade screamed across the surface of the stone he kept wetting with murky water from a wooden tub at his side.

'Why are you sharpening that?' I asked

'In case we need it,' he said.

'What could we possibly need it for?' I asked.

He shrugged in that infuriating way of his, stood, and swiped the sword through the air, cutting off the head of one of the cabbages growing in the vegetable patch.

'I need to get out of here,' he said.

'Why?' I asked.

'Are you kidding me? I feel like I'm dying from the inside out, stuck in these four walls all day long, with only a geriatric and a bimbo for company.'

'Thanks a lot,' I snapped.

'You know what I mean,' he said.

'I don't,' I said. 'I thought we were happy here. And if you feel like you're stuck in four walls, why don't you get out? There's nothing stopping you.'

But there was something stopping him. Jovano knew what he planned to do and he knew it would be better for him if he was never seen. He didn't feel the same protective urge towards me, unfortunately. He knew exactly what he was doing. And poor Christina; she didn't deserve what happened to her.

No one deserves to end their life in that way. If only I'd gone earlier.

Chapter 46
KATIE: 2019

I was home alone, drinking tea and looking forward to some downtime. I turned on the cold tap to fill the kettle to make another pot, but nothing came out. *Does anything in this house work properly?* I was startled when the shrill ring of the phone cut the silence.

'Katie Kovacs?' said a voice I didn't recognise.
'Who's speaking, please?' I asked.
'This is Ann Emberg from Penguin ...'
'Oh, hello,' I said. 'How are you?' I was trying to buy time as I couldn't remember which client's manuscript she was reading.
'I'd like to speak with you about the initial pages you sent me from the debut author.'
I racked my brains for who she meant.
'The book about Heather Parnell.'
I put down my drink and picked up a pen, opening a notebook on the coffee table beside me.
'Oh yes, of course,' I said. I'd completely forgotten I'd sent that. I was just trying to gauge interest at this stage. 'Go on.'
'I must say I really liked it.'
'Thank you,' I said.
'This is definitely something we'd be interested in. I want to take it to the next acquisitions meeting.'
'Is this a wind up?' I said. I thought about Paddy at work. I imagined he and Edward creased up in the corner of a pub, drinking lager and thinking of ways to embarrass me. Asking a female punter to help them play a joke on a friend.
'I'm sorry?' the voice said.

'Is someone taking the mick?'

'No, I can assure you ... I'm really interested.'

It transpired it was not a wind up, and Penguin were indeed interested in publishing a book about Heather Parnell. I told Ann I was ghost writing the story and it didn't put her off. In fact she seemed even more excited. I met her for lunch in Covent Garden at a place serving Vietnamese street food. Round glasses surrounded almond eyes, and a Chanel suit added to the air of wealth and authority. She shook my hand, showed me to a table, ordered rice wine, goi cuon, bun cha and banh xeo.

'I'm so excited about this,' she said. 'It's a brilliant story.'

'Thank you.'

'What's she like?'

'She's ... well ...'

'I imagine meeting her is chilling ...'

'Actually it isn't ... It's all quite normal. She writes. I ask a question now and then. Sometimes she answers, and sometimes she doesn't.'

'There'll be an advance on royalties, of course,' she said.

'Great,' I said, spending it already in my head. *Deposit on a holiday home, new car ...*

'It won't be a great deal but ...'

Maybe enough for a new laptop then?

'We were wondering whether you could have the first draft ready in three months?'

'Three months? I doubt it ... I mean I work and ...'

'Okay, maybe we could try and raise the advance.'

'I could try ...' I found myself saying. I had no idea how I'd find the time.

'That's settled then,' Ann Emberg said, pushing back her chair and reaching to shake my hand. 'Must dash. I have to catch JK this afternoon. We're in talks about her new series.'

I was left wondering how I had got myself into this predicament, and how I was going to write a book as well as work full-time for my clients.

I was almost as shocked as my boss when I asked him if I could go on sabbatical to write my novel.

'What are you talking about, Kovacs?'

'I have a story to tell, and I want to tell it my way with no distractions.'

'Out of the question,' he said. 'You have too many people for the others to manage.'

'Maybe I could go down to two days and move some of my clients sideways.' I was already making a list in my head of who I wanted to keep and who could be moved to Lucinda, Tarquin, and Edward's lists.

When I got home, I shut myself away in the study with my laptop. I could no longer spend hours staring into the sunset as my fingers sat idle at the keyboard.

Now I had to write. I had a story to tell the world, mysteries to solve, and secrets to uncover.

Chapter 47
KATIE: 1988

I woke in my bed to the sound of Mark's stern voice. 'What the hell was she doing out there?'

'I don't know, Mr Amell. She was warned that the tide is dangerous and folk have got lost in the dunes.'

'She's not to go out alone again, do you hear me?'

I wasn't a child who had to be chaperoned everywhere I went. Anger welled up inside me but dissipated as I didn't have the energy to demonstrate it. I tried to speak, but the words were muddled.

Mark was by my side. 'Hush now. Don't try to speak.'

'I saw her,' I said. 'I saw Laura.'

'Laura?' Mark's stern voice asked.

'Your wife, I saw her.'

'She hit her head when she fell,' Mrs Benson said. 'They said there was quite a bit of blood at the site.'

'You need to rest, Katie,' Mark said. 'You've had quite a shock.'

Yes, it was a shock to see the face of his dead wife on a cloaked stranger on the beach, but this had nothing to do with a bump on the head.

'She was there, Mark.'

'Yes, my love. Just rest.'

He spoke to the help when he thought I was sleeping.

'Make sure she doesn't go anywhere alone. Especially the beach.'

'Don't you worry, Mr Amell. I won't let her out of my sight,' said the housekeeper.

And she didn't. I felt suffocated by her constant presence. Whenever I wanted to go for a walk, she was there. I'd put on my coat and slip out of the kitchen entrance and she'd be behind me, following, watching my every move. I complained to Mark that I felt stifled, but he said it was for my own good.

'I'm not a child, Mark,' I said.

'No, but you don't know this area, and you wandered into a dangerous part. You were hurt, but you could have been killed. You were very lucky.'

I didn't feel lucky. I felt smothered.

'Sometimes I enjoy solitude.'

'I don't want to be called back from an important business trip because you've gone missing. They searched for you for hours. They were just about to call out the coast guard when Joseph found you in a pool of blood.'

'It won't happen again. I'll be extra careful.'

'You weren't even wearing a warm coat. Any longer out there and you'd have died of hypothermia. You were lucky not to get pneumonia.'

The fussing and fretting was just because he cared, but when they began to lock me in my room, I gathered something more sinister was afoot.

Chapter 48
KATIE: 2019

The drive home was longer that night, and the roads seemed to twist and wind on forever. By the time I pulled up at the house I was already exhausted. I wanted to type my notes before I went to sleep, so I headed straight to the kitchen to make a strong coffee.

I could tell immediately that something wasn't right. There was an imperceptible shift in the air. The scent of something alien and a presence.

'Hello,' I called out. 'Who's there?'

I was answered by a gurgle, a splutter, a loud crack. My heart pounded, and my legs were woolly. Another splutter, and red and brown liquid gushed from the cold tap and splashed into the sink like a mixture of blood and mud. The pipes had obviously been blocked. The sooner the plumber got here the better. I left it until the water ran yellow, then turned off the tap.

The iPad jingle alerted me to an incoming FaceTime call. It was from an unknown number, but I pressed to receive. The screen hissed and buzzed. The outline of a head appeared, but I couldn't make out who it was. The voice was other-worldly and sounded far away.

'Mark, is that you?'

I was sure a voice called out. I strained to hear what it was saying.

'Katie, I'm coming for you.'

'Who is it?'

'Kaaytiiiie. Kaaaaaytttiiiiieeeee.' An eerie voice shrieked my name.

The connection was cut, and I was left with a blank screen.

Knocking vibrated through me and I jumped. No one had called since I'd moved in. I opened the door, and a familiar face greeted me. She was holding a cup and a bunch of lilies.

'Cup of sugar,' Mollie said.

'Oh, how kind, come in,' I said. 'The kettle has just boiled.'

She stepped inside, looking from left to right as though expecting someone to jump out on her. I led her straight to the kitchen.

'I saw the light on when I passed, and I was just wondering how you're settling in.'

'Oh, I'm fine,' I said. 'I've had some issues with the plumbing. The heating isn't working properly, and the water is temperamental, but it's fine.' I opened a cupboard and took out a cracked vase. I turned on the cold tap, praying it would work without issue. Yellow water ran into the clear vessel. I reached into a drawer for scissors, cut the cellophane, snipped the little food pouch for the flowers and added it, watching the liquids swirl and merge, then placed the flowers in the water. 'Tea or coffee?'

'Whatever you're having.'

'Coffee? I have a chapter to write so I need to stay awake.'

'Ooh, you're writing a novel? I didn't realise you were an author.'

'No, it's a memoir actually. I'm a literary agent. I'm taking time out to write a book.'

'How exciting! Is it your own story?'

'Lord no! No one would be interested in my life story.' That wasn't altogether true. There were some parts of my life which might fascinate those with a taste for the macabre. 'It's the Commune Murders.'

Her eyes grew wide at this. 'Oh, really? That must be heavy going?'

'Yes, it certainly doesn't make light reading. Is instant okay?'

She nodded, and I spooned the coffee into cups.

'Sugar?'

She shook her head. 'No, thank you. I'm trying to watch my weight.'

I poured the water and milk after she'd nodded her assent, shook a few biscuits onto a plate from an open packet, and placed them on a tray to take into the sitting room.

'They say she looks completely different from the photos in the paper. She's changed her identity completely. It shouldn't be allowed, in my opinion. Devils like that running around in public and us having no idea who they are.'

I added a log to the burner and sat on the sofa. She spoke again and my blood ran cold.

'I just wanted to let you know, in case you hadn't heard, there's been a spate of break-ins lately in the county, and someone was seen hanging around outside your house.'

'Oh no, how awful.'

'Nothing has been taken, and no one has been harmed, luckily, but I just wanted you to know so you could be on your guard. I thought of you all on your own out here. It's a very isolated spot. I wouldn't like to be here alone.' She shuddered.

'Strange,' I said. 'Why would someone want to break in if they weren't going to steal something?'

'Yes, none of it makes sense. It's almost as if they're looking for something specific and haven't found it yet.'

'How do they know they've been targeted?' I asked, not daring to hear the answer.

'Well, some have seen the intruder and others have just noticed a broken window, footprints, things moved around.'

'I see.' My mouth went so dry I could hardly form a word.

'Strangely, all the houses have been former vicarages or parsonages, which is why I wanted to alert you to the problem so that you can be on your guard.'

As soon as she said this, the colour must have drained from my face.

'Are you okay?' she asked, a frown crossing her forehead. 'I'm sure it's nothing to worry about.'

'Yes, I'm sure you're right,' I said.

'I better get going.'

'You didn't finish your coffee.'

'Thomas will be waiting for his dinner. You know how men can get when they're hungry.'

Oh, I did know. Mark had suffered from what he called hanger. When we stayed in the apartment, if he came home from work and his dinner wasn't there on the table, he'd erupt into whirlwinds of rage. Berating me, calling me lazy, asking what I'd done all day. He'd be absolutely vile and then apologise, saying he was hungry. I'd forgive him, of course, and then he'd shovel his food down his throat with a hearty appetite, while I pushed mine round my plate and seethed inwardly.

'Be sure and keep everything locked, set the burglar alarm, and leave a light on when you're out,' Mollie said as she left, promising to visit again.

'I always do,' I said.

I thumbed through the local trade papers, picked up the phone, and dialled.

'Hello, yes, I wonder whether you can fit new locks for me and perhaps make the windows more secure?'

'Shouldn't be a problem,' the young female voice on the other end said. 'Let me check his diary. He's free on Friday at ten o'clock. What's your address? I'll get him to pop round.'

'It's The Old Parsonage on the seafront.'

'Just a second, please,' the voice said. There was a pause, muffled speech that I couldn't make out. 'Hello, sorry, I made a mistake, he's busy on Friday.'

'Monday then?' I asked.

'Sorry, he's booked up at the moment.'

'When is he free?' I asked.

'He's booked up for the foreseeable future. Maybe you should try someone else.'

The phone clicked off before I even had the chance to say goodbye. I tried two more firms, but they were all busy. It was obvious to me what the problem was. No one wanted to come here because of the house's past.

Someone had been here. I knew what they were searching for, but they wouldn't find it.

I had hidden it well.

The jar.

Chapter 49
Regression Therapy: JANUARY 1976

Just when I think I'll be left down here forever, he opens the cellar door and tells me to come up.

'Have ye learnt yer lesson?' he asks. I climb the steps with the blanket wrapped round me.

I nod, squinting against the light. The kitchen is dirtier and untidier than it was before. Empty tins sit, their contents congealing; dirty dishes are piled high; pizza boxes and takeaway cartons cover the table. I stand in the corner.

He points to a carrier bag on the side. 'Make yerself useful. Fry that bacon and put it in a sangwich.'

My hand shakes. I put the pan on the stove. I lift a box of matches, take one, and strike it against the side. It falls off and doesn't strike. The head must be wet. I try again and again.

'The matches are wet,' I say.

'Yer fuckin' useless,' he says, pushing back his chair and standing.

I cower beside the cooker, waiting for the first strike.

'Ye have tae pay for ye keep somehow. Upstairs,' he says. 'Yer old enough now.'

I don't ask him old enough for what. I'm assuming he has jobs for me to do, but he sends me into his bedroom and follows me in. There's a big bed the size of Mammy and Daddy's, but it has brown and yellow stains and a sleeping bag in the centre.

'Lie down,' he says.

'I'm not tired,' I say.

'*Dae as yer telt,*' *he says.*

My stomach squirms, and I don't really know why. Just an overwhelming feeling of discomfort and dread.

'*Ye ken whit happens when ye dinnae behave.*'

I don't lie down. My whole body shakes.

'*I'll go back to the cellar,*' *I say. Something tells me I'll be safer down there.*

'*Get on the fucking bed,*' *he says.*

'*No.*' *I want him to lock me in the cellar. I want to be down there in the dark.*

Alone.

He grabs my wrist with one hand and pulls my hair with the other. He flings me on the bed like a bag of bones. I try to fight him. I bite, I claw, I scream and shout, but he's too strong. He slaps me across the face, and it feels like my head will explode. He's too strong and too mean. I can do nothing but lie still.

What he makes me do is unspeakable.

Afterwards, I sit in the dirty bath and scrub and scrub. I will never be clean. I would rather die than do that again. I have to escape.

Chapter 50
KATIE: NOW

When I dared to broach the subject of his mother, Mark had a distracted air.

'The Lodge is ready, isn't it?' I asked him.

'Yes.'

'When will your mother move in?'

'I don't know,' he said, flicking through a document.

'It will be lovely to have the house to ourselves,' I said.

'It's a big enough house for us all to survive in without living cheek by jowl.'

'It is, but I thought the plan was for your mother to move to The Lodge so that we could relax.'

'My mother sets you on edge?' he asked, his voice a thin layer of frost.

'I would prefer it to be just the two of us. It's our honeymoon period after all.' I thought the word 'honeymoon' might conjure up sexy afternoons in bed, eating snacks from trays, and drinking champagne.

'Some of us have to work, Katie,' he said. His brows met in the middle, showing his irritation.

'I know,' I said. 'But surely you're allowed a little time off to spend with your new wife?'

'Don't be demanding,' he said. 'You're putting me under pressure, and I don't appreciate it.'

'Oh, I'm sorry,' I said. 'That really wasn't my intention. I just want to feel close to you again.' *As I had before we moved in with your mother* was left unsaid.

He spoke with her later that day. I was standing outside the library, and they were both inside.

'The Lodge is ready,' he said.

'Is it?' she said with a disinterested air.

'So whenever you want to move your things …'

'There's no rush,' she said. 'Is there?'

'No, of course not,' he said.

There is, there is.

'Unless your new wife wants rid of me? Unless you want rid of your poor old mother?'

I do, I do.

'Mother, you're neither poor nor old,' he said, laughing. 'And I certainly don't want rid of you.'

I do, I wanted to scream. I'd never feel comfortable with her here. I'd never feel like this was my home.

Footsteps clattered on the tiles and I fiddled with some flowers on the hall table.

'Would Madam like me to change the water?' Mrs Benson asked, a defiant look in her eyes.

She always appeared as though she'd just telepathically transported from somewhere else. Silently. Secretly. I could tell by the smug smirk sitting on her dry lips she knew I'd been eavesdropping.

'Not at all,' I said.

'Katie, is that you?' Mark's voice drifted through the crack in the open door.

'Yes, I was just about to go out into the garden.'

'Come in here and have some tea,' he said. 'Mrs Benson, would you have Maisie bring us a fresh pot and a plate of scones?'

'Of course, Mr Amell.' She threw me a look of disdain and disappeared.

I entered the library where Mark was reading a paper and his mother nursed a book. It sat unopened on her knee, and she eyed me quizzically.

'You're very peaky,' she said. 'Perhaps you shouldn't be out of bed yet.'

'I shall go out of my mind if I stay there any longer,' I said.

'Quite,' she said as though she believed I was out of my mind anyway. 'Sit down, child, for God's sake. Otherwise you're going to fall down.'

The word 'child' rubbed me up the wrong way. It scratched like sandpaper. I was a woman, not a child. A grown, married woman.

'A bump on the head can cause all sorts of problems.'

'That's true,' Mark said. 'So I took the liberty of handing in your notice at the agency.'

'You did *what*?' I shrieked. 'Mark, you said my leaving work was a temporary thing and that I could go back whenever I pleased. It's the only reason I agreed to leaving for a while. You know I love my job. You know I want to go back.'

'We have to take care of you. You are to carry the Amell heirs.'

Mark and I had not discussed children since we were married, though I'd assumed he would want at least one. But I wasn't sure I was cut out for motherhood, and to me all that seemed a long way off.

'You'll want to get started with that right away,' his mother butted in, 'if you are to have a football team.'

She laughed mirthlessly, and I coughed and tried to smile, but inside I was seething.

'A five-a-side team will do,' Mark said, and I stared at him in shock. 'I'm teasing, Katie. You must learn to realise when people are pulling your leg.' Why did everything feel like a criticism? Why did I feel like I never measured up?

That inner voice chided me again: *second wife, second best, second rate.*

Chapter 51
HEATHER: LETTER TO KATIE 2019

The day Jovano hit Christina, things really took a downward turn. I'd never seen him like that. It wasn't like the rage I witnessed when he killed Adrik and Karma. This was something new.

We were having breakfast in the kitchen with Christina. The radio was playing 'Do You Really Want To Hurt Me?' She was singing along in her usual tuneless way. I'd buttered crumpets, and Jovano was sharpening a knife at the back door. The familiar jingle signalled the local news. I'm not sure when I became aware Christina had stopped listening and was staring at me with her mouth open. At the same time Jovano's knife clattered to the ground as he reached to turn off the radio. It was too late. Even before she spoke, the look in Christina's eyes told me she'd heard every word and now knew the police were searching for me in connection with the Commune Murders …

'I'm just popping out,' she said.

'To make a phone call to the police?' Jovano asked. The menace in his voice was unmistakable.

'No,' her voice wavered. Fear filled her eyes.

'I can't let you do that,' Jovano said.

'It was an accident,' I said. 'We didn't mean to hurt anyone.'

He hit her once on the side of the head, and she was knocked out cold.

'Here, help me,' he said, curling his hands under her arms and dragging her to the cellar stairs. 'Let's get her down here.'

'What the fuck are you doing?' I shouted.

'Heather, do you want to go to prison?'

'Of course not.'

'Then do as I say.'

We struggled down the cellar steps.

'I don't understand,' I said. 'Why are we bringing her down here?'

'We can't leave until we're ready,' he said. 'Now she knows they're after us, we can't trust her. You saw her face. She was going to call the police. You know she was. We couldn't have that. She'll have to stay down here until we're ready to go.'

'And then we'll let her go back upstairs?'

'Of course. Now tie her hands and feet.'

'Do we have to do that?'

'Yes, or she'll escape. Do you know what they do to people like us in jail?'

I wanted to say *I'm not like you*, but I couldn't. I was complicit in his crimes. I had held the shovel. I had dug the holes. He pulled string from his pocket, and I swallowed the feeling that Jovano had planned this all along.

As I was tying the string round her ankles, I noticed the bottom of Christina's shoes. The scuff marks bore the shape of a ghoulish face like a silver-grey version of *The Scream*. It reminded me of my childhood imaginings about the holy souls. My mother used to ask us to offer up our sufferings for the holy souls. If you had a pain in your leg, you'd offer it up for the holy souls. If you had an itch you couldn't scratch, you were to offer it up to the holy souls. It didn't help the pain or the itch in the slightest, so I never saw the point of it. Christina's holy *sole* was screaming at me. She was laid so awkwardly I imagined she'd wake with a crick in her neck and a pain down her spine. When I tried to move her to a more comfortable position, she stirred.

'We need to bring her something comfortable to lie on,' I said.

'She isn't going to be here long,' he said. 'Stop being so soft.'

'I just don't like this,' I said.

'It won't be for long. I promise.'

I chose to believe him.

But Christina was in that cellar for weeks. It was one of the things the media were in a frenzy about. The headlines spoke of the cruelty and incarceration of a vulnerable woman. Her torturous final days.

When she woke up the first time, it scared me half to death. I was creeping round in the dark, pouring water from a jug into her cup and cutting a sandwich into the quarters she liked. If she could have spoken afterwards she'd have said I cared for her. Nurtured her. Was kind to her.

But the way it turned out, that wasn't to be.

Chapter 52
KATIE: NOW

You ask me if I'd like to lie on the couch. I fantasise about you climbing on top of me, kissing me, touching my breasts, and entering me. I can feel my orgasm building as you pound me hard.

'Katie ...'

Your voice brings me back, and my cheeks flush.

'Are you okay?'

'Fine,' I say.

'Shall we begin?'

I lie on the couch and listen to the hum of traffic. 'I thought this room was sound-proofed.'

'I have the window open,' you say. 'It's very warm. I can close it if you like.'

'No, it's fine. I was just saying.'

'You seemed like you were in a world of your own there.'

'Hmm ...?' I'm still distracted by your presence. You smell of something oriental and earthy.

'You looked preoccupied.'

'Oh, er ... yes.' Why do I always feel like you are trying to catch me out?

'Do you want to talk about it?'

Oh no, mister, you aren't getting me that way. I know what you're up to. This is a ploy to get me to admit to having alternative realities and imaginary friends so you can lock me up again. There is no way I'm going back to Satis House.

So what if I had imaginary friends as a child? Who didn't? So what if I lived in my own little world? It was understandable, considering what I'd witnessed in the real world.

'You were telling me about a conversation you had with Mark.' You sit opposite in a black leather chair, your dark hair curled below your collar, big brown eyes ringed with fluttering lashes, a five o'clock shadow enhancing your thick jaw, a pen poised above a notebook.

I feel another twinge. I try to focus on non-erotic thoughts.

'Yes,' I say.

'Do you want to go on with that?'

I don't, but I don't want to tell you I don't; it's easier just to disclose.

'I was in bed when he rang. He woke me from a terrible dream …'

'About Laura again?' you ask.

'Yes, she was shouting at me. Telling me to get out of her house. Telling me I didn't belong there. It was her bed, her dressing table, her bath, even her coat hung up in the hall. It was true. There *had* been a coat belonging to her in the hall. When I'd challenged Mark about it, he had the gardener burn it in a brazier. In the dream, the coat turned into Laura, and he burnt her, too. She was screaming that I had murdered her.'

'That must have been very upsetting,' you say.

'Everything to do with Laura was upsetting. I felt like I was second best. Like he wished she was still alive and I was a poor substitute. I tried to tell him how I felt, but he said I was being childish. He took me into the grounds to see her memorial headstone.

'She's buried here?' I asked.

'No,' he said, 'She was cremated, and her ashes were scattered here. It was her favourite spot, but you're missing the point. The point is, Laura is dead. She's no longer the mistress of this house. You are.' It pacified me for a while, but then the old fears and worries resurfaced. Something didn't add up. I couldn't put my finger on it, but every time anyone spoke of her there was a strange atmosphere. Like there was a secret and I was the only one who didn't know it.'

'What did you do?'

'Do?' I ask.

'I'm sensing that you did something.'

Irritation scratches at me. You always read me correctly, and just for once I wish you didn't.

'I went to see the vicar.'

'The vicar?' you ask.

'Yes, the vicar who performed the funeral ceremony. Laura's funeral ceremony.'

'I see.' You say it in that way which lets me know you see right inside me. It's unnerving and infuriating.

I sneaked out one evening after dinner and went to the church. I asked the vicar if I could speak with him about Laura. Even before I said her name he couldn't meet my eyes. 'Please, Father,' I said.

'Okay,' he said. 'Come in. I only have a few moments before I have to prepare for Evensong.' He led me into the presbytery and bid me sit on a winged chair. 'What is it you'd like to know?' he asked.

'No one speaks of Laura. It's weird.'

'What's weird?' he asked.

'Whenever I mention her name there's silence.'

'Perhaps it's respect for the dead, or maybe people are worried it will make you uncomfortable.'

'No, it's more than that.'

''You're being paranoid,' he said. 'Laura died. Her memorial service was held in this very church, and she was buried in the churchyard.'

'I thought she was cremated.'

'Yes, sorry, that's what I meant. Sorry, I was a little confused for a moment. Age, you know.'

He tried a half-hearted laugh, but I could see through him. He wasn't telling the truth.

'Mr Amell scattered the ashes. There were doves, and poetry, and beautiful readings and ...'

'Which crematorium?'

He rose from his seat then and paced the floor. 'This is ridiculous. You're clearly unwell.'

'What date was the service?' I asked him. I wasn't going to allow him to fob me off.

'Pardon?'

'What date was Laura cremated?'

He stammered then, his cool completely lost. 'Well ... I ... it's not something I would know offhand ... I'll need to check.'

'I'll wait,' I said. His breath out was a growl. He stood and stormed from the room. I could hear him on the telephone further down the passage. I tiptoed to the door and pressed my ear against it. I could only grasp parts of the conversation.

'She's asking questions ... yes ... yes ... I've told her that ... Okay ... I don't like this ... yes ... okay.'

The phone clicked into its cradle, and I tiptoed back to my seat. As far as he was aware I'd never left it.

'The memorial service was July 1st 1987,' he said. 'Now if you'll excuse me ...'

'At which crematorium was the service held?'

'Really, Mrs Amell, this is most irregular. Is it completely necessary?'

I stared until he sighed and said, 'It was the one on South Road. If that will be all, I have ...'

'Yes, Evensong, you said. Thank you, Father. I appreciate your time. I'll see myself out.''

I went to the crematorium.

And the service he spoke of never happened.

Chapter 53
HEATHER: LETTER TO KATIE 2019

Over and over, I tried to persuade Jovano to set Christina free. I couldn't bear to think of her locked up in that basement. 'She's old. She could have a heart attack,' I said one morning while forging her signature on her cheque book. 'I don't like it, Jovano. I don't like her being down there.'

'Fucking grow up, Heather. What do you think is going to happen to us? We're fugitives on the run. We have to survive, and if that means an old woman has to be a bit uncomfortable for a while, then so be it.'

'But it's cold down there. She could get hypothermia.'

'Take her a fucking heater down, then.'

So I dragged the electric heater down the stone steps and plugged it into the only socket in the basement. Christina's eyes pleaded with me and burnt guilty holes, which I couldn't fill.

'What are you doing, child?' she said. 'I know you're not a wrong 'un. I can tell. Just do the right thing and let me go, and I won't say owt about all this.'

'I can't,' I said. 'Jovano …'

'Mark my words, lass, this is not going to end well.'

My stomach agreed with her. It turned over and over. I tried to tell myself we were only doing what was necessary. We hadn't really done anything wrong. Christina was comfortable enough now I'd given her some blankets and a heater. I took her three meals a day and endless cups of tea. I couldn't stand having to empty the pail we'd left for her toilet needs. That was one thing that really didn't sit right with me at all.

'We're treating her like an animal, having to do her business in a bucket. It isn't right,' I said to Jovano.

'It's too awkward to allow her upstairs every time she needs to go,' he said. 'It's fine. Stop fussing.'

What had happened to him? It was as though he no longer had empathy or sympathy for anyone. It was like he'd become a whole different person.

I didn't really know how long she was down there. We continued to cash her pension and raided her bank account. When her son rang, we told him he'd just missed her. 'Oh she's just popped to the shops ... sorry, she's at the bingo ... we'll get her to call you, she went to church.' Every time, he asked us to tell her to ring him.

'What if he starts to suspect?' I said. 'We should really let her talk to him.'

'She might start screaming and telling him. No.'

'But he could come round. What if he sends the police?'

Jovano was lost in his own thoughts. He disappeared for a couple of hours, and when he came back he said he'd had an idea.

Chapter 54
KATIE: NOW

'I want to talk about the phone calls,' I tell you.

'I hoped we'd continue with what happened at the crematorium.'

'You said it was my choice what I tell you and when.'

'It is, Katie. Certainly. Please go ahead.'

'The phone rang, waking me,' I say. 'I couldn't hear anyone at first, just that crackle that lets you know there's someone there, but no voice. No good morning. No how are you? Then Mark spoke. It was just a whisper at first, but of course, I'd know his voice anywhere.'

'What did he say?'

'He asked if I was all right, and I said that I was fine. I was a bit snappy, having being woken so rudely and from such a distressing dream. He said I didn't sound all right, but he'd take my word for it. I asked about Oliver, and he said let's not talk about that. Why would he not want to talk about our son?'

'Why do you think he might not want to talk about him?'

'We have to talk about him,' I say. 'We're his parents.'

'It's a very difficult subject, isn't it? There could be a number of reasons why …'

'Guilt,' I snap. 'Except I'm not sure Mark is capable of guilt or remorse.'

'I'd really like to hear about your visit to the crematorium now?'

'I've already told you the important part.'

'That's okay.'

'I don't know whether you know anything about crematoriums, but a page is provided for each day of the year, and the book remains open at the appropriate page so that the entries may be seen on the anniversary of the date of death for many years to come.'

'So you went to the crematorium to check the book?'

The sun was shining when I got out of the car. I expected it to be a deeply depressing place, but that couldn't be further from the truth. The chimneys were hidden behind a hedge of tall leylandii, and the garden of remembrance was plump with all manner of summer blooms. Birds bathed in the water feature, flapping and tweeting. It was as close to heaven on earth as you could imagine.

The building was a new brick structure interspersed with floor-to-ceiling stained glass windows. I approached the entrance. 'Queen of the May' sang out from the sound system, and a family shuffled, weeping, from the exit. Women in black dabbed at their eyes, and men blew their noses. Inside the entrance, the book stood in a glass case surrounded by candles. I scanned the list of names: Stanley Norman Mould, Richard Steven Errington, Mary Ann Swan, Jon Herron. Nowhere did the name Laura Amell appear.

In fact there was no Laura to be found.

'What do you think that meant?' you ask when I relay that part of the story to you.

'It's obvious what it meant.'

'I'm asking you for your thoughts, though.'

'It's clear that Laura did not die. She was still alive. So where was she?'

'Perhaps you were mistaken about the date? Maybe the vicar was wrong?'

'Oh, for God's sake. I want to go.'

'You may go whenever you wish, Katie. You know that.'

You think you can get away with saying anything because you are a beautiful man. I've met your type so many times. Male and female. They are physically exquisite and know that others admire them, so they push all boundaries because they feel they won't be challenged.

'I don't care how handsome you are, Dr Julius. You won't get away with this,' I say.

'Away with what, Katie? Remember I'm here to help.'

'Fuck off,' I say, getting up. 'I'm aware of what manipulation looks like. I've suffered it enough.'

You speak about me into your Dictaphone as I leave.

'Katie has undoubtedly created a paracosm as a way of orienting herself in real life. She is still experiencing the sleep paralysis and hallucinations. She became defensive when discussing this, and again when being questioned about the things she saw and heard …'

The door closing on the soundproof room stops me from hearing the rest. I vowed I'd stop seeing you after the last time, but there is something about you which draws me back. Perhaps it's the rugged good looks, perhaps it's the dark-brown eyes like muddy pools waiting to drown me, or perhaps I'm just inquisitive to see whether you are any better than all the others.

Can you succeed in helping me where all the others have failed?

Chapter 55
KATIE: NOW

'What about when you got pregnant for the first time? That's a key moment, I think,' you say, sitting forwards and running your fingers over the paperweight which contains a picture of your child.

'What about it?' I say.

'I thought that might be a good place to start today.'

I look at you, your floppy hair, your white teeth, the self-assured way you carry yourself. So confident. Winning at life. You haven't a clue that everything can come crashing down in the blink of one of those beautiful brown eyes. You haven't known struggle. You haven't known pain. Not real pain. Not like me.

I was surprised to feel really happy and I expected Mark to be overjoyed. After all, it was he and his mother who'd spoken about a football team. I think perhaps it was because he didn't control it. We hadn't 'tried'. It had just happened. I was excited at the thought that Mrs Amell would surely move out and we'd have the house to ourselves. He couldn't expect me to share the house with his mother now. I was going to be the mother of his child.

I'd cooked him his favourite supper and lit a candle at the table. I'd wrapped a set of baby clothes, a bonnet, bootees, and matching cardigan. I'd bought him a card with TO MY DADDY and a picture of a bouncing baby on the front. His face turned white as he opened the package and realisation flooded his cheeks. The white became red, and he jumped to his feet, knocking over a glass of champagne I'd poured in anticipation of a celebration.

'What the fuck is this?' he shouted.

My heart thumped and my legs shook.

'I thought you'd be pleased,' I said, stung by hurt. 'You said you wanted a five-a-side team, and you wanted to start trying right away.'

'But we hadn't started trying,' he said. 'You've tricked me.'

I couldn't believe he was taking this attitude.

'Whose is it?'

'Mark, don't be ridiculous,' I said, my voice rising in shock.

He threw the baby clothes into the middle of the table and stormed out. I lay awake all night, crying into my pillow. Bemoaning the injustice of it. How I'd been so excited and how everything was ruined. I also chided myself for being so insensitive. Why had I not been more considerate of his feelings? Why had I been so selfish? How had I misjudged the situation so completely? At six in the morning, the French doors clicked and I rushed down the stairs to apologise. Mark swayed in front of me. Drunk. Mark never got drunk. He liked to remain in control.

'I'm so sorry, darling,' I said. 'I didn't think …'

'Thas your trouble,' he slurred. 'You never think. You don't think about anyone else but yourself. Selfish is wha you are.' He staggered through the house, bouncing from pieces of furniture, and slept in his dressing room, snores rolling round the upstairs of the house. I had been selfish. I could see it now. I would have to try and make it up to him.

Mark slept off the drink, and I felt sick all day. I reprimanded myself over and over for my self-centred behaviour. I must try harder to make him happy. I hid all the baby clothes I'd bought and tried to pretend it had never happened.

When Mark got up, I expected the cold shoulder, but his attitude had changed completely. 'How are you feeling?' he said. 'Did I hear you being sick? They say that's the sign of a healthy pregnancy.' I stared at him in wide-eyed disbelief.

'What?' he asked.

'You don't mind?' I said.

'It would seem I don't have a choice,' he said. 'I was a bit grumpy yesterday. Let's forget it.' I really thought he owed me an apology for his behaviour and his unkind words, but I was just so relieved he had come round to the idea of me being pregnant. He continued, 'Don't think you can use this as an excuse to be lazy. It's not an illness. Generations of women have done it before you. You aren't the first woman to bear a child.'

'I'm the first woman to bear your child,' I said, nuzzling his neck. He peered at me sideways and chewed the inside of his mouth. Doubt gripped me. 'Aren't I?' I asked.

'What do you mean?' he snapped. He sat up and pulled away from me.

'I said I'm the first woman to bear your child.'

'Yes,' he said. 'Of course you are. What the hell are you getting at? Why does everything have to be an issue with you, Katie?'

'It doesn't, I just thought I read something on your face.'

'Well, once again you're wrong. Why do you always have to overthink everything? And don't play the victim, Katie.'

'I'm not. I'm just standing up for myself.'

'It's called causing issues where there are none. It's called being confrontational.'

'I wasn't, I'm not. Let's not argue.'

'We weren't arguing. You were.'

I must stop being so difficult, I thought.

'Maybe it's the hormones,' I said.

'Don't start using that as an excuse for your poor behaviour.'

I seethed inside, but bit my tongue. I probably was being unreasonable. It probably was my hormones. Mark shouldn't have to put up with this. I must try harder. I must be a better wife.

'You're going to be an amazing father,' I said, changing the subject. I waited for the compliment to be reciprocated, but it didn't come. 'Do you think I'll be a good mother?' I asked. He stared, as if gazing through me.

'You're always so needy and insecure, Katie. It's very draining. I hope the pregnancy isn't going to be blighted by this.'

My heart sank again. I was needy. I was insecure. I must allow him to enjoy the pregnancy. I must try harder to hide it.

Chapter 56
KATIE: NOW

'The pregnancy was a troubled one?' you ask.

'Not at first, but our sex life was over as soon as I announced it. Mark's excuse was he didn't want to hurt the baby, but I felt like he didn't fancy me anymore. He'd always liked small breasts and a tiny frame.'

I was beginning to resemble a pregnant cow. I was undressing one evening when he raised his eyebrows and tutted.

'What is it?' I asked.

'Nothing,' he said. 'It's nothing to do with me.'

'What do you mean, nothing to do with you? What's wrong?'

'It's nothing.' He paused and pulled off his socks, flinging them towards the washing basket and missing. He left them there for me to pick up, even though I'd told him bending down was causing me pain. 'I just didn't think you'd be the type to let yourself go.'

'What do you mean?'

'Well, you've always been one to stay in shape.'

'I'm pregnant, Mark!' I said, incredulous.

'Yes, but that doesn't mean …' He stopped himself.

'No, go on, don't hold back on my account.'

'Okay, you asked for it. It doesn't mean you have to put weight on everywhere else. The baby is in your tummy, but your bottom, legs, and breasts are expanding at an alarming rate.' My face must have shown my hurt and horror.

'Look, I'm only telling you for your benefit. I know you wouldn't like to let yourself go. You wouldn't want me to ignore it, would you?'

'Maybe I want you to just adore me whatever size and shape I am.'

'Oh, don't be ridiculous! That's such a childish attitude. You really need to grow up.'

He was right. I could be immature. I had put on too much weight. I had used the pregnancy as an excuse to binge on all the things I enjoy. It wasn't necessary to have gained seven pounds by week fifteen.

'And another thing, I wasn't going to mention it, but you're beginning to smell.' I now shrieked. I was obsessed with cleanliness, and the thought of having BO was a phobia of mine.

'*Smell?* Of what?'

'I don't know, it's a dirty, musky smell.'

'But I bathe twice a day.'

'I'm just telling you for your own good. You don't want other people talking about you behind your back.' Oh God, I certainly didn't. I sniffed at my armpits but couldn't smell anything.

'I suppose you're immune to it,' he said. 'Trust me, it isn't pleasant. Oh, and I've bought you some tea-tree oil for those spots on your face.' He really knew how to make a girl feel ugly. I already felt fat, bloated, itchy, sore, and low. I was concentrating on my baby to stop me from feeling depressed. The magazines told me she was about the size of an apple, covered in hair, and weighed about the same as a bag of salad. She was now sensitive to light and noise, so I didn't want any arguments to reach her. No matter how much Mark upset me, I would not retaliate. He didn't mean it, I told myself. He was just trying to be helpful. He just wasn't very tactful, that's all.

'Wasn't this around the time when Shelly started to hurt you?' you ask.

'Yes, this was when the physical abuse began.'

'Do you want to talk about that?'

'No.'

'Okay, do you want to continue to tell me about the pregnancy?'

I pause for a while, just looking at you. No emotion shows on your face, but I know you are fascinated by me.

'Instead of being upset and angry, I dreamt of holding my beautiful baby girl, parading her in the pram, watching her grow into a chubby toddler, pushing her on the swings, brushing her blonde curls, and holding her hand on her first day of school. Of course, Mark wanted a boy. Don't all men want a son to follow in their footsteps?'

'I'm not sure,' you say. 'As long as the baby is healthy, I suppose that's the most important thing.'

'But you must have been happy to have your little boy.' I nod towards the paperweight.

'I'd have been equally happy if he'd been a little girl,' you say.

'Would you, though?'

'Yes, I would.'

'You were lucky,' I say.

'Yes, I was,' you say. 'I am.'

Chapter 57
HEATHER: LETTER TO KATIE 2019

Jovano disappeared from time to time, and I'd go down into the cellar to sit with Christina. I'd tell her the stories my dad told us, and she'd listen in silence. Sometimes she'd stare into the distance. Always, she'd beg me to let her go.

'Please stop asking,' I said. 'I can't. I want to, but I can't. If you keep asking, I won't be able to come down any more. You're making me feel bad.'

'I'll tell you another story,' I said. So I told her the story of the Pollard's Boar.

When I'd finished the tale, Christina shuddered. A tear rolled down her cracked cheek, and she turned her face to the wall.

Chapter 58
KATIE: 2019

I was in the supermarket. I didn't really want anything in particular, I was just wandering the aisles, hoping for inspiration, when I felt a tap on my shoulder and turned to see Mollie.

'Hello,' she said. 'How have you settled in?'

'Great, thanks,' I said. 'Just trying to find some nice wine and something for dinner.'

'In the stationery aisle?' she said.

'Just killing time,' I said.

'I know what you mean,' she said. 'I'm bored to death.'

I don't know what made me say the next thing. It was almost as though my tongue took on a life of its own.

'Why don't you come to dinner tonight? You and your husband and the kids if you can't get a babysitter.'

'Oh, well … I don't know …'

'Please,' I said. I was shocked at how desperate I sounded, but my pleading tone must have had an effect because she said:

'Do you know what, I'd love to. We'd love to. Thomas's mum might have the kids. We haven't been out for ages.'

'Is seven o'clock okay?' I said, panicking about what to cook.

'Perfect.'

'Should I take your number?' I removed my phone from my pocket. She took it from me and tapped her number in, saving it under Moll and Tom. She then rang her number from mine. 'I have yours now, too.'

'What do you like to drink?'

'Anything alcoholic,' she said and laughed. 'Red wine is my fave, but I'll drink toilet water if there's nothing else on offer.'

'See you at seven,' I said.

She plucked a packet of Post-it notes from the shelf and dropped them into her trolley.

'I'm looking forward to it,' she said, then sped away with a wave of her right hand.

I bought enough food to feed an army, and made my way home, both excited and anxious about having company in the house. I hadn't cooked for anyone else in a very long time. I'd get out some cookery books, or maybe do a YouTube tutorial and make something special.

I spent the afternoon making monkfish and chorizo with *patatas bravas* and ham and cheese croquettes. I opened a lovely Rioja and left it to breathe while I showered, dried my hair, and applied some light makeup. I didn't want it to appear as if I'd made too much effort. It was just an informal dinner. I sat on the bed for five minutes browsing Facebook, wondering whether Mollie was on it. It dawned on me that I'd invited a couple I didn't know. I searched her name and came across her profile. Her cover photo was of her two children, and her profile pic was one of those airbrushed ones from Snapchat where people resemble aliens. I scrolled through her recent posts. There were the usual questions about school kit, memes about struggling through motherhood without a guidebook, mindless quizzes asking questions about which Disney princess she'd be. There were likes and comments from friends called Tara and Emma, and political rants from the 'loony' left and 'fascist' right on her timeline. I clicked through the rest of her photos. There were family ensembles, beach shots, pictures of her holding a cocktail. Then a wedding photo. Her wedding photo.

When I saw the face of her husband my heart stood still, my mouth went dry, and my legs numbed. I zoomed in to make sure.

It was him.

It was definitely him.

Oh God! In ten minutes' time he'd be knocking on my door.

Chapter 59
KATIE: NOW

You look through me as though I'm not there. It's like my very existence is halted just by your ignoring me. You think you're more important than me. You'd never admit to that. You're far too liberal. A do-gooder. I imagine your tweets are full of virtue signalling. 'Look at me, I'm beautiful, intelligent, but also kind and thoughtful.' The type of tweets which make me want to troll them, picking on every point you make to imagine you squirming at your laptop. Enraged that everyone in the world doesn't fall at your designer-clad feet.

'Do you want to continue to tell me about the pregnancy?' you say.

I don't. I want to scream and kick and tell you to fuck off, but it's easier just to talk. I don't have the energy to fight any longer.

I was fifteen weeks pregnant when the pain started. I went straight to the doctor who said it was 'round ligament pain and nothing to worry about'. He told me to put my feet up and rest. Mark came in from a particularly long business trip, his hair unusually dishevelled, and he was fractious like a tired toddler.

'It's okay for some sitting about all day while the rest of us earn a crust.'

'I am pregnant, darling. It's very tiring.'

'Tiring,' he spat with disdain. 'I just knew you'd act like the first woman ever to have a baby. I could have bet money on you using it as an excuse to be lazy.' This was really unfair. I had always wanted to work, and it was Mark who'd put an end to my career. I wasn't happy about it, but it was futile to point this out to Mark, and I really didn't want to argue.

'I've had some pain,' I said. 'The doctor told me to rest.' I hoped Mark would then show concern and rush towards me, hugging my growing tummy, but he walked past me, telling me to call Mrs Benson and order tea for him in the library.

I got up to go to the toilet, and a wave of nausea washed over me. I felt like I was going to faint. It was a relief to sit, but when I did so I noticed the spots of blood. Small and round like raindrops dripping onto the tiled floor. I screamed in terror, and Mrs Benson came running. A sneer sat on her lips as she witnessed my fear and my shame. Doctor Foulds was sent for, but by the time he arrived I was writhing in agony on the bed, and my baby was nothing more than a stain on the silk sheets. The magazine had been right. My baby girl was no bigger than an apple. I tried not to look, but I caught a glimpse before they took her away. I cried for a month. Wailing in darkness, the curtains closed, the drapes drawn round the bed to block out any daylight. The servants tiptoeing round me in large circles. Mark hardly came near. At least I don't remember his presence at that time. I just remembered him coming in one day, tearing open the curtains, dragging back the covers from the bed, and snapping at me to get up.

'You've wallowed long enough,' he said. 'Stop being so selfish. You aren't the only person who has lost a child. My mother has lost her first grandchild. I've lost my son and heir.'

'She was a girl,' I snarled.

'Jesus, Katie. Pull yourself together. You're losing your grip on reality.' I lost count of the number of times I heard that phrase over the years. 'There will be other children. The doctor said we can start trying straight away, and there's no reason why you can't carry the pregnancy to full term. The chances are there was something wrong with the child. It was probably for the best.' I wanted to spring at him, to claw out his eyes, to tear at his flesh. How dare he say that losing my perfect little girl was for the best. The man was a monster.

I realised eventually he was right. I felt guilty for the amount of animosity I'd held towards Mark when he'd been so good to me. He had been so patient. No wonder he'd lost his temper and told me enough was enough. I did wallow. I was pathetic. It happened to a lot of people. Miscarriages were common. I came to realise that more than most.

The second pregnancy lasted only eight weeks, and this time I kind of expected to lose it, given what had happened with Angel. That's what I had secretly called my first daughter. Mark wanted to name her Elizabeth after his grandmother. It was a name I hated, so in my eyes she was Angel and she'd always be an angel. I mourned the second baby, Eva-Lily, but the grief didn't compare to that of Angel.

The third pregnancy lasted thirteen weeks. Unlucky for me. Olivia would have looked like a baby. She'd have had fingers and toes and been as big as a lemon. Whenever I saw lemons in the market I thought of Olivia. This was when Mark seemed to reject me completely. It was like his love for me had been contaminated by the losses and had changed to hatred, contempt, and disdain. He could barely look at me.

It was torturous. When I said I was pregnant for the fourth time, he showed little or no interest. It was as though he didn't believe I could carry a baby to term and wasn't going to invest anything in this pregnancy. *I'll show him*, I thought. I did everything right. I ate all the right foods and avoided those it was suggested pregnant women avoid. I didn't touch a drop of alcohol. I avoided smoke of any kind. I wouldn't even go to London to see a show because of the pollution.

'You've gone quite mad,' Mark said after trying to talk me into going to the theatre with Tarquin and Cynthia. 'Honestly, Katie, you're obsessed, and it has become incredibly boring.'

'You'll thank me when we have a healthy child,' I said. He stared at me like I had two heads. He didn't let it stop him getting on with his social life. He didn't stop going to London, Paris, New York, Tokyo. It suited me. It meant I could concentrate on the baby without his interference.

When Oliver was born, I was quite alone. I felt the pains as I was pruning roses in the garden. My back had been aching for a couple of days, but I was fed up with sitting around inside the house. I pricked my finger on a thorn and was sucking at the blood when a searing pain shot through me and water splashed onto my shoes. I realised my waters had broken and went into the house to call Doctor Foulds and Jenny, the midwife. I drank a glass of water and lay down on the bed. The doctor's phone was engaged, and Jenny's rang to answerphone. I left a message and then waited for the contractions to bring my baby closer to me.

I had refused the twenty-week scan (I'd read there could be unknown risks) so I didn't know the sex of my baby. I prayed for a boy. A brother to my darling angels.

At twenty past two in the morning, Oliver was born. A beautiful boy. Seven pounds exactly. He had a shock of dark hair and blue eyes surrounded by dark lashes. His skin was the colour of a ripe peach, and he smelled of sunshine on warm hay. He was perfect.

Mark was a jealous father. He said I was obsessed. I was sure his mother would try to come in and take over, but to my surprise she never came near. She moved out of the house into The Lodge. Part of me was relieved that I didn't have to put up with the 'You don't want to do it like that' criticisms, but another part of me was deeply hurt. Oliver was her first grandson and Mark's heir. If she met me in the village pushing the pram, she walked the other way as if she hadn't seen me. Her behaviour was bizarre. I just couldn't understand it. When I tried to broach the subject with Mark, he made me feel like it was all my fault.

'For God's sake, Katie,' he'd explode.

'Why does she never come near me?'

'Isn't it obvious?' Mark would say.

'Not to me it isn't,' I'd say.

'You really have no idea, do you?'

'No, Mark. Did she want a girl? Is that it?'

'No, that isn't it,' he'd say.

'Well, what? I haven't done anything to warrant being ignored in that way, and your son certainly hasn't.'

'For fuck's sake,' he'd shout and then storm out for hours or days on end. I learned to bite my tongue. I learned not to bring up the subject of his mother and why she didn't want anything to do with her grandson.

The day came to register Oliver's birth, but I was ill. I'd been suffering debilitating migraines. Mark would have to do it alone. He was, as usual, reluctant and bad-tempered about it, but I told him it was a legal requirement and he couldn't get out of it. He eventually consented to go. 'Remember, we agreed no middle name.' I didn't quite trust him not to add Mark, even though I was adamant his name was to be purely Oliver.

'Please will you get me some new nursing bras while you're in town?'

'I certainly won't,' he said.

'I need them, Mark.'

'I am not going into a store to ask for nursing bras, so you can get that idea right out of your head.'

'It's a perfectly natural request,' I said, tears prickling my eyes.

'There's nothing natural about you,' he muttered. Why did he always have to be so mean? It should have been the best time of my life and it was marred by his need to drag me down and hurt me.

'Do you think that it was Mark's sole intention, to drag you down and hurt you?' you ask.

'Oh, that's just typical. A typical male response. Oh, I'm sure he never meant to punch me in the face. I'm sure he never meant to call me a stupid bitch. I'm sure it was all a big misunderstanding. I was just too sensitive.'

'That isn't what I said or what I meant.'

'I'm so sick and tired of the patriarchy. So bored with the needs and wants of men. Why does everything have to come back to you lot?'

'Take a breath,' you say. 'Obviously, I've said something which triggers a feeling in you. Stay nice and calm now.'

'I am calm,' I say.

'Do you lose your temper often?' you ask.

'Only when I encounter morons,' I say.

'Tell me about Oliver,' you say.

Chapter 60
HEATHER: LETTER TO KATIE 2019

One day when I took down her supper, Christina wasn't herself. She didn't speak to me. Her skin was grey. The light had gone from her eyes, and she sat slumped against the wall. I held a cup and plate towards her.

'I made your favourite,' I said.

She ignored me.

'Cup of tea and a toasted teacake.'

'I don't want it,' she said, acting like a sulky child.

'You have to eat,' I said.

'Why?'

'Because you'll get sick.'

'What do you care? You don't care whether I'm sick or hurt.'

'That's not true.'

'Oh, really?' she said. 'What's this, then?' she rolled up her sleeve to show me a smattering of bruises in different shades of purple, black, and yellow.

'How did you get those?' I asked.

'You know,' she said.

My stomach churned.

'You need to let me out of here or you're going to regret it. I'll tell the authorities it wasn't your fault and that you were good to me.'

'I can't. I'm sorry.'

She rocked backwards and forwards and repeated a rhyme over and over. I thought perhaps she was losing her mind.

'There was a man and he went mad,
He jumped into a paper bag.
The paper bag was too narrow,
He jumped into a red wheelbarrow.
The wheelbarrow set on fire
He jumped into a cow byre.
The cow byre was too nasty
He jumped into an apple pasty,
The apple pasty was too sweet,
He jumped into Chester-le-Street,
Chester-le-Street was full of stones,
So he fell down and broke his bones.'

She chanted it over and over, and every time I shuddered. As I set down her plate, she grabbed my arm and said, 'He's evil. Truly bad to the core.'

I drew back.

'You're mistaken,' I said coldly. 'We don't wish you any harm. We're just trying to survive.'

'You're a fool,' she said. 'You don't know. You don't know anything at all.'

I felt unnerved, and the rhyme went round and round in my head: 'Chester-le-Street was full of stones, He fell down and broke his bones.'

Jovano wasn't mad or bad. I truly believed this until the next time I went into the cellar.

Chapter 61
KATIE: NOW

Oliver grew into a totally adorable toddler. No temper tantrums, no naughtiness, just a perfect angel. He kept me entertained with his chatter and laughter and songs. My favourite time of day was when he was bathed and in pyjamas, tucked up in bed while I read to him tales of *The Velveteen Rabbit* and *The Tiger Who Came to Tea*.

One thing blighted my perfect time with him. Well, two things. I was neurotic about his health, and this got on Mark's nerves. Every time I tried to talk to him about my worries, he shut me down.

'But, Mark, I'm worried.' I tried again one afternoon when Oliver's temperature was raised and his food lay untouched on the dining room table. Mark had vetoed the need for a highchair. 'He hasn't eaten a thing. I'd like to call Doctor Foulds.'

'I'd like to call Dr Foulds,' he snapped. 'In fact, I'd like to call a head doctor. A shrink. You're not right in the fucking head. You seriously need to get a grip, Katie. You're losing it.'

'That's so unkind, Mark. I'm just a normal mother worried about her son.' He rolled his eyes and stormed from the room, slamming the door. Why could he not be more understanding and sympathetic? Why did no one understand? I had hoped that when Oliver was born Mark would bond with his son and he'd become an amazing father, but you'd think he was jealous of my relationship with him. I'd read about cases of fathers who were jealous of their children and the amount of their partner's time they took up. I didn't expect Mark to be one of them. I thought we would spend cosy family weekends, walks in the park, trips to the fair, the cinema, the swimming baths, but whenever I suggested doing any of those things, Mark was too busy or too tired to come. Half the time he appeared exasperated, and the other half he looked like he hated me. I couldn't understand where it had all gone wrong. The miscarriages had definitely taken their toll. I grieved. We grieved. But now that we had a son, surely things should have improved? If anything, however, they were much, much worse.

Mark ruined Oliver's fourth birthday for me. I'd ordered a beautiful cake from Harrods. A prehistoric scene featuring dinosaurs (Oliver loved dinosaurs) with a big green number four in the centre, a compsognathus sitting in the triangle of the number four and a velociraptor ready to jump from the top. I imagined him squealing with delight when he saw it. I'd had the staff blow up balloons in the shape of his age and a banner with Birthday Boy written in blue. I'd bought him a swing set for the garden, a slide, a Mercedes car which was battery-powered. He'd have hours of fun driving round the gardens in it. It had cost a fortune, but we could afford it. As I passed the kitchen I heard Mark speaking to Mrs Benson.

'Who helped with this charade?' he hissed.

'I'm sorry, Mr Amell, but it's what the mistress ordered.'

'Send it back,' he said. How could he begrudge his only son a wonderful birthday? What had happened to him?

He caught me creeping back to the parlour.

'Katie, have you lost your fucking mind?'

'I wish you wouldn't swear in front of Oliver,' I said. 'I'm not having him going to school talking as though he's from a rough London council estate.'

'How much did that lot cost?' Mark shouted.

'What does the cost matter?' I asked. 'It's not like we can't afford it.'

'Send it back,' he screamed at me. 'Send the fucking lot back.'

'It's his birthday,' I cried. 'Surely you don't begrudge your son a birthday present?'

'I'm warning you, Katie. All this had better be gone when I get back.'

'What do you mean, 'Get back'? Where are you going? You can't miss his birthday, Mark.'

Mark rushed towards me then and grabbed my face, pinching me hard.

'Get rid of this shit before I get back, or you're out on the street.' My mind whirled. I couldn't believe he was being so cruel. So unreasonable. What kind of man ruins his four-year-old son's birthday? I had to pack everything away, send it all back to the store, and Oliver had nothing for his birthday except a small pink piglet I managed to hide. Oliver called him Piggy and went to sleep with him every night after that.

Every time I tried to do something special for Oliver, Mark resisted. It was like he didn't want to acknowledge his son's existence. It was like he was so jealous of him he couldn't bear me to even speak of him. It didn't even need to be anything special. The day I went to register him for school, Mark had a fit. We'd been talking about it for months. At least I had been trying to get Mark to see that we'd need to put his name down soon or all the places would be gone in all the best schools. Mark wouldn't hear of making an appointment to speak with the headteacher of St Leonard's, so I did it myself. He was furious when he found out. I wouldn't have needed to go behind his back if he'd listened to me and made the appointment when I told him to do so. The fact was, I'd changed my mind about St Leonard's anyway. The headteacher had no business calling Mark and telling him our whole conversation. Also, she was rude. She practically threw me out. All because I questioned her about their Ofsted results, their bullying policy, their teacher training. Surely all parents want to know these things? Surely that isn't unusual? I only wanted the best for my son. Just like every other parent.

Initially, she was warm and welcoming, asked me to take a seat and offered me tea. There was a bit of small talk about the weather, and then she took my details. She typed my name and Oliver's details into a desktop computer, and I asked her questions about the school. I'd just asked her about how her teachers kept abreast of the latest developments in pedagogical practice when she looked up from her computer and removed her glasses. Her eyes had become slices, and her lips pursed. She pressed a button on her desk and a voice asked:

'Yes, Mrs Frobisher?'

'Please call Mr Amell at the Old Parsonage, Alice? The number is in the directory.'

'Why are you calling my husband?'

'Mr Amell asked us to get in touch if you came to make an appointment to view the school,' she said. I couldn't believe Mark was being so controlling.

'So that's what it has come to? A woman can't make a decision without the permission of her husband?' My cheeks burned and my voice rose. 'It isn't the 1950s, you know.'

'Please stay calm, Mrs Amell,' she said. You'd think she was talking to an escaped lunatic she didn't want to rile.

'I'll stay fucking calm when people stop treating me like I'm a child or a possession of my husband. Oliver is my son, too. Just because Mark is an important person in the village doesn't mean he owns me.'

'Of course not,' she said. 'Shall we have that tea?' Her assistant arrived, pushed open the door with her hip, carried a tea tray to the desk, placed it down, and backed away. They exchanged a glance and my blood bubbled.

'Milk? Sugar?' the head asked, pouring tea from the pot into two china cups.

'No thank you,' I said. 'I'm going to go.' As I got up to leave, the head put out her hand as though to shake mine. I ignored her and stormed out. By the time I'd got to the car park, Mark's car was screeching across the gravel driveway. He jumped from the vehicle, his face an explosion of red anger.

'What the fuck do you think you're doing?'

'Someone had to show an interest in Oliver's schooling, and it wasn't going to be you. How many times have I asked you to make an appointment with the head? How many opportunities have I given you to do this with me? Don't blame me for wanting to get things organised. If you didn't procrastinate everything, it would have been sorted by now.'

'Get in the fucking car,' Mark said, spitting at me with ferocity.

'I have my own car,' I said defiantly.

'Jasper will pick your car up. Now get in, Katie. I'm not joking.' Why did he always have to treat me like a child? Why could he never be on my side for once? He even rang the head to apologise for me, like I was a small child who had embarrassed herself at a friend's birthday party.

This became my life. I couldn't move without someone telling Mark where I was or what I was doing. I had no privacy. No life of my own. It got to the point where I felt like I couldn't leave the house with Oliver. He grew pale and became sickly, which fed my anxiety. I called Doctor Foulds who smiled at me kindly and listened to my worries. He assured me I didn't need to be anxious, but still I fretted.

I suppose every new parent obsesses a little about their first child. Especially if there have been miscarriages. It's probably perfectly natural, but it caused problems between Mark and me. He was mean. He hated spending money on Oliver. He hated me even mentioning his name. I think he was jealous.

I eventually found a school for Oliver. It was the village school, a state school away from those stuck-up teachers and parents. It had an excellent reputation and Ofsted had rated it outstanding. Everyone was so friendly. They chatted in the yard while we waited for our children to arrive, carrying bags and looking worried about lost jumpers. Oliver was always last. I was always the last person standing, waiting patiently for his perfect blond head to appear. And then everything changed.

I couldn't put my finger on when it started, but I remember walking into the yard one day. It was spitting on to rain, and a number of the parents had left it until the last minute to get out of their cars and descend on the yard. The north wind blew leaves and chip papers into small whirls, and people pulled up their hoods to protect their ears from the chill. I spotted Luke's mum and trotted across the yard to stand with her.

'Afternoon. How are you? They're late out today.'

Usually, she'd moan about how they were always late out when the weather was bad. She'd say you'd think the teacher knew they were freezing and wanted to punish them. But today there was just a tight-lipped, 'Yes.' And she turned away to chat to Ava's mum. I waved at Kelsey's dad, and he returned a barely perceptible nod. He usually flirted with me and tried to get me to go for coffee with him. What had happened to make them ignore me like this? Surely Oliver hadn't been mean to one of their children? Oliver wasn't like that. He was a perfect angel. That wasn't me being one of those parents who think their child is an angel when really they're a little menace. Oliver really was no trouble at all. Then it dawned on me what this was. This was Mark. Mark had been telling tales. Mark had intervened. My eyes stung and my heart sank. The reception teacher came out to dismiss the children, flanked on both sides by men, as though she thought I might cause trouble.

'Mrs Amell?' she said, lightly touching my elbow. 'Would you mind coming inside?'

Chapter 62
Regression Therapy: FEBRUARY 1976

I've got used to making him something to eat. He munches greedily on whatever I put on the table in front of him. I will never get used to the things he makes me do on the bed. Just once he made me do it in the kitchen, too, but I grabbed a fork and stuck it in his chest. The look of shock on his face was priceless. He stamped on my foot for that misbehaviour. It swelled like a balloon, and now I limp. The bones crack and crunch as I try to walk, and I retch with the pain. When he sees me limping he hits me, so I have to try and put weight on my foot as normal, which is agony. I cry only when I'm alone.

I've been watching him. He has no idea. He hides things in his bedroom. I've seen him lift the floorboards when he thinks I'm asleep. The next time he goes out, I'm going to see what he has hidden there.

'I'll be gone all day today,' he says. 'See you dae anything ye shouldnae dae, and ye'll get it.'

He loosens his belt and removes it from his trousers. I shake. He threads the belt through the hole and tucks the end back into the loop. The door slams shut behind him, and I breathe a sigh of relief. I hobble up the stairs and into his room. I try not to think about the things that happen there. I move the small cabinet, as I've seen him do, and work the fingers of my good hand into the space between the boards. It lifts out easily. I put my hand in the space, but disappointment fills me as I can feel only dust. I yank out my arm and raise another board and another. There, shoved right to the back, is a metal box. My face is flat against the floor and my arm stretched as far as it will reach. It seems like ages before my fingers can move the box. I'm anxious I'll push it further away. Gently, gently, it's moving towards me.

An engine roars, brakes squeal and a car door opens. Panic fills me. I leave the box, shove the floorboards back into their place, and try to clear the dust I've created with my hand. I move the cabinet back in its place just as his key turns in the lock. My heart is thumping, and my legs feel like they'll give way. I move as quickly as I can and flush the toilet chain, then make my way back downstairs, expecting him to be sitting at the table waiting for his square sausage.

There's a rustle from the pantry, a scratching and a scraping.

'I'll put the sausage on,' I say.

His shape appears in the doorway of the pantry. Only it isn't him. It's another man.

'Who the fuck are you? Where's Tam?'

Chapter 63
KATIE: NOW

I always knew children could be cruel, but I didn't expect the parents to be cruel, too. That shocked me. How they could hurt a defenceless young boy, I'll never know. Why would they want to? What had Oliver ever done to them?

It was his fifth birthday, and I'd decided he'd have a big party with all his classmates. I sent out invitations. Careful to invite everyone in the class. I couldn't bear the thought of any child feeling left out. Even if I didn't particularly like the mothers or fathers, I wouldn't ignore any child. How awful it is to be discounted? For everyone to be talking in anticipation for weeks at school, and for everyone to then be chatting in excitement for weeks afterwards about what had occurred there. It was soul-destroying to be the only one unable to join in with the conversation. It was humiliating. I would never do that to a child. So I was careful to make sure no one was excluded.

I'd ordered a clown, a magician, a petting zoo. This was going to be the most talked about party in the village ever. I had caterers make the food rather than have the kitchen staff spend days in preparation. Everything was set. The house was decorated. Oliver was dressed in his best designer shirt and trousers. He looked so grown-up with his hair cut neatly and brushed to try to disguise the cowlick I loved so much. My heart was bursting with love and pride for him as he opened his gifts, flinging his arms round me and thanking me for being so generous. His father skulked in the background. His petty jealousy rearing its ugly head once again.

'If you are continuing with this charade, I'm going to go out,' he said.

'If you insist on twisting your face about everything, then you might as well,' I said. But I was hurt that once again he'd decided to abandon Oliver on his birthday and leave me to face everything alone.

The magician arrived and set up on the table I'd put aside for him. The petting zoo was erected, and the animals were all in their pens. The food was served and covered in clingfilm, ready for the onslaught of small fingers and plastic forks. 3 p.m. arrived, and no chimes emanated from the doorbell. 3:30, and I was checking my watch, then checking the invitation to make sure I didn't have the time wrong. 4 p.m. ticked past. 4:30. Where were they? By 6 p.m., I finally gave in and realised no one was coming. Not one friend. The children I could forgive. They didn't know any better. But the parents? I'd never forgive the parents for what they put Oliver and me through that day. Have you ever tried to console a devastated five-year-old when he realises he has no friends? Have you ever given a party and had no one turn up? Do you know how soul-destroying that is? How could they do that to him? How could they do that to me? Why?

I rang for Mrs Benson. Usual manners and etiquette were forgotten.

'Get rid of this lot before we return,' I snapped.

'Yes, ma'am,' she said, a sly smile tickling the corners of her mouth.

At 6.30, I put on our coats and took Oliver to the cinema to see a film about cartoon monsters who were scared of humans. I didn't blame them. Humans are shitty. Oliver pretended he didn't care. He munched on popcorn and devoured ice-cream while kicking his legs because he was satisfied with an excellent film.

We returned home, and Mrs Benson had been as good as her word. There was no trace of a party that had been held in our house. Even a party no one had attended. I was left with an awful feeling. One which itched at me in the small hours and a gripping fear stronger than any I'd ever experienced.

Oliver was home-schooled after that. I wasn't going to embarrass myself in the yard any more. Speaking to people who talked about me behind their hands and giggled when they thought I wasn't watching. I wasn't going to make an effort with people who believed the lies Mark told about me. It was hurtful, but all that mattered was Oliver. His happiness was more important than my own. As long as he was okay, I was okay. Mark could continue his campaign of humiliation and vitriol. I wasn't about to let it get to me.

I taught my son in a project-based way. We learned about nature by visiting parks. We collected pine cones and conkers, we observed frogspawn and squirrels. We learned about history by visiting places of interest, museums, and heritage sites. Art lessons were creative and messy. One afternoon we'd get the train up to the Tate and another we'd do potato prints on the breakfast bar. Mark would come home to gifts of green handprints and silver pinecone stacks. Until realisation dawned that the artistic creations were unappreciated. That saddened me more than anything else.

Mark heard me telling Dr Monroe that Oliver was really creative.

'He takes after me,' I said.

'Without a doubt,' Mark said, but he didn't say it like he was giving me a compliment. He was insulting both Oliver and me.

People probably wondered why I stayed when all Mark seemed to do was to run me down, but I loved him. And where could I have gone? I wanted Oliver to have two parents. I didn't want him to come from a broken home.

Then we had a huge fight. Our biggest to date. I was sitting in the library, reading his clients' latest bestseller. It was a psychological thriller about a woman whose husband had an affair with her best friend and tried to drive her mad by gaslighting. That would never happen in my marriage. I didn't have any friends. Mark had seen to that.

Oliver had been bathed and put to bed. Mark came and sat in the seat opposite me. This was a rare thing. He generally avoided my company now.

'I've been thinking,' he said. I put down the novel and took off my glasses. 'Why don't you go back to work?' I shook my head, not believing what he'd just said.

'But it was you who made me leave work,' I said.

'Yes, and now I'm suggesting that it would probably do you good to go back.'

'You hated me working,' I said.

'That was before,' he said.

'I can't go back,' I said.

'Maybe not full-time at first,' he said. 'But you could ease yourself back in gradually. You loved your job.'

'I did,' I said. 'But I love what I do now.'

'It isn't good for you, Katie.'

'Since when have you been worried about what's good for me?' I said, a rare moment of bravery.

'You are to go back to work,' he commanded this time.

'You can't tell me what to do, Mark. I'm not a child. I have Oliver to look after. Oliver is the most important thing now. Going back to work will interfere with that. Who will school him?'

'For God's sake, Katie,' he shouted, running one hand through his hair.

'What, Mark? What is it? Are you jealous? Don't you like the time Oliver and I spend together? Do you resent it? You want me to spend all my time thinking about you, looking after you like I did before Oliver came along?' I sounded spiteful now, but I couldn't stop myself.

The violence was incidental. It's what he did after that that broke me. It was cruel and heartless. I just don't know how he could do what he did.

'What did Mark do, Katie?' you ask.

'You know what he did … he took Oliver from me.'

Chapter 64
HEATHER: LETTER TO KATIE 2019

I woke the next morning with anxiety pressing down on my chest. A black cloud hovered above me and nothing I did would chase it away. I tried to think nice thoughts: Jovano and me on a beach somewhere, the sun shining on my sausage-skin legs, the wind whipping his newly grown hair into saw-toothed sculptures. Trekking in the mountains or wandering through sunlit everglades side by side. Free. But with every positive thought came a wave of disquiet.

I shouted his name, but silence came back at me. I padded downstairs and into the kitchen. The cat yowled from outside the back door, so I turned the key and let her in. Her ear was torn, and her fur was thick with blood.

'Come here,' I said, trying to get her to come to me so I could look at her injuries.

She backed into the corner of the kitchen and hissed at me.

'Come on, I'm not going to hurt you. I want to help.'

She arched her back, puffed up her hair, flattened her ears, and opened her mouth, her fangs ready to strike. I ignored her then, thinking it would be best to wait for her to calm down.

A daddy longlegs floated above my head. Starfishing across the ceiling. I resisted the urge to reach for a broom to sweep it away. I imagined Jovano's reaction to my killing his favourite creature. It squeezed into a corner, playing dead, and I eyed it as I filled a pan with water and placed it on the stove.

I made breakfast of poached egg on toast and a cup of tea to take down to Christina. A jar sat on the counter. A strange fishlike thing in pink liquid. What the hell had Jovano been doing?

My hands shook, and the teacup rattled against the saucer. I turned the key and pushed open the cellar door. Christina was sitting on the floor with her head down.

'I've brought breakfast,' I said.

She didn't move.

'Come on, Christina. Please don't sulk. It won't be for much longer. I made your favourite. Just how you like them.'

She lifted her head, and all I could see was a mass of red. Was it paint? All over her face, dripping off her chin, down her front, and onto the floor. I realised it was blood. I would never forget her eyes. That tortured expression. Pain, fear, terror.

'What happened?' I asked, putting down the tray and rushing towards her. 'What did you do?'

She shook her head from side to side, and tears rolled down her cheeks.

'Speak to me, Christina. What happened?'

A noise came from her. As she opened her mouth, more blood spilled out. The sounds coming from her were demonic.

Fear gripped me. 'Christina, you're scaring me. What's wrong?'

She moaned and rocked. Rocked and moaned. I ran up the stairs calling for Jovano. He eventually came back.

'Where have you been? I've been looking all over for you. There's something wrong with Christina. Something terrible. She's bleeding really badly. We have to phone an ambulance.'

'No we don't,' Jovano said. 'She's fine.'

'She isn't fine, I said. 'She really isn't. Please, you have to listen to me. Something is terribly wrong. Come and see.'

He came with me down the cellar steps. When Christina saw us, she cowered in the corner as the cat had done. I think if she could have hissed, she would have.

'You see,' I said to him.

'She's fine,' he said.

'She isn't fine.' Panic had gripped me now. He wasn't listening. 'Christina, show him your mouth. Show him what's wrong.'

With that, she opened her mouth, and I could see inside. Her tongue was missing. Cut off. Cut out. I screamed.

'Shut the fuck up, Heather. Someone will hear.'

'What happened? What …?'

'She was going to tell the coppers. She's telling them fuck all now.'

I couldn't believe what I was hearing.

'What are you saying? What did you do? Oh God, no! No, Jovano, you didn't?' This was unspeakable.

Christina's eyes followed me out of the cellar, fat with tears.

'What were you thinking?' It was one thing killing Karma and Adrik in self-defence, but this …

'I got sick of listening to her,' he said.

'You can't just cut someone's tongue out because you don't like what they say.' How could he try to justify these actions?

'She could get us into a lot of trouble, Heather.'

'You've got yourself into trouble,' I said. 'I'm going to the police. I'm going to hand myself in. This has gone far enough. This has gone far too far. I'm going to ring an ambulance and the police.'

'You go near that fucking phone and I'll chop your tongue out as well.'

Fear crept down my spine, chilling me to my toes.

'Jovano, please. Be reasonable. You haven't thought this through.'

'Oh, but I have. I have thought it through. I know exactly what I'm doing.'

My whole body shook. It wouldn't stop. What the hell was I to do? I wanted to go to the police. I wanted to get Christina medical help, but I also wanted to keep my tongue. I also wanted to stay alive. How could I go against Jovano now? How could I rescue Christina? She said she'd stand up for me and tell the authorities that I had helped her, that I hadn't been cruel. I hadn't hurt her. Maybe I could get her to write something to that effect. Maybe she'd write a kind of reference to let them know I was innocent. Well, if not innocent exactly, not as guilty as Jovano. I'd try and do that later tonight. Then I'd sneak out and ring the emergency services.

Jovano had to be stopped.

Chapter 65
KATIE: 2019

Panic filled me. The hand on my clock crept closer to the twelve. Any minute now, Mollie and her husband would be knocking on the door. What would he do to me? Maybe he'd do nothing. Pretend he didn't recognise me while his wife and children were there, but then he'd come back in the dead of night and slit my throat as I slept. Maybe he'd drag me into a van and drive me to the woods. Maybe he'd grab me by the throat and squeeze the life out of me, just as he'd tried to do all those years ago.

I wasn't mad. The noises in the night. The feeling that someone had been here. The writing on the mirror. It was him. It had to be him. And now I'd invited him into my home. Oh God, was Mollie in on it? Had she befriended me so her husband could kill me? I ran from room to room, making sure all the doors and windows were locked. I closed the shutters and turned off the lights. A car pulled up the drive. I dropped to the floor and slid under the coffee table in the front room. The door knocker beat against the front door, sending tremors through the house. My hands shook and my heart turned to stone. The knocks again boomed through the house, echoing in the hallway and through every room. Then my name was called.

'Katie, hello. Are you there?' Mollie's voice. 'She's maybe upstairs. We are a little early.'

Their misshapen silhouettes in the glass. The shape of his head. The knocks again, mirroring my heart thumping off my ribcage.

'I'll have a look round the back.'

That's when I smelled it. Burning. From the kitchen. I'd left the pan on the hob, simmering. She'd see it from the kitchen window. I rolled out of my hiding place and ran to the kitchen, heaving the pan off the hob and throwing it into the sink. Steam poured out and misted the window. I threw myself under the breakfast bar, praying she couldn't see me from the window. The knocking on the window set my heart thundering and my knees shaking.

'Hello, Katie. It's Mollie, we're here.'

Footsteps padded back to the front of the house.

'She's in. There's something cooking. The kitchen is full of steam.'

'Did you try the door?' he asked, his tone impatient.

The handle creaked as someone put pressure on it.

'It's locked,' Mollie said.

'Ring her,' his voice said.

Seconds later, my ringtone rang out from the dining room table.

'I can hear it ringing,' Mollie said. 'Do you think something is wrong? Should we break in?'

My heart stopped at this. My blood ran cold, and I thought I would faint from fear.

'Ring her again,' he said. Children's voices. Arguing. 'Stoppit, you two.' Surely he wouldn't do anything where the children were? Maybe I could let them in and pretend I didn't know him. Oh God, why didn't they just go away?

'Try the French doors,' he said, and I remembered with absolute certainty that I hadn't locked them. Any minute now, they'd be in the conservatory and they'd see me hunched under the breakfast bar like some deranged fugitive.

Chapter 66
KATIE: NOW

'What happened, Katie? What did Mark do to Oliver?' you ask.

'It was terrible,' I say. 'I've had bad days. I've had days where I wanted to end it all, but this … it was truly the worst day of my life.

'I had already told myself he was up to something. I shouldn't have fallen for it. I should have fought against it. I think in the pit of my stomach, I knew. I always say you should trust your first instinct. Your first instinct is the most accurate. Everything else that comes into play after that can be misleading. Smoke and mirrors. Downright lies.'

'Tell me about it,' you say. 'Tell me exactly what happened.'

Mrs Benson woke me and feigned excitement. The fact that she was being pleasant should have made me sit up and take notice. She was never willingly nice to me. She did her duty, what was expected of her, but nothing more. Nothing warm or human or helpful beyond the duties of her position.

'Mr Amell said you are to bathe, dress, pack a weekend case and be ready at eleven to go to the station,' she said with a smile. It didn't reach her eyes, but I didn't even know her lips were capable of curling into a pleasant crescent. I certainly hadn't seen it before.

'Where are we going?' I asked, keen to make use of this new-found friendship.

'I don't know, ma'am. My instructions were merely to rouse you and tell you just what I've told you.'

'How exciting!' I said. 'Will you pack a bag for Oliver?'

'Mr Amell said it was just to be the two of you. The child has already gone.' Alarm swept through me. I wanted Oliver to come with us. I thought it would be a lovely family trip. I imagined us taking him to museums and art galleries, zoos and parks.

'Gone where? What do you mean?'

'I'm sure it will be a lovely break for you,' Mrs Benson said ignoring my questions. I didn't want a break from my son. I wanted to spend every waking moment with him. He was the love of my life. But it wouldn't do to cause a fuss when Mark had gone to so much effort on my behalf. Part of me felt grateful he had considered me, and another part felt furious that he knew so little about me that he thought a weekend away from Oliver would be a treat. A weekend away from Oliver would be torturous and I didn't even get to kiss him goodbye. How cruel. I'd spend the whole time wondering what he was doing and worrying about his welfare. When I was here I could control things. Well, not control exactly. That was Mark's preserve, but I could oversee what he was doing. Why didn't I fight against it? I should have just refused to go. If only I had refused to go.

'Is Mr Amell in the dining room?' I asked, thinking I could chat with him and persuade him to allow Oliver to come with us.

'No, he's left already. He went on ahead as he had some business to take care of.' I became excited that I could pick up Oliver and Mark wouldn't be able to refuse once we got there, but what Mrs Benson said next denied me that possibility.

'We are under strict instructions to get you to the airport alone and ready for a romantic weekend.'

I gave in. There was nothing to be gained from complaining about the situation. I would have to go and endure it. I know the servants thought me spoiled and ungrateful. Here was my husband booking a romantic weekend away to treat me, and here I was being petulant about it, but the truth was, I couldn't bear to spend a few hours away from Oliver, let alone a whole weekend.

I should have fought. How I regret not doing so, but it seemed so futile at the time. If only I had listened to my instincts, my inner voice, I'd have taken Oliver away. Far away from that house. Far away from those people. But I didn't, and I paid the ultimate price.

Jarvis drove me to the airport, and my luggage was checked in. I was soon on a first-class flight to Barcelona and missing Oliver like only a mother could. I tried to switch off. I had to endure this weekend, so I might as well make the most of it and enjoy it the best I could. The cabin crew came round with champagne, and I didn't say no. By the time we touched down, I was nicely mellow and eagerly anticipating the time ahead.

Mark met me at the airport, and his first words were, 'You're drunk.' I felt like he'd slapped me. I'd had the best part of a bottle of Laurent Perrier, but I certainly wasn't drunk. I was merry and warm and genial.

'I'm not drunk, Mark,' I protested. 'I'm just relaxed.'

'Is that what they're calling hammered these days?' His tone was sharp, and I wished I was back home with my son.

'I'm not hammered,' I said. I snatched my bag from him and proceeded towards the exit.

'You're going the wrong way,' he said. 'You who is stone-cold sober.' Sarcasm oozed from him, and I wanted to slap him hard. I sighed a deep sigh. So much for a congenial, peaceful weekend. Mark was ready for war, and now I felt hurt and resentful.

'Can we just stop this?' I asked.

'I didn't start it,' he said.

'I apologise if you think I had too much to drink on the plane, but I was just trying to get in the mood.'

'That is a non-apology, if ever I heard one. You're sorry if I think you had too much to drink. Not sorry you got drunk. And you had to get drunk to spend the weekend with me. Thank you. That makes me feel really special.'

'You're putting words in my mouth,'' I said. 'That isn't what I said.'

'It's exactly what you said,' he said, then hailed the driver, who took the bag from him and placed it into his open boot. The car burst with silence all the way to the hotel. The driver pulled up beside the hotel foyer. I cracked open the door, stormed out, and stomped up to reception.

'The room for Mr and Mrs Amell,' I said to the pretty Catalan girl.

'Good afternoon, Mrs Amell, I trust your journey was trouble-free …?'

'If only …' I said.

'Pardon me, Madam?'

'Nothing, never mind,' I said. 'Could you have my bag sent up, please?'

'Of course, Mrs Amell. Room 601 on the top floor. The penthouse suite.'

'Thank you,' I said. I snatched the key and marched to the lift.

I was relieved the room had twin beds. I certainly didn't want to sleep with Mark, the way I was feeling. Crisp white sheets and a spotless en-suite bathroom and dressing room eased my frustrations, and when I gazed out at the view from the balcony it took my breath away. Our own private pool had a deck which boasted the best view in Barcelona. The whole city sat at my feet. My anger melted away, and I opened the champagne in the bucket beside the bed. I'd poured us both a glass and added a strawberry when Mark came in. I was expecting him to say something along the lines of, 'Don't you think you've had enough?', but he took the glass from me, clinked his against mine, and said, 'Cheers. I've got some catching up to do.' He downed that glass in one gulp and poured himself another.

'It's a beautiful hotel,' I said. 'Thank you.' I kissed the top of his head. He drank his champagne and poured another, kicking off his shoes and lying on the bed. 'Forty winks, and we'll go and grab a bite before we do a tour of the city.'

'Great,' I said. 'I could do with a nap myself.'

I must have fallen straight to sleep. When I awoke it was with a headache and a fuzzy feeling. It was dark. Mark was nowhere to be seen. I called his name and was met with silence. I rang his phone, but it went straight to voicemail. My vision was blurred as I tried to see the time on my watch. Surely it couldn't be ten o'clock? I'd slept for hours. It felt as though I'd just closed my eyes for a moment.

The door opened, and Mark staggered in. He rested his eyes on me, and a nasty expression crossed his face.

'So you've surfaced?' he said, shaking off his jacket and loosening his tie.

'You should have woken me,' I said. 'Where have you been?'

'Never mind where I've been. I couldn't wake you. You were drunk.'

'And now you are.' I got up and gathered my toiletries so I could shower.

'What the fuck are you doing?'

'I'm having a shower and getting ready to go out,' I said.

'You're doing nothing of the sort,' he snapped. 'Get back into bed.'

'Don't tell me what to do, Mark. If I want to go out, I'll go out.'

'I said, get back into bed.' He grabbed hold of me then and pushed me towards the bed. I lost my balance and fell backwards. Luckily, I had a soft landing. Had I been a foot to the right I'd have banged my head on the bedside table.

'For God's sake, Mark. Stop,' I said. 'Just stop.'

'You fucking stop,' he said. I decided to get into bed just to keep the peace. There'd be plenty of time to explore in the morning, and I couldn't face a fight. Long after his snores growled round the room, I lay awake, my heart thumping, my mind racing. Going over and over the conversation. The way his lip curled, the way he'd regarded me with disdain. It was as though he hated me. What on earth had I ever done to provoke such vitriol?

'How did the rest of the weekend go?' you ask.

'The next morning, he woke and it was like nothing had happened. There wasn't even an apology for pushing me. He whistled in the shower and ordered breakfast in the room. Omelettes and ham sandwiches, coffee, and croissants. While I ate, he pored over a map of the city, picking out places of interest for us to visit. It was like we were newlyweds. Totally in love. It was almost as though Mark had a split personality.'

'So you had an enjoyable time?'

'I was on edge, but we saw some incredible art and architecture and ate at some fabulous restaurants. But I still couldn't wait to get home.'

The journey home was torturous. All I wanted was to see Oliver. I couldn't wait to see his face, to have him fling his arms round my neck and tell me how much he'd missed me. I imagined he'd drawn pictures of us swimming in shark-infested waters and building sandcastles on the beach, a child's-eye view of what a weekend break should be. We rode up our driveway and my stomach turned in excited anticipation, much more so than it had on my outward journey.

Mrs Benson greeted us at the door with another rare smile and the news that the vicar was in the library to see my husband.

'I'm going to wash and change,' I said. If I said I was going straight to see Oliver I'd have been met by exasperation. I went straight to his rooms on the first floor. Calling his name, I ascended the stairs two at a time in my eagerness.

'Oliver, Mummy's home. Where are you?' I opened the door to his room, expecting him to be recumbent, wearing headphones, his fingers at work on the Xbox controller. The room was empty. And by empty, I mean *empty*.

Everything belonging to Oliver had gone.

Chapter 67
HEATHER: LETTER TO KATIE 2019

When it came down to it, there was nothing I could do. I wanted to help Christina, of course I did, but I couldn't. It was too late.

The next morning, I took her water. I doubt she could have eaten anything with her injuries. I thought she was asleep at first. Then I thought she was sulking because of what Jovano had done. When I realised, I didn't scream. No sound would come. Nausea gripped me and I ran to the bucket, heaving and retching, hot bile rising in my throat and splashing into the pail. People have told me dead people's faces are peaceful. There was nothing peaceful about Christina's face. I see it every night in my dreams. A mask of fear and pain. Tortured. I think she must have bled to death or had a heart attack. Now there was nothing I could do to help. There was that overwhelming feeling of wanting to turn back the clock. That all-powerful 'if only' feeling. But now it was done, and I couldn't undo it. I thought this was the worst thing, but what happened next was even more vile.

I eventually found my tongue and told Jovano Christina was dead. He didn't even react. How could anyone be so cold and unmoving? How could he feel nothing?

'I have a list of things you need to buy,' he said.

'Are you mental? I asked. As I sat in the kitchen and looked out of the window onto the garden, I noticed a bird sitting on the top of a wheelbarrow. 'Where did that come from?' I asked him.

'Where did what come from?'

'The wheelbarrow.'

'The shed. We need to clean up the mess,' he said.

I stared at the list: bleach 4 litres, rubble sacks, rubber gloves.

'What do we need these for?' I was consumed with panic. I could barely speak. 'What mess?'

'Grow up,' he snapped. 'We need to take care of the body.'

My eye was drawn to the falchion on its perch on the living room wall.

'What are we going to do?' My blood ran cold as we descended the steps to the cellar, the falchion tapping on the floor.

The rhythmic tap, tap, tapping of an old man and his walking stick.

Chapter 68
KATIE: NOW

I searched through his wardrobes, and not one item of his clothing remained. None of his toys, books, school things. Nothing. What had they done with them? Where had they taken Oliver?

I ran to the library where Mark sat with the vicar, sipping tea.

'Where is he?' I screamed. 'What have you done with him?' I raged against Mark. The vicar looked startled and spilt drops of his tea onto his knee. He placed his teacup into its saucer and pulled a hanky from his pocket, wiping the wet patch.

'I'd better go,' he said.

'Katie, you're making a scene,' Mark said.

'Where's my son, Mark? Where's Oliver? What have you done with him?' Mark rang the bell, and Mrs Benson appeared as though she'd been floating outside, listening and ready to spring into action.

'Call Dr Foulds,' Mark said.

'He's already on his way, sir. I took the liberty when I heard the commotion,' she said.

'Why?' I shouted. 'Why have you called the doctor? What's happened? Where's Oliver? Tell me.'

'Perhaps it would be better if we continue this meeting at another time,' Mark said to the vicar. The vicar seemed relieved. He gathered up his gloves and hat before bidding a hasty good day. Mrs Benson showed him out, and Mark turned to me, grabbing my wrist.

'I've never been so embarrassed,' he said, his lip curling in a snarl.

'What have you done with Oliver?'

'Katie, you aren't well. You haven't been well for a long time.'

'What are you talking about, 'not well'? There's nothing wrong with me. I'm perfectly healthy. I know what you're trying to do,' I said. 'You're trying to say I'm not well enough to care for my son so you can take him away from me. I'm not going to let you get away with this.'

'You are mentally ill.'

'There's nothing wrong with me. It's you, Mark. You're insane. I've been reading about it. You're a narcissistic sociopath.' He laughed then, throwing back his head to reveal two black fillings. Rage swelled within me.

'You're mad, quite mad,' Mark said. 'Everyone knows it.'

'You mean you've tried to convince everyone of it? You aren't going to get away with this.'

Mrs Benson showed Dr Foulds into the library. A smirk sat on her lips, and I could have flown at her and clawed it from her face. She was loving what was happening.

'How are you feeling?' Dr Foulds asked me.

'How do you think?' I snapped. 'They've taken Oliver somewhere. They're trying to say I'm an unfit mother. I know exactly what they're up to. Don't let them do this to me, Doctor. I'm a good parent.'

'I'm going to give you a shot; it's for your own good,' Dr Foulds said.

'Please don't,' I said. 'I can't sleep now. I need to find Oliver. I need to stop them.'

'You're overwrought,' he said. 'You're no good to anyone in this condition. Let me give you a shot. Sleep tonight, and we'll see how everything is in the morning.'

'No,' I said. 'Get away from me.' I must have sounded deranged then, but who wouldn't in those circumstances?

'Did he give you a shot?' you ask.

'Yes. The last thing I remember is being held by Mark and Mrs Benson while Dr Foulds gave me an injection. He told me it was all for the best, and everything turned black.'

I awoke during the night to someone calling my name. I followed the voice to the beach and I saw her. Laura. Mark's dead wife. I realise what it sounds like, but she wasn't dead. For some reason, they wanted people to believe she was, but she was there. I spoke to her.

'You're letting them win. You have to play the long game. Don't let them get away with this,' she said.

'I won't,' I said.

'You'll find any information you need among Mark's things. That key he has around his neck, it's for a secret drawer in his desk. You need to open that drawer. You'll find everything in there you need to know. But you must be clever about it. Stop the hysteria. Now get back to the house before they notice you're missing.'

People would have blamed the drugs. They'd have said I was hallucinating. I wasn't I know I wasn't.

That night, I prepared a drink for Mark laced with Valium. While he was sleeping, I intended to steal the key from the chain around his neck, open the drawer, and find out where he had taken my son. I took my chance when he rang for his evening brandy.

'I'll get that,' I said.

'You seem to be feeling much better today,' he said.

'Yes, I'm feeling much more myself,' I said.

'It's good to have you back.' He smiled smugly as though he'd single-handedly cured me of some foul and fatal disease.

I'd crushed the tablets to a powder and now I shook them into his drink and stirred it until they were dissolved. I added ice and handed his drink to him. He stared at it for a second, and I thought I'd been discovered, but he sipped. I breathed a sigh of relief.

'Will you ask Mrs Benson to bring charcuterie into the library? I'm suddenly peckish,' he said.

When I returned, he'd drunk the brandy and was pouring himself another. By the time Mrs Benson brought the snacks, he was sleeping in the chair, his newspaper on his lap, his glasses skewed on his face. Mrs Benson failed to hide her shock at finding her beloved employer in such a state.

'Mr Amell is exhausted,' I said. 'Don't disturb him.'

'I'm not surprised,' she said, suggesting I was exhausting. I ignored her insolence. I covered him with a throw, and when he didn't stir, I tried to unfasten the chain around his neck. He turned over, so it was harder to reach the clasp. My hands shook, but I eventually managed to prise the clasp open, remove his chain, and get the key. I crept out of the room and across the hall to his office. The door creaked as I opened it; it sounded like a shriek in the silent night air. I padded across the floor to his desk, feeling with shaking fingers, not daring to switch on the light. A clatter from the hallway and my heart thumped. One of the maids had dropped something. Mrs Benson was hissing a rebuke to her. I slipped the key into the lock and turned. The drawer was stiff, but it eventually opened, revealing the contents. I flicked through the documents: birth certificates, marriage certificate, death certificates. But there was one certificate missing. Surely not. It couldn't be! I put my hand up to my mouth in shock, and then I spun round and he stood in the doorway.

'What the hell are you playing at?' Mark asked. 'Did you really think I'd fall for your pathetic trick? Just as well I didn't drink it.'

'I ...I don't know what you're talking about ...'

'There are Valium missing from your supply, and the residue is still on the glass. I've put the glass in the safe with a little note. If anything happens to me, everyone will know it was you who killed me.'

'I didn't try to kill you ...'

'Save it. You're fucking insane.'

'Why is there no death certificate for Laura?'

'What?' he spat.

'Everyone's birth certificates are here. The family death certificates are there. Why is there no death certificate for Laura?'

'You're actually fucking crazy,' he said.

'I want my son. I want Oliver back.' Mark laughed, and I leapt at him, clawing chunks of skin from his face and neck. He slapped me and I fell backwards, a pain shooting through my hip.

'You're mad. You need locking up,' he said, stepping over me and closing the door behind him. I lay in a heap, crying in anger, frustration, and fear. I knew what I had to do. I would go to the police. Somebody had to listen to me.

Chapter 69
KATIE: NOW

'Can we go back to 1995?' you ask. 'You were telling me about going to the police.'

I sigh. Bored. I'm sick of myself and I'm sick of my story, but I started this so I suppose I must finish it.

The officer at the front desk didn't look much older than thirteen. This was a definite sign I was getting old.
'How can I help you, madam?' he asked.
'It's my son,' I said. 'He's missing.'
'How old is he?'
'He's six years old.'
'I'll get someone to come and take some details,' he said. 'If you'd just like to take a seat.'

I sat on a hard metal chair opposite the reception area. My stomach churned and my hands trembled. If Mark knew I was here he'd go mad. Everything was about appearances with him. Keeping up appearances. No one should know anything going on in the Big House as they called it in the village. The people in the Big House were beyond reproach. The people in the Big House were superior to the rest of the village. Their children didn't run the streets, eating sugar and staying out after dark. Their children didn't have dirty noses and scraped knees. Their children didn't go missing.

A young woman came out of the door next to the glass reception area. She shook my hand and said, 'DS Swinburn. If you'd like to come with me, Mrs Amell, and I'll take some details.' She led me through another door and down a short corridor to a room on the right, which held a table and two chairs. I sat opposite her, and she opened a notebook. 'If I can just take some details,' she said, 'starting with your name and address.' Frustration and impatience filled me, but I went through the necessary rigmarole required.

'You say your six-year-old son is missing. Can you explain the circumstances leading up to his disappearance?'

'My husband and I have just returned from a long weekend in Barcelona. When we got back to the house, Oliver was gone.'

'Have you searched the whole house, the grounds, contacted friends and other family members?'

'You don't understand, Oliver doesn't have any friends. I had to take him out of school. Yes, I've looked everywhere for him. They've got rid of everything. All his clothes, his toys, his books …' My anguish must have shown on my face, and I tore at the skin of my arms with my nails.

'They?' the sergeant asked.

'The staff, Mrs Benson, my husband, and his mother. They're all in on it. Don't you see? That's why he took me away, that's why Mrs Benson was so nice to me. She's never been nice before. She knew. They all knew.'

'I'm not really sure I understand. You're saying your husband and his staff have taken your son? Why would they do that?' she asked, her pen poised above her notebook but writing nothing.

'They've been trying to take him away from me for years,' I said. 'They're going to try and say I'm an unfit mother.'

'Why would they do that?'

'Because I've had some problems. I've been ill at times. I had serious postnatal depression, but I would never neglect or harm my son. He's my life.'

'And where do you think they've taken your son?'

'If I knew that, I wouldn't be here. I need you to find him for me and bring him back. Please help me.'

'We'll do everything we can, Mrs Amell.'

She showed me back to reception, and Mark was there shouting at the desk sergeant.

'There you are,' he said, then turned towards me and enveloped me in a hug. 'I was worried about you. Why didn't you tell me where you were going?' He continued, 'My wife isn't well. She has delusions.'

'Stop lying,' I screamed. 'There's nothing wrong with me.' I must have appeared demented. I'd played into his hands. The DS looked us both up and down.

'I'd like to call at The Parsonage if you don't mind, sir.'

'You'd be welcome anytime,' Mark said. 'Come this evening, Sergeant.'

'I will,' she said sharply. I couldn't decide whether she completely believed him and thought I was a nuisance, or whether she disbelieved him and wanted to check out whether he was lying. It gave me hope. Hope that she might listen to what I'd said and do something about it. I hoped she might help me find Oliver.

Then Mark turned on the charm. He shook the hand of the DS. 'If I could just have a quick word,' he said. He was going to convince them I was a raving lunatic and they shouldn't listen to anything I said. I could have screamed with frustration when, after a quick private chat, she put her hand on his shoulder in sympathy for him. 'I'm so sorry to have bothered you,' he said.

'No bother at all,' DS Swinburn said. 'We're here to help.'

'Let's get you home,' Mark said to me, taking off his mac and placing it lovingly round my shoulders. A show of affection for the officers' benefit. I didn't want to go home. I didn't feel safe there, but where else would I have gone?

When we got back to the house, his mother was there. She fidgeted with her napkin and pushed the soup around her bowl. The maid took it from her, and the soup had barely been touched.

'Should I ask Cook to make you something else, Mrs Amell?' she asked.

'No, I'm not hungry,' Mark's mother said. She was never a woman who had a hearty appetite, but she wasn't usually wasteful either. She and Mark looked at each other throughout dinner. Their stolen glances and mouthed conversations were completely obvious. The door opened, and when the butler announced the arrival of Dr Foulds, I wasn't surprised. Mark stood and, shaking the doctor's hand, bid him join us for dinner.

'I've eaten, thank you,' he said.

'Let's go into the drawing room,' Mark said. 'Mrs Benson, arrange for tea to be brought?'

'Of course, Mr Amell.'

'Shall we?' Mark said.

'Actually, I have the beginnings of a headache. Please excuse me?' I said.

'Darling, I'm sure Dr Foulds has something to help with that, come join us.' He held my elbow firmly and led me to the drawing room, pinching me when I tried to resist.

We were seated, the tea had been brought and poured, Mark began to speak. 'We've asked Dr Foulds to join us tonight, Katie, because we're worried about you.'

'Don't think I don't know what you're up to,' I said. Mark pretended to be wounded. His mother tutted, sighed, and shook her head.

'My poor son,' she said. 'What he's had to put up with.'

My voice rose along with my temper. 'What he's had to put up with?' I shrieked. 'Are you fucking kidding me?'

'Katie, please,' Mark said. 'Let's not make another scene.'

'Oh, God forbid we make a scene,' I said. 'God forbid any of us express a feeling. Dear God, no. Let's not do that.'

Dr Foulds spoke calmly and quietly, taking my hands in his. 'Katie, everyone is worried about you. You've been under a lot of strain.'

'They caused the strain,' I said. I snatched my hands away and pointed towards Mark and his mother. 'They've taken my son!'

'You see,' Mrs Amell said. 'It's just as I told you. She doesn't accept any responsibility for her behaviour. She's deranged.'

'For *my* behaviour?' I said. 'That's rich. What about *your* behaviour? What about your precious son's behaviour?'

'Have you been taking your medication?' Dr Foulds asked.

'It's not about me, it's about them. This is them and what they're trying to do. Don't you see?'

'Is that a no?'

'No,' I said.

'Why, Katie?' he asked. 'Why have you not taken your meds? They're there to help you.'

'Because I don't trust him,' I said.

'Why don't you trust your husband?' the doctor asked me.

'Because he's taken my child,' I said. 'Have you seen the film *Gaslighting*? They're trying to make me and everyone else think I'm mad. Don't fall for it.'

Mrs Amell drew a noisy breath in and shook her head. 'She's insane. Psychotic.'

'That really isn't helpful, Mrs Amell,' Dr Foulds said. He then turned to me.

'What makes you have these thoughts?'

'He's jealous of my relationship with Oliver. He's got rid of him. I'll be next.'

'That's ridiculous, Katie, and you know it,' Mark said.

'Is it? Is it, Mark? You've never shown any interest in our son. What have you done for him? I've done all the parenting, and now you're trying to say I'm not fit to look after him. You're trying to take my son away from me.'

'I'm going to take you to Satis House, Katie. It's a state-of-the-art facility with the best medical care. We'll have you good as new in no time,' said Dr Foulds.

'I'm not going anywhere,' I said. 'I know exactly what they're trying to do. She has never wanted me here.' I pointed at his mother. 'She didn't want Laura either. Ask them what happened to her. Ask them what they did to her. They got rid of her, and now they're going to get rid of me.'

'Nobody is getting rid of you. All we want to do is to help you. You're suffering from a psychiatric disorder. You have delusions. Hallucinations, even.'

'You're as bad as them,' I said. 'I thought you were on my side.'

'I am, Katie. I am on your side.' The doctor wasn't, though. He had conspired with them to abduct me. They kidnapped me and bundled me into a van, taking me to a lockup with mad people so they could steal my son and turn him against me.

'Why would they want to steal your son and turn him against you?' you ask when I tell you the rest of the tale.

'Because Mark was truly evil,' I say.

'You really believe that?'

'I know it. Mark was the Devil. He had no conscience, no empathy. He was the one suffering from psychosis, not me. He was a psychopath.'

'So what did you do?'

'I did the only thing I could do. I took care of him.'

Chapter 70
Regression Therapy: FEBRUARY 1976

My eyes are wide open and I'm shaking. Is the man standing before me someone who could help me? Or will he hurt me, too?

'Tam has gone out,' I say.

'Where's my money?' the man asks.

'I don't know,' I say. 'I don't know where he keeps the money.'

He swipes his arm across the table, knocking everything onto the floor; he pulls open drawers and empties the contents, he runs upstairs, his footsteps clattering on the floorboards. He runs from room to room, turning everything upside down. I'm shaking, and my stomach's heaving. I think I'm going to collapse in a heap. He bowls back into the kitchen and seizes me by the throat, lifting me and pinned me to the wall.

'Where's my fucking money?'

I can't breathe and I feel like I'm going to die. My eyes are bulging, and I'm going to pass out. He lets go abruptly, and I drop to the floor, putting my hands to my throat and coughing. He sits, defeated.

'I don't know anything about any money,' I whisper. 'Please help me.'

There is a sound of an engine roaring and brakes screaming, footsteps running. He appears, and the man jumps to his feet. Tam looks from me to the man and back again. Then an emotion I've never seen before on him crosses his face. Fear. The man jumps up and grabs Tam by his neck.

'I'm getting yer money, Boab. Honest tae God.'

'Where is it?'

'It's taken longer than I thought, right enough, but I'm just waitin' on selling sumptin.'

'What?'

He looks at me then back at the man. He's red in the face and spluttering.

'There's a man comin' the night tae pick her up and ye'll have yer money.'

'Yer selling her?' he says.

'Aye.'

Selling me? What is he talking about?

'Hang on a minute. Is she the one off the news?'

Tam says nothing.

'Are ye fucking crazy? Everyone's oot looking for her.'

'It's fine. They know whit they're daeing. He's coming the night.'

'How much?'

'I'm gettin' a good price. Ye'll get yer money.'

'Aye, well, ye owe me interest,' the man says, gripping Tam tighter.

Tam jerks his head back, then forwards fast until it connects with the man's nose. There's a crack and a splash of blood. The man screams then dives for Tam. They're rolling around on the kitchen floor, punching, kicking.

I see the open front door and take my chance.

Chapter 71
KATIE: NOW

'I had to play the game or I'd never have been allowed out of the facility. I pretended I was making progress when really there was nothing wrong with me. I told them exactly what I thought they wanted to hear.'

'Is that what you're doing to me now?' you ask.

'I'm sorry?'

'Is that what you're doing to me now, telling me what you think I want to hear?'

'No, not at all. This is the truth.'

'Okay, continue,' you say.

'Whenever I had a session with a therapist, I just accepted the things that Mark and his mother said were wrong with me. It killed me, but I did so because they would never allow me out of there if I didn't.'

'How long were you at Satis House?'

'I don't know exactly. It's all a bit of a blur. I don't have a very good concept of time. More than a few months, possibly a year.'

'Do you want to talk about your time there?'

'Not really.'

'It might help,' you say.

'It might not,' I say.

The building was terrifying. A red-brick monstrosity with a tower in the centre which reminded me of the lookout posts Nazi soldiers shot prisoners from. The arched windows were like raised eyebrows, the driveway an invitation to imprisonment. I wanted to fight, to kick and scream and rail against the doctors' decision, but Mark and his mother had convinced them I was insane and they'd only lock me in solitary, in a padded cell where guards dropped food and drink but never spoke.

The reception area had polished floors and smelled of disinfectant and dead dreams. Dark wood surrounded the walls and doors. A huge staircase reached up onto a gallery. People in white uniforms led noisy patients to rooms above. Screeching pierced the air, and strange warbling sounds mixed with the rattle of medicine trolleys. The receptionist welcomed us with a smile that didn't reach her eyes. 'Mrs Amell is in room 66,' she said after checking in a huge ledger in front of her on the desk. I cried, the realisation hitting me that they were going to leave me there.

'Come along, Katie. Let's not have any fuss. You're here to get better,' Mark snapped. I wanted to scream at him that he was a heartless bastard. I wanted to scratch his eyes out, but that that would be playing into his hands. He'd have loved to have painted me as the screeching she-devil, uncontrollable and feral.

'There's nothing wrong with me,' I said. 'You know there isn't, Mark. You're a manipulative, self-serving, evil, toxic …'

'Come along, now, Mrs Amell, Let's get you settled in,' said a nurse to my right, taking me by the elbow. 'Say your goodbyes.' Mark leant towards me, trying to plant a kiss on my cheek. I shrugged him off, and my shoulder caught his eye. He winced and held his palm to his face in an exaggeration of being hurt.

'Go to Hell,' I said. The receptionist shook her head in sympathy for Mark. I bridled in disgust and allowed the nurse to lead me away. She had a fierce grip on my upper arm. We reached the room which was to be mine and she released her hold. I had four bruises the shape of purple grapes. I rubbed at my arm and threw her a filthy look, which she ignored. Instead she checked something on a clipboard and strode away down the corridor.

The room was sparse. It had a wardrobe, a cast-iron bed, and a small chest of drawers. I peered through the bars on the window at the garden. A dry water feature boasted gargoyles whose faces had been eroded by the weather. Lips curled into snarls, eye sockets crumbled, leaving brains exposed. I watched Mark cross the driveway to climb into the car, my eyes boring into his back, the strength of my hatred willing him to turn around, but he didn't. He slipped easily into the passenger seat and was driven away to his house without his nuisance of a wife. I imagined him bringing in my replacement. A pretty blonde who hung on his every word. Mrs Benson would dote on her, and Mrs Amell would revere her. I would be spoken about in hushed tones like a disgraced relative or mad old aunt.

I wondered whether Laura had been treated in the same way. What had happened to her? My imagination had taken hold again. I was having one of my *delusions* as Mark and his mother would call them. If only I hadn't taken Mark into my confidence about the problems I had had as a child. If only I'd kept my own counsel. He could never have used my past against me. I should have been more careful. I should have bitten my tongue. My mam always said I was too big in the gap.

The nurse who'd bruised my arm returned. 'Come,' she said. 'Tour.' She spoke very few words, as though I wasn't worth the effort of speech. She led me through the long corridor and pointed out the dining hall, communal areas, stairs to the garden. A different nurse disappeared through a small door in the wall and a distant scream pierced the air. I caught a glimpse of a winding staircase before she closed the door and locked it behind her.

'Where does that lead to?' I asked.

'That's out of bounds to patients,' the nurse said curtly. 'Let's get you back to your room.' Once there, she handed me a vial of pills and a glass of water. 'Take these,' she said.

'What are they?'

'Your medication.'

'But what are they?'

'Never you mind what they are. You're one for the questions, aren't you? You'd be wise to temper that inquisitive nature while you're here. Yours is not to reason why. Just get them down your neck.' She stood over me while I took the tablets. I can't explain why I was so afraid of her or even describe just how afraid I was, but I felt I must do exactly as she told me or my life would be miserable for my time there. If I'd known then what I know now I'd have never have taken the tablets, and I would have made attempts to escape that night and run away as far away as possible from Satis House, from Mark, from his mother, and from the whole of my previous life. But I didn't know. I couldn't know what was in store.

We were herded into the dining hall for dinner, and there I met some of the other residents. Some wandered past, talking to themselves, trapped in their own little worlds and conversing only with the voices in their heads. Others wept and self-harmed publicly. One woman spun on her bottom and moaned constantly. She stopped spinning, then rocked backwards and forwards. Mark and his mother thought I belonged here! It was a zoo. It was like watching caged animals. It was a maelstrom of madness. I sat next to a woman who introduced herself immediately.

'I'm Kelly,' she said. 'And this is Charlene.' She pointed over her right shoulder. 'We're twins,' she continued. 'As you can see, we're conjoined. We haven't spent a second apart since we were born.'

I reflected on what it must be like to be physically attached to someone else. Never to be able to have a single private moment. 'I don't know how you manage to live like that. It's enough to drive you crazy.'

'Who are you calling crazy?' she asked, her voice rising.

'No, I wasn't, I was just saying … I was just trying to be friendly.'

Nurse Prentice, who had been the one to nip my arm, stepped forwards and asked Kelly what the problem was.

'She called me crazy.' She pointed towards me.

'She's new,' Prentice said.

'She didn't ought to call me crazy,' Kelly said. 'Not if she wants to wake up tomorrow.'

'I didn't call you crazy,' I tried to reason. 'But now that you come to mention it …'

She started screaming then, a high-pitched sound like a whistling kettle. My ears felt like they were bleeding, and my head spun. I blocked my ears with my hands and others around me did the same. Kelly launched herself towards me. With nails like claws she grabbed my face and tried to sink her teeth into my nose. I turned, and she caught my cheek. I pushed her away with some force, and she flew backwards. She became a wild cat then. Screaming, slapping, biting, spinning. Four nurses rushed towards her, overpowered her, pinned her to the floor, and plunged a needle into her thigh. Within seconds she was floppy as a worm on a hook. The others had become overexcited but instantly calmed when they saw how the staff had subdued Kelly. Some shuffled back to their rooms in silence. Others wailed mournfully. I ate my dinner and then went back to my room. I examined my face in the cracked mirror on the door of the wardrobe. I had four scratches on my cheek, and my hair looked like tufts of grass in sand dunes. Hands shaking, I reached in the drawer for a brush and noticed my makeup bag was missing. I'd have to report it to the nurse on duty.

Within minutes of taking the meds, a calmness washed over me and I drifted into sleep. I woke when it was still dark to the sound of the sea and an eerie voice calling my name.

'Kaaaayytie, Kaaaaayyyyttie.'

I sat up and rubbed my eyes. Shadows danced across the walls of the room, and for a second I had no clue where I was. I looked round, expecting to see the golden curtains and sash windows. Realisation dawned, and my heart sank. The curtains danced in the draught which blew into the room from the open window. I had no idea how it was opened. The bars had stopped me from allowing any fresh air into the room earlier, yet now a gale blew through, rattling the door and bringing goose bumps to my arms and chest. I tugged the blanket and sheet up round my bare shoulders.

A flicker of movement in the corner of my eye told me a rodent was sharing the room with me. I shuddered. Its eyes glistened in the moonlight, and it scurried into a hole in the wall. Another eerie moan reverberated round the room, and a face appeared at the window. A white face, dark eyes, a hook nose. Staring right at me. My heart thundered, and my hands shook. It hooted before it flew off into the night. An owl. Nothing more than an owl. I chided myself for being silly. My imagination was running away with me once more. I settled down to try to sleep when the voice began again.

'Kaaaayyyytie, Kaaaaayyyytie.'

I turned back the covers and reached into my bag for a dressing gown. I pulled it round me, pushed my feet into slippers and padded towards the door. The nurse had locked it behind her, but strangely, when I tried it, the knob turned and the door swung open. The corridor was lit only by moonlight shining in the Gothic-style windows. Stripes of blue light crossed the floor in front of me. I crept towards the voice. It grew louder and more desperate. Why was no one else coming to her aid? It was definitely a female voice, and she certainly sounded distressed, haunted even. Where were all the other inmates and the staff?

I passed dormitories where patients lay unconscious in bunks, knocked out by different variations of medication, sharing the room with a dozen other people. Thank God I had a room of my own, I'd have hated to have had to share. Especially with some of the fragments of humanity that populated this place.

The moaning escalated. Louder and louder. I crept down the staircase and into the library. The door of the library opened out onto a walled garden. We were only allowed out there when heavily supervised, and the doors were kept locked at all other times. I pressed the handle and was surprised when the door swung open with a creak. I looked around me, expecting the staff to descend on me and pounce, inject me with sedatives and drag me back to bed, but no one came. The moaning was definitely coming from outside. The moonlight bounced off a figure on the lawn which moved swiftly out of the gate at the bottom of the garden. I ran after it. How unusual for the gate to be open. The high walls bore barbed wire to keep us inside and others out. Though why anyone would want to break in is a mystery. I closed the gate so no one would be able to see from the building that it was unlocked. I padded through the sand dunes and out onto the beach. Ripples from the waves lapped the shore like molten silver. The horizon rose from the sea, a ball of fire. The figure ran ahead of me. 'Stop,' I shouted. 'Wait.'

The moaning had ceased now, but music and children singing floated across the night air. The figure ran ahead of me and up towards the clifftop. 'Please stop,' I shouted, worried they'd fall. The hood blew down in the wind, and the hair flailed behind her. It was a woman. The shape was familiar. The wind gathered speed, and she was blown from side to side. The wind took my breath, and my shouts were lost. She turned towards me, and I caught a glimpse of her face. It was Laura. I called her name, but the wind stole it.

'Laura, come back. It's dangerous.'

What was Mark's wife doing out on the clifftop here at night? They said she was dead. Why did I keep seeing her? I watched her get closer and closer to the brink. Trying not to breathe in case a minuscule movement sent her to her death, I inched forwards. 'Laura, please move back.' I felt dizzy and sick. I was trying to keep my eyes on her, but the moon kept disappearing behind a cloud. When I got to the edge, there was no sign of her. The sea raged and clashed against the rocks below. If she had fallen in she'd definitely be dead now. But they said Laura had died years ago. How could she be here on the cliffs at night? Surely I couldn't have imagined it.

The wind tore at my night clothes, and rain lashed down. I turned at the sound of a shout behind me. Three nurses ran towards me. 'What are you doing out here, Amell?' snapped Prentice.

'I heard someone calling my name,' I shouted into the wind. She grabbed me roughly and dragged me back to the house.

'You know the rules. You are not allowed outside of the building after supper, and no one is allowed out of the boundary wall,' Prentice barked at me and shoved me along the corridor to my room.

'I saw someone.'

'What were you doing on the edge of the cliff?'

'Nothing, I told you. Someone called my name. I was worried they'd be blown into the sea.'

'So, where are they?'

'I don't know. They disappeared.'

'Rubbish,' Prentice said. 'Rubbish and lies.'

'You can understand why they said that to you?' you say. 'Bearing in mind that Laura is dead.'

'But she wasn't dead. I've told you that,' I say. 'Have you been listening to anything?'

'I'm listening, Katie.'

They were all liars. The next day, they rang Mark and told him I'd tried to commit suicide. I heard the conversation and could do nothing to defend myself. 'Mr Amell, we have some quite distressing news about your wife … em … Katherine.' He gasped at the other end of the phone. 'She's fine, please don't upset yourself.' A sigh. Relief? Or something else? 'We found her on the very edge of the cliffs. It would have taken only a slightly more vicious wind to take her right over the top.' I couldn't hear his response. 'Yes, yes … it doesn't bear thinking about. … Oh yes, rest assured, we'll be keeping a much closer watch on her from now on. There will be no repeat of this incident.'

My heart sank. I was going to be even more of a prisoner now.

Chapter 72
KATIE: 1988

Laura came to me again. They tried to say the bump on the head had caused damage, but I knew she was there. Again I woke to the sound of moaning, but this time she was in the room beside me. I saw the room perfectly. This did not have the wishy-washy quality of a dream. Nothing changed. Faces didn't mutate into frightening demons. The room was exactly as it was when I went to sleep, but when I awoke, Laura was there. Her face the image of the photo on the windowsill. The same hooded cloak she'd worn that night on the beach partially covered her hair, which curled like seaweed. She smelled of the ocean. She leant towards me.

'You need to leave,' she said. 'You're in grave danger.'

I couldn't speak. I couldn't move.

'Katie, you need to listen to me. You need to leave.'

Eventually, a scream escaped from my lips. And once I'd started, I found I couldn't stop. Nurses came running, lights flashed on, but Laura had slipped out of the doors, down the corridor, and out of sight.

'It was Laura,' I said. 'Laura was here. She spoke to me. She told me to leave.'

There was nothing wrong with me, but they insisted I speak to the doctor the next day. If only I hadn't confided in them about my childhood conditions. They were just like all the adults from my childhood, the ones who thought I was an attention-seeker or a lunatic.

Chapter 73
KATIE 1995

That night, I dreamt of Oliver. He was being bundled into the back of a van. A man in black shoved a pillowcase over his head. Oliver kicked and screamed and pulled at the pillowcase, managing to remove it and biting the man on the arm. The man slapped him across the face, and Oliver cried out for me. I saw his face. He was sobbing and asking for me over and over again. He'd known nothing but love from me, and now he was being mistreated by this awful man. How could Mark and his mother do this to their own flesh and blood? They were truly evil. I had to get out of here and find my son.

I awoke, distressed, to the sound of moaning. My bedroom door was ajar, and it had been closed. I looked out of the window. A small figure stood on the grass below, beckoning to me. I shoved my feet into my slippers and wandered down the corridor. As I passed the small door that led to the winding staircase, the same scream I'd heard the first night escaped. The door lay open. Stone steps spiralled upwards. Tiny slit windows let in little light from the moon. I crept upwards, my heart thudding against its cage. Wondering what would happen if I was caught. The same voice called my name.

'Kaaaayyytie, Kaaaaayyyyttttie.'

Further up I crept, twisting, curling up towards the top of the tower until I came to a door. A solid arched door with iron hooks for handles. I turned the hook, sending squeals across the night. I pulled, and the door creaked open, revealing the room at the top of the turret. I couldn't believe who was standing inside.

I racked my brains to think how this could have happened. Nothing made sense. I could understand why people thought Laura was dead. I had been to the graveyard myself and seen the stone with my own eyes. I'd met people who were present at the funeral. I'd seen a copy of the death notice in the local paper. Short of seeing the body laid out in the morgue, I had borne witness to the death of Laura Amell. Yet here she was, standing before me. Not a ghostly figure on a beach, that could be mistaken as an apparition caused by a bang on the head. Not an amorphous shape in the distance. Here, standing before me: flesh, blood, and bones. My mouth opened and closed, but no sound came out. Then eventually, I managed one word.

'Laura?'

'Yes.'

'Mark's wife?'

'Unfortunately, yes.'

'But how? When? How?'

'Exactly the same as you, I should imagine. Make me believe I'm going mad. Convince everyone else I'm mad. Lock me up in here and forget about me.'

'But … but … the headstone … the death notice … people went to your funeral. How did they …?'

'Mark has a way of making sure everyone does his bidding. He's powerful in the village and beyond. Everyone has a weak spot. Even the vicar. And Mark has a talent for manipulation as you've probably learned.'

My brain felt like it was being kneaded. Every vein tingled. I suspected Laura hadn't died but I thought it could be my imagination running away with me.

'It's perfect for them. No one knows I'm here.'

'So I'm not married to him? He's a bigamist?

'Yes.'

My legs finally gave way, and I sat on the cold, hard floor, my brain grasping for some truth to cling to.

'Why are you locked away here?' I asked.

'Come on, Katie. Why do you think?'

If this got out, they'd be finished. It was false imprisonment. And fraud. Mark and his mother would both go to prison. Supposing they couldn't bribe the police, the Crown Prosecution Service, or the jury members? This made me more and more afraid for Oliver. Where was he? What had they done with him?

She jumped at a clatter in the distance and I scrambled to my feet.

'You have to go now,' she whispered. 'Come back tomorrow night. I have stolen a key and I'll leave the door open. Hurry before you're caught, or everything will be ruined. You're my only hope.'

I ran down the staircase, my feet missing the stone steps a couple of times and my heart racing, fearing I'd fall and break my ankles. I tiptoed back down the corridor and into my room where I lay awake, watching the sun chase the moon into the shadows and hearing the cock crow three times before drifting into a troubled sleep.

Chapter 74
HEATHER: LETTER TO KATIE 2019

Jovano made me dig a hole in the garden. 'Surely we aren't burying her here?' I said.

'Just dig,' he said.

As the spade plunged into the dirt, dislodging insects and creatures, I thought about the tale of the Lampton Worm. It was another story Dad brought with him from our previous life and told around the campfire in the dark.

Young Lampton went fishing and caught a worm, which he threw in a well. It grew and grew until it could wrap itself three times round Penshaw Hill. It ate sheep and cows and uprooted trees. Many gallant knights tried to slay it, but each time it was cut in two it came together again. Lampton consulted an old witch who told him how to slay the worm. She said that when he had conquered the worm he should slay the first living thing he should meet, and that if he did not, the Lords of Lampton for nine generations would not die peacefully in their beds. Young Lampton told his father he would blow a bugle when the worm was dead, and he should let slip one of the hounds so it would run to him and be the first living thing he would meet. Unfortunately, the father forgot what he was told and was so overjoyed when the bugle was blown and his son had killed the monster that he ran towards his boy. The son could not raise his sword against his father and waited for one of the hounds, then plunged his weapon into its side as it came lolloping through the wood. That night, there were great celebrations in Lampton Castle, but for nine generations not one of the Lords of Lampton died peacefully in his bed.

When I was in the commune, I captured worms from the garden and flung them into the well, willing them to turn into monsters and wrap themselves round the mansion to crush the commune leaders. I cut one in half once as an experiment, to see if it could knit itself back together. It didn't, but it carried on wiggling as though it were now two separate beasts. Something which looked like a vein protruded from the bottom of one half. I read somewhere in adulthood that the brain half can regenerate and grow a new tail, but the tail half just dies. Apparently, though, biologists at a university somewhere decapitated a worm, and it regenerated its head, its brain, and all its memories.

'The body will have to be dismembered,' Jovano said. 'We'll get rid of it bit by bit.'

'So we aren't burying it? Why did we dig a hole?' He ignored my question.

He made me buy bleach from the corner shop. He said we'd use it neat to clean up the bodily fluids.

It was like some horror farce you might sneak into at the cinema because your parents thought it unsuitable. I just had to forget that these pieces were Christina. I had to think of them as joints of meat. It was the only way I could get through this. So I used Christina's wheelbarrow, wheeled the parts to the big bridge, and flung them into the river. I imagined their journey out to sea. The limbs bobbing in some kind of cannibal soup.

I dreamt that like the Lampton Worm Christina's head grew back, her tongue came next, then her arms and legs. She got up and walked out of the cellar. Now she could tell the authorities I wasn't the one. I didn't do it.

I struggled to sleep after that. Though the nightmares were no worse than reality. We continued to live in her house, use her electricity, eat her food, and cash her pension.

All the time, the tongue in the jar was buried in the garden.

Chapter 75
KATIE: 1995

The next evening, I waited until everyone was asleep. The random noises of the night rolled round the corridors. I padded towards the bottom of the staircase and waited for Laura to call my name. Silence. I waited and waited. Nothing. I pushed open the door at the bottom and climbed the spiral staircase. I was reminded of the childhood tale of Rumpelstiltskin my father used to tell us.

A miller made the claim his daughter could spin straw into gold, so the king locked the girl in a tower room filled with straw and a spinning wheel. He told her that if she hadn't spun the straw to gold by morning, he would cut off her head. A strange little man arrived, and the girl offered him various gifts to help her. On the third day, she had no more gifts to give him, so he told her he would spin the straw to gold if she promised to give him her firstborn child.

The king married the miller's daughter, and they had a child. The strange little man arrived to claim his prize. The queen offered him all her wealth if she could keep her child. He eventually agreed to give up his claim to the child if she could guess his name. She guessed every name she could think of, but every one of them was wrong.

She was wandering the woods when she came to a mountain cottage.

The strange little man hopped about his fire, singing, 'Tonight, tonight, my plans I make, tomorrow, tomorrow, the baby I take, the queen will never win the game, for Rumpelstiltskin is my name.'

The next day, the queen gave a couple of wrong guesses before she guessed his name correctly. Rumpelstiltskin was so angry he drove one foot into the floor, then seized the other foot and tore himself in two.

After hearing the story, I had nightmares for weeks about strange little men stealing my family members. Being reminded of this tale drove fear through my whole body.

My shadow crept along the wall beside me, scaring me as it flickered in the light from the wall sconces. At the top of the staircase, I pushed open the door to the room Laura had been in the night before. The creak scraped through the night, and my heart pounded. I kept imagining one of the staff catching me and dragging me back to bed. No one came. The door opened, and I peered into the room, half expecting to see a small, strange man on a spinning wheel.

Nothing. No one. The room was completely empty. Laura was gone.

I didn't know where they'd taken her or what they had done with her, but after she disappeared I knew I had to play the game. I had to be a model patient, obedient, placid, and compliant if I was to get out of here.

And they eventually allowed me home.

Once home I began to plan what I should have done a long time before.

I wasn't sure whether to make it look like an accident or whether to make it look like a suicide. Of course, his mother suspected. I'd have liked to have done away with her, but it would have aroused suspicion. After what they had done to Oliver, and the way they treated me, they deserved the worst.

Mark came to pick me up from the clinic, and hugged me in front of the staff. He told me he'd missed me so much and was delighted I'd made enough progress to be allowed home. I didn't believe a word that came out of his mouth, but I acted well. The subdued, remorseful, and penitent wife. He drove me home, chatting inanely about new beginnings, fresh starts. The man was a walking cliché. I smiled and nodded in all the right places. He must have been inwardly cheering at the new Stepford wife he'd created.

When we got back to the house, I went straight up to bed, claiming a headache. In truth, I wanted to plan what I had to do. It would be a huge risk. If he suspected, or if it went wrong, I'd be hauled straight back to Satis House, and this time I wouldn't get out.

I waited patiently until his mother was out of town. I gave Mrs Benson and the rest of the staff a rare day off and told Mark I was going to prepare him a delicious meal to thank him for everything he'd done for me. The words almost choked me, but I must be a hell of an actress because he wasn't a bit suspicious.

'That's wonderful, darling,' he said and I cringed as he pulled me into an embrace. 'I'm so pleased we're back to normal.'

Normal, pah! We'd never been normal. The man was a maniac. A sociopathic narcissist.

I'd chosen Oliver's birthday as the day he would have 'the accident.' I made a meal of lobster paella, laid the table with candles and flowers. A perfect romantic setting. I dressed in his favourite outfit of mine, which was probably my least favourite. I looked like his mother in my twinset and pearls.

I'd been down to the cellar earlier to pour oil onto the steps below the reach of the light. You had to descend a number of steps before you could reach the switch. I'd told Mark this was dangerous.

He said, 'Only the staff go down there.'

His disregard for the hired help inadvertently helped seal his own fate. By the time he saw the danger it would already be too late. So it was just a matter of luring him down there and getting the timing of everything right.

When he came downstairs and I was nowhere to be seen, he shouted, 'Katie, where are you?'

'I'm down here,' I said. 'We've run out of Beaujolais, and I wanted to make tonight special.'

He wouldn't hear me properly and he'd be forced to come to the cellar stairs.

'What did you say?' he asked, just as I'd predicted.

'I'm trying to reach the Beaujolais,' I said. 'Can you help?'

'Oh, for God's sake, that's what we employ staff for.' He cursed.

'I've given the staff the day off so we can have a romantic dinner for two,' I said.

'Okay, I'm coming.' Exasperation was clearly threaded through his voice, but he was trying to be patient with the new 'improved' me.

His shadow fell into the cellar and crept across the floor. His footsteps on the stairs echoed round the room. I counted the steps and held my breath. He hit number nine. He cried out as he slipped and fell. His head hit the stone step with a crunch. I powered up my torch just in time to see his crumpled body. His legs twitching. His eyes pleading with me to help, blood already pooling and spreading beneath him. His mouth opened and closed like a guppy, and his eyes bulged. I watched until the life drained out of him. He was pathetic in his final moments. How could I ever have been afraid of him? I turned off the light, climbed the stairs, and closed the door.

Chapter 76
KATIE: 2019

My spade sliced through the dirt. I pushed down with my foot until it would go no further, pressed down on the handle, and raised the wedge of muck, throwing it aside. Over and over I dug. Down and down until I hit something hard. Down on my knees now, scrubbing the dirt away. I lifted the box out. They didn't think to search in the garden. Didn't think to dig four feet down. This is obviously what they were hunting for. I took the box into the house, placing it on the breakfast bar. Not caring that clumps of dirt stuck to the bottom, beetles, woodlice, and worms wriggling. I opened the lid and peered inside. There it was.

The jar.
The tongue.

Chapter 77
KATIE: 2019

I was crouching under the breakfast bar, and they were knocking on my door. I'd realised Mollie's husband was the man involved in the abduction in Prestwick all those years ago. I knew in my heart he'd found me a long time before. That he'd been following me. Playing with me. Moving things around in my house, making me think I was going mad. Ringing me and pretending to be Mark. Freaking me out. He'd never shown himself until now, so this visit was significant. This was it. He was coming for me. If I was going to stand a chance of defending myself, I had to get out from under the breakfast bar and get a weapon from the drawer.

It was him.

He had populated my nightmares for over forty years. He had the same eyes, the same rat face, the same scar on his cheek. I'd have known him anywhere.

I rolled out from under the breakfast bar and sprang to my feet, banging my head on the corner and crying out.

Mollie's voice again: 'Katie, are you in there?'

Then his voice. 'Maybe she's changed her mind and doesn't want us here.'

'Don't be ridiculous,' Mollie said. 'She's lonely. She's been practically begging me to come to dinner. She just didn't hear us. Try the French doors.'

The handle to the French doors creaked. Any second now they'd be in the conservatory. I tried to focus. I was dizzy from the bang on the head. I pulled the drawer handle and took out a knife, then another. One in each hand would be safest. My hands shook as I pointed them towards where they were coming from.

They were in the conservatory now and making their way towards me, calling out, 'Katie, we're here.'

I reached for the light switch to plunge them into darkness so I could make my escape.

'Shit,' Mollie said.

'What the fuck?' he said.

'The electric has tripped by the look of things,' Mollie said. 'She said she'd been having trouble with the plumbing and electrics.'

He fiddled with his phone, and the torch lit up, casting shadows across the kitchen. His face was demonic. The light splashed in my eyes, piercing them.

Mollie's voice again. 'Katie, are you okay?'

I must have had the appearance of a madwoman, hair half done, tomato juice splashed on my top, a knife in each hand. I reached to switch on the light. It took a second of two for my eyes to focus. He was reaching towards me with what I imagined was a gun, but when my eyes became accustomed to the light, I realised it was a bottle of wine. Mollie reached towards, me but an embrace was made impossible because I was holding the knives.

'Good to see you,' she said. 'Something smells delicious. I hope you don't mind us bringing the kids. Thomas's mother had her book club.'

She thrust a bouquet of flowers towards me, too, and Thomas stepped back rather than hug me. The smile slid from his face as he took in the picture of me holding the knives towards him. The threat unspoken.

I felt like my voice had been stolen.

'Katie,' Mollie said. 'What's wrong? You look like you've seen a ghost.'

'Get back,' I said, thrusting the knife towards them.

The children cowered behind their father.

'What the fuck …?' He glanced at Mollie incredulously. I could tell he was blaming her for getting them involved in this situation.

It wasn't Mollie's fault. If Mollie had turned up on her own or even with the children, they'd have had a lovely night filled with Spanish food, Rioja, and laughter. He was to blame for this. He was the one who'd dragged a schoolchild through the park by her hair and squeezed the life from her throat while I watched in horror. He was the one who'd followed me wherever I went, moved things round my home, wrote messages on the steamed-up mirror, left dead rodents where I could find them, poured rubbish onto my drive, flooded the sink, toyed with the electrics. He was the one who'd tried to muddle my mind. He had no one to blame but himself.

'Katie, you're scaring the children,' Mollie managed to say, her voice shaky. 'I'm going to call Thomas's mother and ask her to pick them up. She won't mind me interrupting her book group.'

'Put the fucking phone down.' I reached to the wall and pulled down the falchion.

Her face changed from shock to anger to fear, and she placed the phone on the table in front of her.

'It's okay, Katie. We're going to do exactly as you say.'

The boy started to cry, and Mollie shushed him and drew him into an embrace. The girl stood behind her father, a sulky expression on her face as though she was just disgruntled she was missing her favourite Netflix drama. I opened the cellar door.

'Get in there,' I said.

'Katie, please,' Mollie begged. 'Just let us go home. We won't tell anyone about this.'

She must have thought I was stupid. Of course they would tell someone. She'd be straight on the phone to the police, and they'd be around to arrest me and throw me in a cell, making sure to take my shoelaces and offer me the services of a solicitor.

There was no way I could let them just walk out of there.

Chapter 78
Regression Therapy: FEBRUARY 1976

I hobble to the door and out into the daylight. The house is on a busy street. People walk past, eyeing me strangely. I must make a bewildering sight. A young girl in shorts, a T-shirt, and a cardigan in the middle of winter. My breath makes clouds in the air. I daren't look behind me in case Tam and the man are following.

A woman holding the hand of a small child stops. 'Are ye all right, Hen?'

I shake my head.

'Are ye lost?'

I nod.

'Should I call someone for ye?'

I nod.

Tam shouts and I turn. He's running towards me.

The woman shoves me behind her, puffs out her chest, and says to Tam, 'My husband's a polis, so ye's best fuck off.'

A siren screams in the distance. I'm waiting for Tam to grab me and take me back, but his eyes widen with fear.

He runs.

Chapter 79
KATIE: 2019

They made me sit in the waiting room for ages. They thought I couldn't see them talking behind their hands. They thought I couldn't hear their whispers. I was taken into a room, and the officer, who introduced herself as DS Sturgeon, asked me, 'I'm told you were going to come to talk to us about today, Ms Kovaks? Apparently you have a crime to report?'

'I do,' I said. 'It's all in here.' I took the manuscript out of my bag and placed it on the desk.

Her eyes widened.

'This is a confession?' she asked.

'It's what happened,' I said. 'You need to read it.'

She seemed lost for words. I stopped myself from saying what my granda used to say: *Devil got your tongue?* I sat waiting patiently.

'Obviously that's going to take some time,' she said.

'I'd guess about ten and a half hours,' I said. 'If you have an average reading speed. 'I'm quite a fast reader and I could read it in eight hours and twenty minutes. Of course, if you're a slow reader it could take you fourteen. Should I call back tomorrow?'

Again, speech eluded her.

'I'm sure you'll want to speak to me when you've read it. I'm certain there will be questions you want to ask me, though it's all in there.'

Eventually, she found her tongue. 'What exactly is it all about?'

'It's hard to describe in a nutshell,' I said.

'Try,' she said.

Chapter 80
KATIE / HEATHER: NOW

So now I'm sitting here talking to you again. They've taken my clothing and put me in this ridiculous sweatshirt and jogging bottoms set. At least they aren't paper, but they're still unsightly on a woman of my age.

I'm imagining blue lights flashing, armed officers prowling and surrounding the house. Hoping against hope they'll find them all alive. Maybe in the cellar. A man, a woman, two children. No one wants to find the dead bodies of innocents. Better perhaps to find the innocents pawing the body of their dead father, weeping and wailing.

'Why did you lock them in the cellar?' you ask.

'I couldn't let him get away,' I say. 'He was the one. The one who abducted me as a child. He held me in that cellar and treated me like an animal. Worse than an animal. The things he did to me were indescribable.'

'I know you suffered, but you can't just exact revenge. You can't just take the law into your own hands. Taking it out on an innocent man.'

'How can you say he was innocent?' I ask.

'Thomas wasn't your abductor,' you say. 'Perhaps there's some physical resemblance, but he wasn't the man who took you from your family and hurt you. It's as well you didn't hurt him. Thank God you had a change of heart.'

'I'm not the monster the media has painted me all these years, but I didn't have a change of heart. I wanted to kill him. I felt so much rage, but Heather wouldn't let me. We just wanted it to stop. I wanted it to stop.'

'What did you want to stop?' you ask.

'The notes, the moving furniture, leaving things in the house, the noises, the phone messages, the messages on the mirror. He was stalking me. He was coming to get me.'

'Will you allow yourself to imagine, just for a moment, that Thomas wasn't the perpetrator, and that the person who abducted you hasn't been stalking you?'

'He was never caught,' I say.

'He wasn't, and that must have been terrible for you.'

'You've no idea just how terrible it was. It haunted me. I used to imagine he was under my bed, in the wardrobe, lying in wait for me on my way to school, behind the library, in the henhouse. Everywhere I went.'

'Yes, you have a long history of mental health problems …'

'… Oh, this again,' I say.

'You were never the same again after the abduction, were you? Understandably so. It was such a traumatic event. And then, of course, there's what happened to Anne Brownlow.'

'I've already told you *that* was an accident. We were playing.'

'You cut out her tongue,' you say.

'It was a game. I didn't mean to do it.'

'The notes say you were given therapy after the incident. They assumed it was a result of the trauma you suffered during your abduction and confinement. But you refused to take any responsibility for what you did. You blamed an imaginary friend. Given the diagnosis, we realise now that these weren't imaginary friends. They were alters.

'You are Heather, and Heather is you.

'You were diagnosed with Multiple Personality Disorder, as you know; today we call it Dissociative Identity Disorder. We know you have many distinct personality states. Sometimes one takes hold of you, and sometimes it's another. It was undoubtedly caused by your childhood trauma.'

'How can you explain what happened to me as trauma? The word is so small for something so big.'

'I agree, there's no word big enough for what you suffered. The alters help you to deal with that, don't they?'

'They are my support system. They protect me.'

'And some of them hurt you. Shelly for example.'

'Shelly is always trying to stop me from meeting people and making friends because she knows I'll eventually get hurt. She comes out when I'm vulnerable. She cuts my arms, and I hate that about her. Sometimes I'm in the room and I can see her doing it, but I can't stop her, and sometimes I have no knowledge of it. I just wake up and the wounds are there.'

'That may explain the blood in the bed as a child.'

'Perhaps.'

'It says in your notes you had many more alters as a child, but that you went through an assimilation process through therapy. It also says you were reluctant to lose the main alters. You said they helped with the suffering.'

'Can you imagine losing a best friend, a family member, a twin? Losing the alters is losing a part of me, and I can't deal with everything alone.'

'I understand.'

'How can you? No one knows what I suffered. I couldn't tell anyone. I came home and I couldn't speak. He told me if I ever told anyone what he did, he would kill my whole family. He'd take me back there and I'd never escape.'

'You've been through a lot in your life, but we can't excuse the crimes you've committed. I'm here to help you, but you have to take your medication, and you have to take responsibility.'

'I expected more of you, but you're just as bad as all the other psychiatrists. And they were as bad as Mark and his poisonous mother. I told you what they did to Oliver.'

'They didn't do anything to Oliver. Oliver was stillborn. You suffered post-pleural psychosis and were committed to a healthcare facility paid for by your husband.'

'They wanted me out of the way so they could take my son. And no one would help me in my search for him.'

'You suffered confusion and delusions. It's understandable, given the traumatic birth. A baby dying is enough to send anyone over the edge.'

'I wasn't over the edge.'

'Can you not remember the funeral?'

As you say this, a moving picture flashes on my inward eye: a woman in a black veil, a tiny white coffin with the inscription 'Born asleep'. Weeping, wailing, pain which cuts deeper than any knife.

'I don't want to talk about this anymore,' I say.

'Let's move on to the commune murders. I know you served your time, but in all of our sessions, you've never once taken responsibility for what happened.'

'Because I wasn't responsible,' I say.

'Jovano is part of your system. He's one of your alters.'

'You're wrong. Jovano is not part of the system. I met Jovano in the commune. How many times do I have to tell you? He is not one of my alters.'

'But there's no record of him,' you say.

'Why will no one listen to me? The system consists of Heather, the host. Katie is the main alter. Shelly is an alter. Jovano is not part of me. He is a different person entirely.'

'So why is there no record of him?' you ask

'Maybe because his parents lived a nomadic life. They didn't register births or deaths. I told you about Heather's father ...' My voice cracks, and my eyes sting. I don't want to show this weakness to you. 'I told you he was buried in the grounds of the commune. That's what they did with their dead. Jovano escaped with us. *He* was there at Christina's. *He* cut out her tongue. It wasn't Heather, it wasn't Katie, it wasn't Shelly. It wasn't one of us.'

'It's known that the disorder is accompanied by memory gaps beyond what could be explained by ordinary forgetfulness. I understand you have trouble remembering certain events?'

'I may dissociate at times, and at other times I'm coconscious, but I don't forget my alters. I may not remember what they do, but I don't forget them. Jovano isn't one of them. It was Jovano who committed the crimes. You have to listen to me.'

You sigh and run your hands through your hair. Your beautiful eyes are wet. Are they tears? Are you crying for me?

I listen to the conversation between you and the detective. You think you're so clever. You think you know everything, but you're wrong about Jovano. He got away with murder.

'I don't understand,' the detective says to you. 'Which parts of the story are true?'

'They're all true in a sense, in that Katie or Heather lived all of them. It's pretty complex, but in a way straightforward, really. Heather went on holiday with her family to Ayrshire when she was seven years old. She was abducted from a park in Prestwick. She was gone for months. No one knew what happened to her, because when she came back she couldn't speak. She eventually started to speak again, but she spoke in different voices and saw things that weren't there. The psychiatrists all had different theories. She saw many health professionals who argued about a diagnosis.

'Piecing together her case history, I'd say her personality split after the terrible trauma of the abduction to help her deal with what she had suffered. Only her alters are aware of the horrific things that had happened to her. Her family decided a new life would be the best thing for them all. They packed up and went travelling. They joined a commune. Heather's father died there, and Heather escaped after attacking two of the elders. Both men were very old and infirm. On the run she met an old woman called Christina Widdecome and lived with her for a while. Christina was found dead in her own cellar with her tongue cut out. Heather was eventually caught and spent three years in a secure facility.'

'Three years for the murder of three people?' The detective is incredulous.

'She was a minor who had suffered a terrible trauma. She was tried on the grounds of manslaughter with diminished responsibility. The defence argued she could be a valuable member of society if given the right medication and support. The medics agreed with this. She was released and given a new identity, Katie. Of course, there was a public outcry about this. You know what the public are like, baying for blood. But her appearance was changed so much even her own mother wouldn't have recognised her. Katie worked in publishing for a short time and then married. She functioned normally for a while and then she suffered many miscarriages and a stillbirth which triggered her dissociative identity disorder. The alters resurfaced to help her cope with the trauma. She'd found a way to detach herself from the painful experiences.'

'By imagining Oliver was still alive?'

'Yes. Her husband said she had conversations with her dead child; he'd hear her reply in a childlike voice as though she was a five-year-old boy. He said it was bizarre, but it's not uncommon in people who have DID.'

'Wow, that's crazy,' the detective says.

'She was in and out of hospital for years, but I don't think she was properly medicated for a long time. Her husband was killed in an accident, and she moved away.'

'It says in this manuscript she killed him,' the detective says.

'The coroner recorded a verdict of accidental death. There's obviously some guilt surrounding his death. Katie frequently talks to him, holds telephone conversations with him … people with DID – like schizophrenics – are rarely dangerous to anyone but themselves, you know. We see a distorted picture in the media. I despair every time I see a news report about someone with schizophrenia. They invariably demonise the mentally ill.'

'I wouldn't say she was harmless,' the detective says.

'She's been much more sinned against than sinning, in my opinion,' you say.

'I can't understand how she ended up in a convent,' the detective says.

'After the death of her husband, she volunteered with the Little Sisters of the Poor. She spent time with them in prayer and service. She took formal discernment where she had a live-in experience in one of their homes. She immersed herself in their life in its totality, accepting their spirituality and traditions. The alters wrote to her, and she wrote to them. The book in front of you is the result of that.'

I'm pleasantly surprised to hear you defending me, but you've got so much of it wrong. You think Jovano was one of my alters, but he wasn't – he was real. Jovano committed the murders, and I got the blame. I was an easy target. It's depressing how mental health disorders are still so misunderstood.

They paint me as a serial killer. A delinquent and madwoman. They think I killed Adrik and Karma and Christina, but I didn't. I was one of Jovano's victims, but when you have a history of mental health issues, no one ever believes you. There is no record anywhere of Jovano's existence, but I have a single photograph of me and him taken by my father before he died. We're sitting side by side in the shadow of the beech tree. A daddy longlegs crawls on his forearm, and his blond hair is alight in the midday sun. I sit beside him with my head resting on his shoulder, my eyes turned towards him in adoration.

The alters and I have been misjudged and misunderstood our whole life. We did hurt Anne Brownlow, but it was an accident, and they thought we were lying. We were playing The Pollard's Boar. We didn't mean to hurt her.

We hurt Mark, but he was selfish, abusive, and controlling. That was self-preservation. He treated us appallingly. Always gaslighting us and making us feel that our feelings weren't valid. Always putting us down in front of his friends.

When your footsteps die away, we look out of the window at the beech tree in the grounds spreading his wings across the sky ready to take flight. We imagine large clusters of daddy longlegs congregating on him. A mishmash of bodies and legs, resembling a small furry animal. One breaks from the pack and scurries away on its six flexible stilts, with every step grappling his way over the obstacles in his path.

Perhaps we'll go back to not speaking. Life was so much simpler then. We imagine ourselves on a beach. Stepping into the frothy sea. Wading up to our waist and disappearing under the salty water.

The Little Mermaid swimming back to the ocean, mournfully sinking beneath the waves and becoming nothing but foam.

Acknowledgements:
I hate writing this part. Not because I don't like thanking people, but because I'm anxious I'll leave someone out. The best way to avoid this is just to say thank you to everyone who made this book possible and leave it at that, but then I'll feel guilty. I think it's the Catholic upbringing. Okay here goes …

In no particular order …

Thank you to:

Conrad for believing in this book and for putting up with my insane demands. You can take the scold's bridle off now.

Emmy Ellis for the perfect cover.

Loulou Brown for editorial advice.

Karen Ankers for editorial advice.

Shelagh Corker for proofreading early drafts and Sue Scott for proofreading later copies.

All at TBC who read and commented. Special thanks to Helen Boyce and Tracy Fenton.

Caroline Mundy and Sharon Thomas who supported me during my MA, read passages and offered advice.

Lesley McEvoy who helped with something I can't disclose because it'll ruin the plot.

Katharine Sands for advice about literary agents.

Kerry Richardson who is my writing rock and responsible adult.

My amazing friends and family who support me in everything I do. I can't mention them all because our family is bigger than the mafia, and I'm lucky enough to have so many good friends.

My three fabulous parents who have made stories a massive part of our lives, and to whom I'm eternally grateful for everything.

My children, without whom I'd be rich and famous by now. But at least we have love. Love you toinfinity Roxanne, Leonni, Levi, Kaii, Eskiah and Callum.

To Stephen, my chief morale officer, who makes me laugh every day and helps to keep both my chins up.

Last but not least, to the readers. If you've bought this book, borrowed it, begged it or stole it thank you for making the writing worthwhile. (Actually, if you stole it can you give it back. I need the royalties for a facelift.)

Printed in Great Britain
by Amazon